THE
OUTLET

ANDY ADAMS

1st WORLD
LIBRARY
Literary Society

The Outlet

Andy Adams

© 1st World Library – Literary Society, 2004
PO Box 2211
Fairfield, IA 52556
www.1stworldlibrary.org
First Edition

LCCN: 2005901128

Softcover ISBN:1-4218-1106-5
Hardcover ISBN:1-4218-1006-9
eBook ISBN:1-4218-1206-1

Purchase *"The Outlet"*
as a traditional bound book at:
www.1stWorldLibrary.org/purchase.asp?ISBN=1-4218-1106-5

1st World Library Literary Society is a nonprofit
organization dedicated to promoting literacy by:

- Creating a free internet library accessible from any
  computer worldwide.
- Hosting writing competitions and offering book
  publishing scholarships.

The Outlet
contributed by Tim, Ed & Rodney
in support of
1st World Library Literary Society

CONTENTS

PREFACE

At the close of the civil war the need for a market for the surplus cattle of Texas was as urgent as it was general. There had been numerous experiments in seeking an outlet, and there is authority for the statement that in 1857 Texas cattle were driven to Illinois. Eleven years later forty thousand head were sent to the mouth of Red River in Louisiana, shipped by boat to Cairo, Illinois, and thence inland by rail. Fever resulted, and the experiment was never repeated. To the west of Texas stretched a forbidding desert, while on the other hand, nearly every drive to Louisiana resulted in financial disaster to the drover. The republic of Mexico, on the south, afforded no relief, as it was likewise overrun with a surplus of its own breeding. Immediately before and just after the war, a slight trade had sprung up in cattle between eastern points on Red River and Baxter Springs, in the southeast corner of Kansas. The route was perfectly feasible, being short and entirely within the reservations of the Choctaws and Cherokees, civilized Indians. This was the only route to the north; for farther to the westward was the home of the buffalo and the unconquered, nomadic tribes. A writer on that day, Mr. Emerson Hough, an acceptable authority, says: "The civil war stopped almost all plans to market the range cattle, and the close of that war found the vast grazing lands of Texas fairly covered with millions of cattle which had no actual or determinate value. They were sorted and branded and herded after a fashion, but neither they nor their increase could be converted into anything but more cattle. The demand for a market became imperative."

This was the situation at the close of the '50's and meanwhile there had been no cessation in trying to find an outlet for the constantly increasing herds. Civilization was sweeping westward by leaps and bounds, and during the latter part of the '60's and early '70's, a market for a very small percentage of the surplus was established at Abilene, Ellsworth, and Wichita, being confined almost exclusively to the state of Kansas. But this outlet, slight as it was, developed the fact that the transplanted Texas steer, after a winter in the north, took on flesh like a native, and by being double-wintered became a marketable beef. It should be understood in this connection that Texas, owing to climatic conditions, did not mature an animal into marketable form, ready for the butcher's block. Yet it was an exceptional country for breeding, the percentage of increase in good years reaching the phenomenal figures of ninety-five calves to the hundred cows. At this time all eyes were turned to the new Northwest, which was then looked upon as the country that would at last afford the proper market. Railroads were pushing into the domain of the buffalo and Indian; the rush of emigration was westward, and the Texan was clamoring for an outlet for his cattle. It was written in the stars that the Indian and buffalo would have to stand aside.

Philanthropists may deplore the destruction of the American bison, yet it was inevitable. Possibly it is not commonly known that the general government had under consideration the sending of its own troops to destroy the buffalo. Yet it is a fact, for the army in the West fully realized the futility of subjugating the Indians while they could draw subsistence from the bison. The well-mounted aborigines hung on the flanks of the great buffalo herds, migrating with them, spurning all treaty obligations, and when opportunity offered murdering the advance guard of civilization with the fiendish atrocity of carnivorous animals. But while the government hesitated, the hide-hunters and the railroads solved the problem, and the Indian's base of supplies was destroyed.

Then began the great exodus of Texas cattle. The red men were easily confined on reservations, and the vacated country in the Northwest became cattle ranges. The government was in the market for large quantities of beef with which to feed its army and Indian wards. The maximum year's drive was reached in 1884, when nearly eight hundred thousand cattle, in something over three hundred herds, bound for the new Northwest, crossed Red River, the northern boundary of Texas. Some slight idea of this exodus can be gained when one considers that in the above year about four thousand men and over thirty thousand horses were required on the trail, while the value of the drive ran into millions. The history of the world can show no pastoral movement in comparison. The Northwest had furnished the market - the outlet for Texas.

CHAPTER I.

OPENING THE CAMPAIGN

"Well, gentlemen, if that is the best rate you can offer us, then we'll drive the cattle. My boys have all been over the trail before, and your figures are no inducement to ship as far as Red River. We are fully aware of the nature of the country, but we can deliver the herds at their destination for less than you ask us for shipping them one third of the distance. No; we'll drive all the way."

The speaker was Don Lovell, a trail drover, and the parties addressed were the general freight agents of three railroad lines operating in Texas. A conference had been agreed upon, and we had come in by train from the ranch in Medina County to attend the meeting in San Antonio. The railroad representatives were shrewd, affable gentlemen, and presented an array of facts hard to overcome. They were well aware of the obstacles to be encountered in the arid, western portion of the state, and magnified every possibility into a stern reality. Unrolling a large state map upon the table, around which the principals were sitting, the agent of the Denver and Fort Worth traced the trail from Buffalo Gap to Doan's Crossing on Red River. Producing what was declared to be a report of the immigration agent of his line, he showed by statistics that whole counties through which the old trail ran had recently been settled up by Scandinavian immigrants. The representative of the Missouri, Kansas, and Texas, when opportunity offered, enumerated every disaster which had happened to any herd to the westward of his line in the past five years. The factor of the International was equally well posted.

"Now, Mr. Lovell," said he, dumping a bundle of papers on the table, "if you will kindly glance over these documents, I think I can convince you that it is only a question of a few years until all trail cattle will ship the greater portion of the way. Here is a tabulated statement up to and including the year '83. From twenty counties tributary to our line and south of this city, you will notice that in '80 we practically handled no cattle intended for the trail. Passing on to the next season's drive, you see we secured a little over ten per cent. of the cattle and nearly thirty per cent. of the horse stock. Last year, or for '83, drovers took advantage of our low rates for Red River points, and the percentage ran up to twenty-four and a fraction, or practically speaking, one fourth of the total drive. We are able to offer the same low rates this year, and all arrangements are completed with our connecting lines to give live-stock trains carrying trail cattle a passenger schedule. Now, if you care to look over this correspondence, you will notice that we have inquiries which will tax our carrying capacity to its utmost. The 'Laurel Leaf' and 'Running W' people alone have asked for a rate on thirty thousand head."

But the drover brushed the correspondence aside, and asked for the possible feed bills. A blanket rate had been given on the entire shipment from that city, or any point south, to Wichita Falls, with one rest and feed. Making a memorandum of the items, Lovell arose from the table and came over to where Jim Flood and I were searching for Fort Buford on a large wall map. We were both laboring under the impression that it was in Montana, but after our employer pointed it out to us at the mouth of the Yellowstone in Dakota, all three of us adjourned to an ante-room. Flood was the best posted trail foreman in Don Lovell's employ, and taking seats at the table, we soon reduced the proposed shipping expense to a pro-rata sum per head. The result was not to be considered, and on returning to the main office, our employer, as already expressed, declined the proffered rate.

Then the freight men doubled on him, asking if he had taken into consideration a saving in wages. In a two days' run they would lay down the cattle farther on their way than we could possibly drive in six weeks, even if the country was open, not to say anything about the wear and tear of horseflesh. But Don Lovell had not been a trail drover for nearly fifteen years without understanding his business as well as the freight agents did theirs. After going over a large lot of other important data, our employer arose to take his leave, when the agent of the local line expressed a hope that Mr. Lovell would reconsider his decision before spring opened, and send his drive a portion of the way by rail.

"Well, I'm glad I met you, gentlemen," said the cowman at parting, "but this is purely a business proposition, and you and I look at it from different viewpoints. At the rate you offer, it will cost me one dollar and seventy-five cents to lay a steer down on Red River. Hold on; mine are all large beeves; and I must mount my men just the same as if they trailed all the way. Saddle horses were worth nothing in the North last year, and I kept mine and bought enough others around Dodge to make up a thousand head, and sent them back over the trail to my ranch. Now, it will take six carloads of horses for each herd, and I propose to charge the freight on them against the cattle. I may have to winter my remudas in the North, or drive them home again, and if I put two dollars a head freight in them, they won't bring a cent more on that account. With the cattle it's different; they are all under contract, but the horses must be charged as general expense, and if nothing is realized out of them, the herd must pay the fiddler. My largest delivery is a sub-contract for Fort Buford, calling for five million pounds of beef on foot. It will take three herds or ten thousand cattle to fill it. I was anxious to give those Buford beeves an early start, and that was the main reason in my consenting to this conference. I have three other earlier deliveries at Indian agencies, but they are not as far north by several hundred miles, and it's immaterial whether we ship or not. But the Buford contract sets the day of delivery for September 15, and it's going to take close figuring to make a cent. The main contractors are all right, but I'm the one that's got to scratch his head and figure close and see that there's no leakages. Your freight bill alone would be a nice profit. It may cost us a little for water getting out of Texas, but with the present outlet for cattle, it's bad policy to harass the herds. Water is about the best crop some of those settlers along the trail have to sell, and they ought to treat us right."

After the conference was over, we scattered about the city, on various errands, expecting to take the night train home. It was then the middle of February, and five of the six herds were already purchased. In spite of the large numbers of cattle which the trail had absorbed in previous years, there was still an abundance of all ages, anxious for a market. The demand in the North had constantly been for young cattle, leaving the matured steers at home. Had Mr. Lovell's contracts that year called for forty thousand five and six year old beeves, instead of twenty, there would have been the same inexhaustible supply from which to pick and choose. But with only one herd yet to secure, and ample offerings on every hand, there was no necessity for a hurry. Many of the herds driven the year before found no sale, and were compelled to winter in the North at the drover's risk. In the early spring of '84, there was a decided lull over the enthusiasm of the two previous years, during the former of which the trail afforded an outlet for nearly seven hundred thousand Texas cattle.

In regard to horses we were well outfitted. During the summer of '83, Don Lovell had driven four herds, two on Indian contract and two of younger cattle on speculation. Of the latter, one was sold in Dodge for delivery on the Purgatory River in southern Colorado, while the other went to Ogalalla, and was disposed of and received at that point. In both cases there was no chance to sell the saddle horses, and they returned to Dodge and were sent to pasture down the river in the settlements. My brother, Bob Quirk, had driven one of the other herds to an agency in the Indian Territory. After making the delivery, early in August, on his employer's orders, he had brought his remuda and outfit into Dodge, the horses being also sent to pasture and the men home to Texas. I had made the trip that year to the Pine Ridge Agency in Dakota with thirty-five hundred beeves, under Flood as foreman. Don Lovell was present at the delivery, and as there was no hope of effecting a sale of the saddle stock among the Indians, after delivering the outfit at the nearest railroad, I was given two men and the cook, and started back over the trail for Dodge with the remuda. The wagon was a drawback, but on reaching Ogalalla, an emigrant outfit offered me a fair price for the mules and commissary, and I sold them. Lashing our rations and blankets on two pack-horses, we turned our backs on the Platte and crossed the Arkansaw at Dodge on the seventh day.

But instead of the remainder of the trip home by rail, as we fondly expected, the programme had changed. Lovell and Flood had arrived in Dodge some ten days before, and looking over the situation, had come to the conclusion it was useless even to offer our remudas. As remnants of that year's drive, there had concentrated in and around that market something like ten thousand saddle horses. Many of these were from central and north Texas, larger and better stock than ours, even though care had been used in selecting the latter. So on their arrival, instead of making any effort to dispose of our own, the drover and his foreman had sized up the congested condition of the market, and turned buyers. They had bought two whole remudas, and picked over five or six others until their purchases amounted to over five hundred head. Consequently on our reaching Dodge with the Pine Ridge horses, I was informed that they were going to send all the saddle stock back over the trail to the ranch and that I was to have charge of the herd. Had the trip been in the spring and the other way, I certainly would have felt elated over my promotion. Our beef herd that year had been put up in Dimmit County, and from there to the Pine Ridge Agency and back to the ranch would certainly be a summer's work to gratify an ordinary ambition.

In the mean time and before our arrival, Flood had brought up all the stock and wagons from the settlement, and established a camp on Mulberry Creek, south of Dodge on the trail. He had picked up two Texans who were anxious to see their homes once more, and the next day at noon we started. The herd numbered a thousand and sixty head, twenty of which were work-mules. The commissary which was to accompany us was laden principally with harness; and waving Flood farewell, we turned homeward, leaving behind unsold of that year's drive only two wagons. Lovell had instructed us never to ride the same horse twice, and wherever good grass and water were encountered, to kill as much time as possible. My employer was enthusiastic over the idea, and well he might be, for a finer lot of saddle horses were not in the possession of any trail drover, while those purchased in Dodge could have been resold in San Antonio at a nice profit. Many of the horses had run idle several months and were in fine condition. With the allowance of four men and a cook, a draft-book for personal expenses, and over a thousand horses from which to choose a mount, I felt like an embryo foreman, even if it was a back track and the drag end of the season. Turning everything scot free at night, we reached the ranch in old Medina in six weeks, actually traveling about forty days.

But now, with the opening of the trail season almost at hand, the trials of past years were forgotten in the enthusiasm of the present. I had a distinct recollection of numerous resolves made on rainy nights, while holding a drifting herd, that this was positively my last trip over the trail. Now, however, after a winter of idleness, my worst fear was that I might be left at home with the ranch work, and thus miss the season's outing entirely. There were new charms in the Buford contract which thrilled me, - its numerical requirements, the sight of the Yellowstone again, and more, to be present at the largest delivery of the year to the government. Rather than have missed the trip, I would have gladly cooked or wrangled the horses for one of the outfits.

On separating, Lovell urged his foreman and myself to be at the depot in good time to catch our train. That our employer's contracts for the year would require financial assistance, both of us were fully aware. The credit of Don Lovell was gilt edge, not that he was a wealthy cowman, but the banks and moneyed men of the city recognized his business ability.

Nearly every year since he began driving cattle, assistance had been extended him, but the promptness with which he had always met his obligations made his patronage desirable.

Flood and I had a number of errands to look after for the boys on the ranch and ourselves, and, like countrymen, reached the depot fully an hour before the train was due. Not possessed of enough gumption to inquire if the westbound was on time, we loitered around until some other passengers informed us that it was late. Just as we were on the point of starting back to town, Lovell drove up in a hack, and the three of us paced the platform until the arrival of the belated train.

"Well, boys, everything looks serene," said our employer, when we had walked to the farther end of the depot. "I can get all the money I need, even if we shipped part way, which I don't intend to do. The banks admit that cattle are a slow sale and a shade lower this spring, and are not as free with their money as a year or two ago. My bankers detained me over an hour until they could send for a customer who claimed to have a very fine lot of beeves for sale in Lasalle County. That he is anxious to sell there is no doubt, for he offered them to me on my own time, and agrees to meet any one's prices. I half promised to come back next week and go down with him to Lasalle and look his cattle over. If they show up right, there will be no trouble in buying them, which will complete our purchases. It is my intention, Jim, to give you the herd to fill our earliest delivery. Our next two occur so near together that you will have to represent me at one of them. The Buford cattle, being the last by a few weeks, we will both go up there and see it over with. There are about half a dozen trail foremen anxious for the two other herds, and while they are good men, I don't know of any good reason for not pushing my own boys forward. I have already decided to give Dave Sponsilier and Quince Forrest two of the Buford herds, and I reckon, Tom, the last one will fall to you."

The darkness in which we were standing shielded my egotism from public view. But I am conscious that I threw out my brisket several inches and stood straight on my bow-legs as I thanked old man Don for the foremanship of his sixth herd. Flood was amused, and told me afterward that my language was extravagant. There is an old superstition that if a man ever drinks out of the Rio Grande, it matters not where he roams afterward, he is certain to come back to her banks again. I had watered my horse in the Yellowstone in '82, and ever afterward felt an itching to see her again. And here the opportunity opened before me, not as a common cow-hand, but as a trail boss and one of three in filling a five million pound government beef contract! But it was dark and I was afoot, and if I was a trifle "chesty," there had suddenly come new colorings to my narrow world.

On the arrival of the train, several other westward-bound cowmen boarded it. We all took seats in the smoker, it being but a two hours' run to our destination. Flood and I were sitting well forward in the car, the former almost as elated over my good fortune as myself. "Well, won't old Quince be all puffed up," said Jim to me, "when the old man tells him he's to have a herd. Now, I've never said a word in favor of either one of you. Of course, when Mr. Lovell asked me if I knew certain trail foremen who were liable to be idle this year, I intimated that he had plenty of material in his employ to make a few of his own. The old man may be a trifle slow on reaching a decision, but once he makes up his mind, he's there till the cows come home. Now, all you and Quince need to do is to make good, for you couldn't ask for a better man behind you. In making up your outfit, you want to know every man you hire, and give a preference to gray hairs, for they're not so liable to admire their shadow in sunny or get homesick in falling weather. Tom, where you made a ten-strike with the old man was in accepting that horse herd at Dodge last fall. Had you made a whine or whimper then, the chances are you wouldn't be bossing a herd this year. Lovell is a cowman who likes to see a fellow take his medicine with a smile."

ANDY ADAMS

CHAPTER II.

ORGANIZING THE FORCES

Don Lovell and Jim Flood returned from Lasalle County on the last day of February. They had spent a week along the Upper Nueces, and before returning to the ranch closed a trade on thirty-four hundred five and six year old beeves. According to their report, the cattle along the river had wintered in fine condition, and the grass had already started in the valley. This last purchase concluded the buying for trail purposes, and all absent foremen were notified to be on hand at the ranch on March 10, for the beginning of active operations. Only some ten of us had wintered at headquarters in Medina County, and as about ninety men would be required for the season's work, they would have to be secured elsewhere. All the old foremen expected to use the greater portion of the men who were in their employ the year before, and could summon them on a few days' notice. But Forrest and myself were compelled to hire entirely new outfits, and it was high time we were looking up our help.

One of Flood's regular outfit had married during the winter, and with Forrest's and my promotion, he had only to secure three new men. He had dozens of applications from good cowhands, and after selecting for himself offered the others to Quince and me. But my brother Bob arrived at the ranch, from our home in Karnes County, two days later, having also a surplus of men at his command. Although he did not show any enthusiasm over my promotion, he offered to help me get up a good outfit of boys. I had about half a dozen good fellows in view, and on Bob's approval of them, he selected from his overplus six more as first choice and four as second. It would take me a week of constant riding to see all these men, and as Flood and Forrest had made up an outfit for the latter from the former's available list, Quince and I saddled up and rode away to hire outfits. Forrest was well acquainted in Wilson, where Lovell had put up several trail herds, and as it joined my home county, we bore each other company the first day.

A long ride brought us to the Atascosa, where we stayed all night. The next morning we separated, Quince bearing due east for Floresville, while I continued southeast towards my home near Cibollo Ford on the San Antonio River. It had been over a year since I had seen the family, and on reaching the ranch, my father gruffly noticed me, but my mother and sisters received me with open arms. I was a mature man of twenty-eight at the time, mustached, and stood six feet to a plumb-line. The family were cognizant of my checkered past, and although never mentioning it, it seemed as if my misfortunes had elevated me in the estimation of my sisters, while to my mother I had become doubly dear.

During the time spent in that vicinity, I managed to reach home at night as often as possible. Constantly using fresh horses, I covered a wide circle of country, making one ride down the river into Goliad County of over fifty miles, returning the next day. Within a week I had made up my outfit, including the horse-wrangler and cook. Some of the men were ten years my senior, while only a few were younger, but I knew that these latter had made the trip before and were as reliable as their elders. The wages promised that year were fifty dollars a month, the men to furnish only their own saddles and blankets, and at that figure I picked two pastoral counties, every man bred to the occupation. The trip promised six months' work with return passage, and I urged every one employed to make his appearance at headquarters, in Medina, on or before the 15th of the month. There was no railroad communication through Karnes and Go liad counties at that time, and all the boys were assured that their private horses would have good pasturage at the home ranch while they were away, and I advised them all to come on horseback. By this method they would have a fresh horse awaiting them on their return from the North with which to continue their homeward journey. All the men engaged were unmarried, and taken as a whole, I flattered myself on having secured a crack outfit.

I was in a hurry to get back to the ranch. There had been nothing said about the remudas before leaving, and while we had an abundance of horses, no one knew them better than I did. For that reason I wanted to be present when their allotment was made, for I knew that every foreman would try to get the best mounts, and I did not propose to stand behind the door and take the culls. Many of the horses had not had a saddle on them in eight months, while all of them had run idle during the winter in a large mesquite pasture and were in fine condition with the opening of spring. So bidding my folks farewell, I saddled at noon and took a cross-country course for the ranch, covering the hundred and odd miles in a day and a half. Reaching headquarters late at night, I found that active preparations had been going on during my absence. There were new wagons to rig, harness to oil, and a carpenter was then at work building chuck-boxes for each of the six commissaries. A wholesale house in the city had shipped out a stock of staple supplies, almost large enough to start a store. There were whole coils of new rope of various sizes, from lariats to corral cables, and a sufficient amount of the largest size to make a stack of hobbles as large as a haycock. Four new branding-irons to the wagon, the regulation "Circle Dot," completed the main essentials.

All the foremen had reported at the ranch, with the exception of Forrest, who came in the next evening with three men. The division of the horses had not even come up for discussion but several of the boys about headquarters who were friendly to my interests posted me that the older foremen were going to claim first choice. Archie Tolleston, next to Jim Flood in seniority in Lovell's employ, had spent every day riding among the horses and had even boasted that he expected to claim fifteen of the best for his own saddle. Flood was not so particular, as his destination was in southern Dakota, but my brother Bob was again ticketed for the Crow Agency in Montana, and would naturally expect a good remuda. Tolleston was going to western Wyoming, while the Fort Buford cattle were a two-weeks' later delivery and fully five hundred miles farther travel. On my return Lovell was in the city, but I felt positive that if he took a hand in the division, Tolleston would only run on the rope once.

A few days before the appointed time, the men began thronging into headquarters. Down to the minutest detail about the wagons and mule teams, everything was shipshape. The commissary department was stocked for a month, and everything was ready to harness in and move. Lovell's head-quarters was a stag ranch, and as fast as the engaged cooks reported, they were assigned to wagons, and kept open house in relieving the home cocinero. In the absence of our employer, Flood was virtually at the head of affairs, and artfully postponed the division of horses until the last moment. My outfit had all come in in good time, and we were simply resting on our oars until the return of old man Don from San Antonio. The men were jubilant and light-hearted as a lot of school-boys, and with the exception of a feeling of jealousy among the foremen over the remudas, we were a gay crowd, turning night into day. But on the return of our employer, all frivolity ceased, and the ranch stood at attention. The only unfinished work was the division of the horses, and but a single day remained before the agreed time for starting. Jim Flood had met his employer at the station the night before, and while returning to the ranch, the two discussed the apportionment of the saddle stock. The next morning all the foremen were called together, when the drover said to his trail bosses:

"Boys, I suppose you are all anxious to get a good remuda for this summer's trip. Well, I've got them for you. The only question is, how can we distribute them equitably so that all interests will be protected. One herd may not have near the distance to travel that the others have. It would look unjust to give it the best horses, and yet it may have the most trouble. Our remudas last year were all picked animals. They had an easy year's work. With the exception of a few head, we have the same mounts and in much better condition than last year. This is about my idea of equalizing things. You four old foremen will use your remudas of last year. Then each of you six bosses select twenty-five head each of the Dodge horses, - turn and turn about. Add those to your old remudas, and cull back your surplus, allowing ten to the man, twelve to the foreman, and five extra to each herd in case of cripples or of galled backs. By this method, each herd will have two dozen prime saddlers, the pick of a thousand picked ones, and fit for any man who was ever in my employ. I'm breaking in two new foremen this year, and they shall have no excuse for not being mounted, and will divide the remainder. Now, take four men apiece and round up the saddle stock, and have everything in shape to go into camp to-night. I'll be present at the division, and I warn you all that I want no clashing."

A ranch remuda was driven in, and we saddled. There were about thirty thousand acres in the pasture, and by eleven o'clock everything was thrown together. The private horses of all the boys had been turned into a separate inclosure, and before the cutting out commenced, every mother's son, including Don Lovell, arrived at the round-up. There were no corrals on the ranch which would accommodate such a body of animals, and thus the work had to be done in the open; but with the force at hand we threw a cordon around them, equal to a corral, and the cutting out to the four quarters commenced.

The horses were gentle and handled easily. Forrest and I turned to and helped our old foreman cut out his remuda of the year before. There were several horses in my old mount that I would have liked to have again, but I knew it was useless to try and trade Jim out of them, as he knew their qualities and would have robbed me in demanding their equivalent. When the old remudas were again separated, they were counted and carefully looked over by both foremen and men, and were open to the inspection of all who cared to look. Everything was passing very pleasantly, and the cutting of the extra twenty-five began. Then my selfishness was weighed in the balance and found to be full weight. I had ridden over a hundred of the best of them, but when any one appealed to me, even my own dear brother, I was as dumb as an oyster about a horse. Tolleston, especially, cursed, raved, and importuned me to help him get a good private mount, but I was as innocent as I was immovable. The trip home from Dodge was no pleasure jaunt, and now I was determined to draw extra pay in getting the cream of that horse herd. There were other features governing my actions: Flood was indifferent; Forrest, at times, was cruel to horses, and had I helped my brother, I might have been charged with favoritism. Dave Sponsilier was a good horseman, as his selections proved, and I was not wasting any love and affection on Archie Tolleston that day, anyhow.

That no undue advantage should be taken, Lovell kept tally of every horse cut out, and once each foreman had taken his number, he was waved out of the herd. I did the selecting of my own, and with the assistance of one man, was constantly waiting my turn. With all the help he could use, Tolleston was over half an hour making his selections, and took the only blind horse in the entire herd. He was a showy animal, a dapple gray, fully fifteen hands high, bred in north Texas, and belonged to one of the whole remudas bought in Dodge. At the time of his purchase, neither Lovell nor Flood detected anything wrong, and no one could see anything in the eyeball which would indicate he was moon-eyed. Yet any horseman need only notice him closely to be satisfied of his defect, as he was constantly shying from other horses and objects and smelled everything which came within his reach. There were probably half a dozen present who knew of his blindness, but not a word was said until all the extras were chosen and the culling out of the overplus of the various remudas began. It started in snickers, and before the cutting back was over developed into peals of laughter, as man after man learned that the dapple gray in Tolleston's remuda was blind.

Among the very last to become acquainted with the fact was the trail foreman himself. After watching the horse long enough to see his mistake, Tolleston culled the gray back and rode into the herd to claim another. But the drover promptly summoned his foreman out, and, as they met, Lovell said to his trail boss, "Arch, you're no better than anybody else. I bought that gray and paid my good money for him. No doubt but the man who sold him has laughed about it often since, and if ever we meet, I'll take my hat off and compliment him on being the only person who ever sold me a moon-eyed horse. I'm still paying my tuition, and you needn't flare up when the laugh's on you. You have a good remuda without him, and the only way you can get another horse out of that herd is with the permission of Quince Forrest and Tom Quirk."

"Well, if the permission of those new foremen is all I lack, then I'll cut all the horses I want," retorted Tolleston, and galloped back towards the herd. But Quince and I were after him like a flash, followed leisurely by Lovell. As he slacked his mount to enter the mass of animals, I passed him, jerking the bridle reins from his hand. Throwing my horse on his haunches, I turned just as Forrest slapped Tolleston on the back, and said: "Look-ee here, Arch; just because you're a little hot under the collar, don't do anything brash, for fear you may regret it afterward. I'm due to take a little pasear myself this summer, and I always did like to be well mounted. Now, don't get your back up or attempt to stand up any bluffs, for I can whip you in any sized circle you can name. You never saw me burn powder, did you? Well, just you keep on acting the d --- fool if you want a little smoke thrown in your face. Just fool with me and I'll fog you till you look like an angel in the clouds."

But old man Don reached us, and raised his hand. I threw the reins back over the horse's head. Tolleston was white with rage, but before he could speak our employer waved us aside and said, "Tom, you and Quince clear right out of here and I'll settle this matter. Arch, there's your remuda. Take it and go about your business or say you don't want to. Now, we know each other, and I'll not mince or repeat any words with you. Go on."

"Not an inch will I move until I get another horse," hissed Tolleston between gasps. "If it lies between you and me, then I'll have one in place of that gray, or you'll get another foreman. Now, you have my terms and ticket."

"Very well then, Archie; that changes the programme entirely," replied Lovell, firmly. "You'll find your private horse in the small pasture, and we'll excuse you for the summer. Whenever a man in my employ gets the impression that I can't get along without him, that moment he becomes useless to me. It seems that you are bloated with that idea, and a season's rest and quiet may cool you down and make a useful man of you again. Remember that you're always welcome at my ranch, and don't let this make us strangers," he called back as he turned away.

Riding over with us to where a group were sitting on their horses, our employer scanned the crowd without saying a word. Turning halfway in his saddle, he looked over towards Flood's remuda and said: "One of you boys please ride over and tell Paul I want him." During the rather embarrassing interim, the conversation instantly changed, and we borrowed tobacco and rolled cigarettes to kill time.

Priest was rather slow in making his appearance, riding leisurely, but on coming up innocently inquired of his employer, "Did you want to see me?"

"Yes. Paul, I've just lost one of my foremen. I need a good reliable man to take a herd to Fort Washakie. It's an Indian agency on the head waters of the North Platte in Wyoming. Will you tackle the job?"

"A good soldier is always subject to orders," replied The Rebel with a military salute. "If you have a herd for delivery in Wyoming, give me the men and horses, and I'll put the cattle there if possible. You are the commandant in the field, and I am subject to instructions."

"There's your remuda and outfit, then," said Lovell, pointing to the one intended for Tolleston, "and you'll get a commissary at the ranch and go into camp this evening. You'll get your herd in Nueces County, and Jim will assist in the receiving. Any other little details will all be arranged before you get away."

Calling for all the men in Tolleston's outfit, the two rode away for that remuda. Shortly before the trouble arose, our employer instructed those with the Buford cattle to take ten extra horses for each herd. There were now over a hundred and forty head to be culled back, and Sponsilier was entitled to ten of them. In order to be sure of our numbers, we counted the remaining band, and Forrest and I trimmed them down to two hundred and fifty-four head. As this number was too small to be handled easily in the open, we decided to take them into the corrals for the final division. After the culling back was over, and everything had started for the ranch, to oblige Sponsilier, I remained behind and helped him to retrim his remuda. Unless one knew the horses personally, it was embarrassing even to try and pick ten of the best ones from the overplus. But I knew many of them at first hand, and at Dave's request, after picking out the extra ones, continued selecting others in exchange for horses in his old band. We spent nearly an hour cutting back and forth, or until we were both satisfied that his saddle stock could not be improved from the material at hand.

The ranch headquarters were fully six miles from the round-up. Leaving Sponsilier delighted with the change in his remuda, I rode to overtake the undivided band which were heading for the ranch corrals. On coming up with them, Forrest proposed that we divide the horses by a running cut in squads of ten, and toss for choice. Once they were in the corrals, this could have been easily done by simply opening a gate and allowing blocks of ten to pass alternately from the main into smaller inclosures. But I was expecting something like this from Quince, and had entirely different plans of my own. Forrest and I were good friends, but he was a foxy rascal, and I had never wavered in my determination to get the pick of that horse herd. Had I accepted his proposal, the chance of a spinning coin might have given him a decided advantage, and I declined his proposition. I had a remuda in sight that my very being had hungered for, and now I would take no chance of losing it. But on the other hand, I proposed to Forrest that he might have the assistance of two men in Flood's outfit who had accompanied the horse herd home from Dodge. In the selecting of Jim's extra twenty-five, the opinion of these two lads, as the chosen horses proved, was a decided help to their foreman. But Quince stood firm, and arguing the matter, we reached the corrals and penned the band.

The two top bunches were held separate and were left a mile back on the prairie, under herd. The other remudas were all in sight of the ranch, while a majority of the men were eating a late dinner. Still contending for his point, Forrest sent a lad to the house to ask our employer to come over to the corrals. On his appearance, accompanied by Flood, each of us stated our proposition.

"Well, the way I size this up," said old man Don, "one of you wants to rely on his own judgment and the other don't. It looks to me, Quince, you want a gambler's chance where you can't lose. Tom's willing to bank on his own judgment, but you ain't. Now, I like a man who does his own thinking, and to give you a good lesson in that line, why, divide them, horse and horse, turn about. Now, I'll spin this coin for first pick, and while it's in the air, Jim will call the turn. . . . Tom wins first choice."

"That's all right, Mr. Lovell," said Quince, smilingly. "I just got the idea that you wanted the remudas for the Buford herds to be equally good. How can you expect it when Tom knows every horse and I never saddled one of them. Give me the same chance, and I might know them as well as the little boy knew his pap."

"You had the same chance," I put in, "but didn't want it. You were offered the Pine Ridge horses last year to take back to

Dodge, and you kicked like a bay steer. But I swallowed their dust to the Arkansaw, and from there home we lived in clouds of alkali. You went home drunk and dressed up, with a cigar in your mouth and your feet through the car window, claiming you was a brother-in-law to Jay Gould, and simply out on a tour of inspection. Now you expect me to give you the benefit of my experience and rob myself. Not this summer, John Quincy."

But rather than let Forrest feel that he was being taken advantage of, I repeated my former proposition. Accepting it as a last resort, the two boys were sent for and the dividing commenced. Remounting our horses, we entered the large corral, and as fast as they were selected the different outfits were either roped or driven singly through a guarded gate. It took over an hour of dusty work to make the division, but when it was finished I had a remuda of a hundred and fifty-two saddle horses that would make a man willing to work for his board and the privilege of riding them. Turning out of the corrals, Priest and I accompanied the horses out on the prairie where our toppy ones were being grazed. Paul was tickled over my outfit of saddle stock, but gave me several hints that he was entitled to another picked mount. I attempted to explain that he had a good remuda, but he still insisted, and I promised him if he would be at my wagon the next morning when we corralled, he should have a good one. I could well afford to be generous with my old bunkie.

There now only remained the apportionment of the work-stock. Four mules were allowed to the wagon, and in order to have them in good condition they had been grain-fed for the past month. In their allotment the Buford herds were given the best teams, and when mine was pointed out by my employer, the outfit assisted the cook to harness in. Giving him instructions to go into camp on a creek three miles south of headquarters, my wagon was the second one to get away. Some of the teams bolted at the start, and only for timely assistance Sponsilier's commissary would have been overturned in the sand. Two of the wagons headed west for Uvalde, while my brother Bob's started southeast for Bee County. The other two belonging to Flood and The Rebel would camp on the same creek as mine, their herds being also south. Once the wagons were off, the saddle stock was brought in and corralled for our first mounts. The final allotment of horses to the men would not take place until the herds were ready to be received, and until then, they would be ridden uniformly but promiscuously. With instructions from our employer to return to the ranch after making camp, the remudas were started after the wagons.

On our return after darkness, the ranch was as deserted as a school-house on Saturday. A Mexican cook and a few regular ranch hands were all that were left. Archie Tolleston had secured his horse and quit headquarters before any one had even returned from the round-up. When the last of the foremen came in, our employer delivered his final messages. "Boys," said he, "I'll only detain you a few minutes. I'm going west in the morning to Uvalde County, and will be present at the receiving of Quince and Dave's herds. After they start, I'll come back to the city and take stage to Oakville. But you go right ahead and receive your cattle, Bob, for we don't know what may turn up. Flood will help Tom first, and then Paul, to receive their cattle. That will give the Buford herds the first start, and I'll be waiting for you at Abilene when you reach there. And above all else, boys, remember that I've strained my credit in this drive, and that the cattle must be A 1, and that we must deliver them on the spot in prime condition. Now, that's all, but you'd better be riding so as to 'get an early start in the morning."

Our employer walked with us to the outer gate where our horses stood at the hitch-rack. That he was reticent in his business matters was well known among all his old foremen, including Forrest and myself. If he had a confidant among his men, Jim Flood was the man - and there were a few things he did not know. As we mounted our horses to return to our respective camps, old man Don quietly took my bridle reins in hand and allowed the others to ride away. "I want a parting word with you, Tom," said he a moment later. "Something has happened to-day which will require the driving of the Buford herds in some road brand other than the 'Circle Dot.' The first blacksmith shop you pass, have your irons altered into 'Open A's,' and I'll do the same with Quince and Dave's brands. Of the why or wherefore of this, say nothing to any one, as no one but myself knows. Don't breathe a word even to Flood, for he don't know any more than he should. When the time comes, if it ever does, you'll know all that is necessary - or nothing. That's all."

CHAPTER III.

RECEIVING AT LOS LOBOS

The trip to Lasalle County was mere pastime. All three of the outfits kept in touch with each other, camping far enough apart to avoid any conflict in night-herding the remudas. The only incident to mar the pleasure of the outing was the discovery of ticks in many of our horses' ears. The pasture in which they had wintered was somewhat brushy, and as there had been no frost to kill insect life, myriads of seed-ticks had dropped from the mesquite thickets upon the animals when rubbing against or passing underneath them. As the inner side of a horse's ear is both warm and tender, that organ was frequently infested with this pest, whose ravages often undermined the supporting cartilages and produced the drooping or "gotch" ear. In my remuda over one half the horses were afflicted with ticks, and many of them it was impossible to bridle, owing to the inflamed condition of their ears. Fortunately we had with us some standard preparations for blistering, so, diluting this in axle-grease, we threw every animal thus affected and thoroughly swabbed his ears. On reaching the Nueces River, near the western boundary of Lasalle County, the other two outfits continued on down that stream for their destination in the lower country. Flood remained behind with me, and going into camp on the river with my outfit, the two of us rode over to Los Lobos Ranch and announced ourselves as ready to receive the cattle. Dr. Beaver, the seller of the herd, was expecting us, and sending word of our arrival to neighboring cowmen, we looked over the corrals before returning to camp. They had built a new branding-chute and otherwise improved their facilities for handling cattle. The main inclosure had been built of heavy palisades in an early day, but recently several of smaller sized lumber had been added, making the most complete corrals I had ever seen. An abundance of wood was at hand for heating the branding-irons, and every little detail to facilitate the work had been provided for. Giving notice that we would receive every morning on the open prairie only, we declined an invitation to remain at the ranch and returned to my wagon.

In the valley the grass was well forward. We had traveled only some twenty miles a day coming down, and our horses had fared well. But as soon as we received any cattle, night-herding the remuda would cease, and we must either hobble or resort to other measures. John Levering was my horse-wrangler. He had made two trips over the trail with Fant's herds in the same capacity, was careful, humane, and an all-round horseman. In employing a cook, I had given the berth to Neal Parent, an old boyhood chum of mine. He never amounted to much as a cow-hand, but was a lighthearted, happy fool; and as cooking did not require much sense, I gave him the chance to make his first trip. Like a court jester, he kept the outfit in fine spirits and was the butt of all jokes. In entertaining company he was in a class by himself, and spoke with marked familiarity of all the prominent cowmen in southern Texas. To a stranger the inference might be easily drawn that Lovell was in his employ.

As we were expecting to receive cattle on the third day, the next morning the allotment of horses was made. The usual custom of giving the foreman first choice was claimed, and I cut twelve of solid colors but not the largest ones. Taking turns, the outfit roped out horse after horse until only the ten extra ones were left. In order that these should bear a fair share in the work, I took one of them for a night-horse and allotted the others to the second, third, and last guard in a similar capacity. This gave the last three watches two horses apiece for night work, but with the distinct understanding that in case of accident or injury to any horse in the remuda, they could be recalled. There was little doubt that before the summer ended, they would be claimed to fill vacancies in the regular mounts.

Flood had kept behind only two horses with which to overtake the other outfits, and during his stay with us would ride these extras and loans from my mount.

The entire morning was spent working with the remuda. Once a man knew his mount, extra attention was shown each horse. There were witches' bridles to be removed from their manes, extra long tails were thinned out to the proper length, and all hoofs trimmed short. The horses were fast shedding their winter coats, matting the saddle blankets with falling hair, and unless carefully watched, galled backs would result. The branding-irons had been altered en route, and about noon a vaquero came down the river and reported that the second round-up of the day would meet just over the county line in Dimmit. He belonged at Los Lobos, and reported the morning rodeo as containing over five hundred beeves, which would be ready for delivery at our pleasure. We made him remain for dinner, after which Flood and I saddled up and returned with him. We reached the round-up just as the cutting-out finished. They were a fine lot of big rangy beeves, and Jim suggested that we pass upon them at once. The seller agreed to hold them overnight, and Flood and I culled back about one hundred and twenty which were under age or too light. The round-up outfit strung the cattle out and counted them, reporting a few over seven hundred head. This count was merely informal and for the information of the seller; but in the morning the final one would be made, in which we could take a hand.

After the cut had started in for the ranch, we loitered along, looking them over, and I noticed several that might have been thrown out. "Well, now," said Flood, "if you are going to be so very choice as all that, I might as well ride on. You can't use me if that bunch needs any more trimming. I call them a fine lot of beeves. It's all right for Don to rib the boys up and make them think that the cattle have to be top-notchers. I've watched him receive too often; he's about the easiest man I know to ring in short ages on. Just so a steer looks nice, it's hard for the old man to turn one back. I've seen him receiving three-year-olds, when one fourth of the cattle passed on were short twos. And if you call his attention to one, he'll just smile that little smile of his, and say, 'yes, he may be shy a few months, but he'll grow.' But then that's just old man Don's weakness for cattle; he can't look a steer in the face without falling in love with him. Now, I've received before when by throwing out one half the stock offered, you couldn't get as uniform a bunch of beeves as those are. But you go right ahead, Tom, and be sure that every hoof you accept will dress five hundred pounds at Fort Buford. I'll simply sit around and clerk and help you count and give you a good chance to make a reputation."

Los Lobos was still an open range. They claimed to have over ten thousand mixed cattle in the straight ranch brand. There had been no demand for matured beeves for several years, and now on effecting this sale they were anxious to deliver all their grown steers. Dr. Beaver informed us that, previous to our arrival, his foreman had been throwing everything in on the home range, and that he hoped to deliver to us over two thousand head from his own personal holdings. But he was liberal with his neighbors, for in the contingent just passed upon, there must have been over a hundred head in various ranch brands. Assuring him that we would be on hand in the morning to take possession of the cattle, and requesting him to have a fire burning, on coming opposite the camp, we turned off and rode for our wagon. It meant a big day's work to road-brand this first contingent, and with the first sign of dawn, my outfit were riding for Los Lobos. We were encamped about three miles from the corrals, and leaving orders for the cook to follow up, the camp was abandoned with the exception of the remuda. It was barely sun-up when we counted and took possession of the beeves. On being relieved, the foreman of Los Lobos took the ranch outfit and started off to renew the gathering. We penned the cattle without any trouble, and as soon as the irons were ready, a chuteful were run in and the branding commenced. This branding-chute was long enough to chamber eight beeves. It was built about a foot wide at the bottom and flared upward just enough to prevent an animal from turning round. A heavy gate closed the exit, while bull-bars at the rear prevented the occupant from backing out. A high platform ran along either side of the branding-chute, on which the men stood while handling the irons.

Two men did the branding. "Runt" Pickett attended the fire, passing up the heated irons, and dodging the cold branding-steel. A single iron was often good for several animals, and sometimes a chuteful was branded with two irons. It was necessary that the work should be well done; not that a five months' trip required it, but the unforeseen must be guarded against. Many trail herds had met disaster and been scattered to the four winds with nothing but a road brand to identify them afterward. The cattle were changing owners, and custom decreed that an abstract of title should be indelibly seared on their sides. The first guard, Jake Blair, Morg Tussler, and Clay Zilligan, were detailed to cut and drive the squads into the chute. These three were the only mounted men, the others being placed so as to facilitate the work. Cattle are as innocent as they are strong, and in this necessary work everything was done quietly, care being taken to prevent them from becoming excited. As fast as they were released from the chute, Dr. Beaver took a list of the ranch brands, in order to bill of sale them to Lovell and settle with his neighbors.

The work moved with alacrity. As one chuteful was being freed the next one was entering. Gates closed in their faces and the bull-bars at the rear locked them as in a vice. We were averaging a hundred an hour, but the smoke from the burning hair was offensive to the lungs. During the forenoon Burl Van Vedder and Vick Wolf "spelled" Flood and myself for half an hour at a time, or until we could recover from the nauseous fumes. When the cook called us to dinner, we had turned out nearly five hundred branded cattle. No sooner was the midday meal bolted than the cook was ordered back to camp with his wagon, the branded contingent of cattle following in charge of the first guard. Less than half an hour was lost in refreshing the inner man, and ordering "G - G" Cederdall, Tim Stanley, and Jack Splann of the second guard into their saddles to take the place of the relieved men, we resumed our task. The dust of the corrals settled on us unheeded, the smoke of the fire mingled with that of the singeing hair and its offensive odors, bringing tears to our eyes, but the work never abated until the last steer had passed the chute and bore the "Open A."

The work over, a pretense was made at washing the dust and grime from our faces. It was still early in the day, and starting the cattle for camp, I instructed the boys to water and graze them as long as they would stand up. The men all knew their places on guard, this having been previously arranged; and joining Dr. Beaver, Jim and I rode for the ranch about a mile distant. The doctor was a genial host, and prescribed a series of mint-juleps, after which he proposed that we ride out and meet the cattle gathered during the day. The outfit had been working a section of country around some lagoons, south of the ranch, and it was fully six o'clock when we met them, heading homeward. The cattle were fully up to the standard of the first bunch, and halting the herd we trimmed them down and passed on them. After Flood rode out of this second contingent, I culled back about a dozen light weights. On finishing, Jim gave me a quiet wink, and said something to Dr. Beaver about a new broom. But I paid no attention to these remarks; in a country simply teeming with prime beeves, I was determined to get a herd to my liking. Dr. Beaver had assured Lovell that he and his neighbors would throw together over four thousand beeves in making up the herd, and now I was perfectly willing that they should. It would take two days longer to gather the cattle on the Los Lobos range, and then there were the outside offerings, which were supposed to number fully two thousand. There was no excuse for not being choice.

On returning to Los Lobos about dusk, rather than offend its owner, Flood consented to remain at the ranch overnight, but I rode for camp. Darkness had fallen on my reaching the wagon, the herd had been bedded down, and Levering felt so confident that the remuda was contented that he had concluded to night-herd them himself until midnight, and then turn them loose until dawn. He had belled a couple of the leaders, and assured me that he would have them in hand before sun-up. The cook was urging me to supper, but before unsaddling, I rode around both herd and remuda. The cattle were sleeping nicely, and the boys assured me that they had got a splendid fill on them before bedding down. That was the only safe thing to do, and after circling the saddle stock on the opposite side of camp, I returned to find that a stranger had arrived during my brief absence. Parent had fully enlightened him as to who he was, who the outfit were, the destination of the herd, the names of both buyer and seller, and, on my riding in, was delivering a voluble dissertation on the tariff and the possible effect on the state of putting hides on the free list. And although in cow-camps a soldier's introduction is usually sufficient, the cook inquired the stranger's name and presented me to our guest with due formality. Supper being waiting, the stranger was invited to take pot-luck with us, and before the meal was over recognized me. He was a deputy cattle inspector for Dimmit County, and had issued the certificate for Flood's herd the year before. He had an eye for the main chance, and informed me that fully one half the cattle making up our herd belonged to Dimmit; that the county line was only a mile up the river, and that if I would allow the herd to drift over into his territory, he would shade the legal rate. The law compelling the inspection of herds before they could be moved out of the county, like the rain, fell upon the just and the unjust. It was not the intent of the law to impose a burden on an honest drover. Yet he was classed with the rustler, and must have in his possession a certificate of inspection before he could move out a purchased herd, or be subject to arrest. A list of brands was recorded, at the county seat, of every herd leaving, and if occasion required could be referred to in future years. No railroad would receive any consignment of hides or live stock, unless accompanied by a certificate from the county inspector. The legal rate was ten cents on the first hundred, and three cents on all over that number, frequently making the office a lucrative one.

Once the object of his call was made clear, I warmed to our

guest. If the rate allowed by law was enforced, it meant an expense of over a hundred dollars for a certificate of inspection covering both herd and saddle stock. We did not take out certificates in Medina on the remudas as a matter of economy. By waiting until the herd was ready, the two would be inspected as one, and the lower rate apply. So I urged the deputy to make himself at home and share my blankets Pretending that I remembered him well, I made numerous inquiries about the ranch where we received our herd the year before, and by the time to turn in, we were on the most friendly terms. The next morning I offered him a horse from our extras, assuring him that Flood would be delighted to renew his acquaintance, and invited him to go with us for the day. Turning his horse among ours, he accepted and rode away with us. The cattle passed on the evening before had camped out several miles from the corrals and were grazing in when we met them. Flood and the Doctor joined us shortly afterward, and I had a quiet word with Jim before he and the inspector met. After the count was over, Flood made a great ado over my guest and gave him the glad hand as if he had been a long-lost brother. We were a trifle short-handed the second day, and on my guest volunteering to help, I assigned him to Runt Pickert's place at the fire, where he shortly developed a healthy sweat. As we did not have a large bunch of beeves to brand that day, the wagon did not come over and we branded them at a single shift. It was nearly one o'clock when we finished, and instead of going in to Los Lobos, we left the third guard, Wayne Outcault, "Dorg" Seay, and Owen Ubery, to graze the cattle over to our camp.

The remainder of the afternoon was spent in idleness and in the entertainment of our guest. Official-like, he pretended he could hardly spare the time to remain another night, but was finally prevailed on and did so. After dark, I took him some distance from camp, and the two of us had a confidential chat. I assured him if there was any object in doing so, we could move camp right to or over the county line, and frankly asked him what inducement he would offer. At first he thought that throwing off everything over a hundred dollars would be about right. But I assured him that there were whole families of inspectors in Lasalle County who would discount that figure, and kindly advised him, if he really wanted the fee, to meet competition at least. We discussed the matter at length, and before returning to camp, he offered to make out the certificate, covering everything, for fifty dollars. As it was certain to be several days yet before we would start, and there was a prospect of a falling market in certificates of inspection, I would make no definite promises. The next morning I insisted that he remain at some near-by ranch in his own territory, and, if convenient, ride down every few days and note the progress of the herd.

We were promised a large contingent of cattle for that day. The ranch outfit were to make three rodeos down the river the day before, where the bulk of their beeves ranged. Flood was anxious to overtake the other outfits before they reached the lower country, and as he assured me I had no further use for him, we agreed that after receiving that morning he might leave us. Giving orders at camp to graze the received beeves within a mile of the corrals by noon, and the wagon to follow, we made an early start, Flood taking his own horses with him. We met the cattle coming up the river a thousand strong. It was late when the last round-up of the day before had finished, and they had camped for the night fully five miles from the corrals. It took less than an hour to cull back and count, excuse the ranch outfit, and start this contingent for the branding-pens in charge of my boys. Flood was in a hurry, and riding a short distance with him, I asked that he pass or send word to the county seat, informing the inspector of hides and animals that a trail herd would leave Los Lobos within a week. Jim knew my motive in getting competition on the inspection, and wishing me luck on my trip, I wrung his hand in farewell until we should meet again in the upper country.

The sun was setting that night when we finished road-branding the last of the beeves received in the morning. After dinner, when the wagon returned to camp, I instructed Parent to move up the river fully a mile. We needed the change, anyhow, and even if it was farther, the next morning we would have the Los Lobos outfit to assist in the branding, as that day would finish their gathering. The outside cattle were beginning to report in small bunches, from three hundred upward. Knowing that Dr. Beaver was anxious to turn in as many as possible of his own, we delayed receiving from the neighboring ranches for another day. But the next morning, as we were ironing-up the last contingent of some four hundred Los Lobos beeves, a deputy inspector for Lasalle arrived from the county seat. He was likewise officious, and professed disappointment that the herd was not ready to pass upon. On his arrival, I was handling the irons, and paid no attention to him until the branding was over for the morning. When he introduced himself, I cordially greeted him, but at the first intimation of disappointment from his lips, I checked him.

Using the best diplomacy at my command, I said, "Well, I'm sorry to cause you this long ride when it might have been avoided. You see, we are receiving cattle from both this and Dimmit County. In fact, we are holding our herd across the line just at present. On starting, we expect to go up the river to the first creek, and north on it to the Leona River. I have partially promised the work to an inspector from Dimmit. He inspected our herd last year, and being a personal friend that way, you couldn't meet his figures. Very sorry to disappoint you, but won't you come over to the wagon and stay all night?"

But Dr. Beaver, who understood my motive, claimed the privilege of entertaining the deputy at Los Lobos, and I yielded. We now had a few over twenty-four hundred beeves, of which nineteen hundred were in the Los Lobos brand, the others being mixed. There was a possibility of fully a hundred more coming in with the neighboring cattle, and Dr. Beaver was delighted over the ranch delivery. The outside contingents were in four bunches, then encamped in different directions and within from three to five miles of the ranch. Taking Vick Wolf with me for the afternoon, I looked over the separate herds and found them numbering more than fifteen hundred.

They were the same uniform Nueces Valley cattle, and as we lacked only a few over a thousand, the offerings were extremely liberal. Making arrangements with three of the four herds to receive the next day, Vick and I reached our camp on the county line about sunset. The change was a decided advantage; wood, water, and grass were plentiful, and not over a mile farther from the branding-pens.

The next morning found us in our saddles at the usual early hour. We were anxious to receive and brand every animal possible that day, so that with a few hours' work the next forenoon the herd would be ready to start. After we had passed on the first contingent of the outside cattle, and as we were nearing the corrals, Dr. Beaver overtook us. Calling me aside, he said: "Quirk, if you play your cards right, you'll get a certificate of inspection for nothing and a chromo as a pelon. I've bolstered up the Lasalle man that he's better entitled to the work than the Dimmit inspector, and he'll wait until the herd is ready to start. Now, you handle the one, and I'll keep the other as my guest. We must keep them apart and let them buck each other to their hearts' content. Every hoof in your herd will be in a ranch brand of record; but still the law demands inspection and you must comply with it. I'll give you a duplicate list of the brands, so that neither inspector need see the herd, and if we don't save your employer a hundred dollars, then we are amateurs."

Everything was pointing to an auspicious start. The last cattle on the delivery were equal to the first, if not better. The sky clouded over, and before noon a light shower fell, settling the dust in the corrals. Help increased as the various bunches were accepted, and at the end of the day only a few over two hundred remained to complete our numbers. The last contingent were fully up to the standard; and rather than disappoint the sellers, I accepted fifty head extra, making my herd at starting thirty-four hundred and fifty. When the last beef had passed the branding-chute, there was nothing remaining but to give a receipt to the seller for the number of head received, in behalf of my employer, pending a later settlement between them.

Meanwhile competition in the matter of inspection had been carefully nursed. Conscious of each other's presence, and both equally anxious for the fee, the one deputy was entertained at my camp and the other at Los Lobos. They were treated courteously, but given to understand that in the present instance money talked. With but a small bunch of beeves to brand on the starting day, the direction in which the herd was allowed to leave the bed-ground would be the final answer. If west, Dimmit had underbid Lasalle; if the contrary, then the departure of this herd would be a matter of record in the latter county. Dr. Beaver enjoyed the situation hugely, acting the intermediary in behalf of his guest. Personally I was unconcerned, but was neutral and had little to say.

My outfit understood the situation perfectly. Before retiring on the night of our last camp on the county line, and in the presence of the Dimmit inspector, the last relief received instructions, in the absence of contrary orders, to allow the herd to drift back into Lasalle in the morning. Matters were being conducted in pantomime, and the players understood their parts. Our guest had made himself useful in various ways, and I naturally felt friendly towards him. He had stood several guards for the boys, and Burl Van Vedder, of the last watch, had secret instructions to call him for that guard.

The next morning the camp was not astir as early as usual. On the cook's arousing us, in the uncertain light of dawn, the herd was slowly rising, and from the position of a group of four horsemen, it was plainly evident that our guest had shaded all competition. Our camp was in plain view of Los Lobos, and only some five or six miles distant. With the rising of the sun, and from the top of a windmill derrick, by the aid of a field-glass, the Lasalle inspector had read his answer; and after the work in the morning was over, and the final papers had been exchanged, Dr. Beaver insisted that, in commiseration of his departed guest, just one more mint-julep should be drunk standing.

When Don Lovell glanced over my expense account on our arrival at Abilene, he said: "Look here, Tom, is this straight ? - twenty dollars for inspection? - the hell you say! Corrupted them, did you? Well, that's the cheapest inspection I ever paid, with one exception. Dave Sponsilier once got a certificate for his herd for five dollars and a few drinks. But he paid for it a month in advance of the starting of the herd. It was dated ahead, properly sealed, and all ready for filling in the brands and numbers. The herd was put up within a mile of where four counties cornered, and that inspector was a believer in the maxim of the early bird. The office is a red-tape one, anyhow, and little harm in taking all the advantage you can. - This item marked 'sundries' was DRY goods, I suppose? All right, Quirk; I reckon rattlesnakes were rather rabid this spring."

CHAPTER IV.

MINGLING WITH THE EXODUS

By noon the herd had grazed out five miles on its way. The boys were so anxious to get off that on my return the camp was deserted with the exception of the cook and the horse-wrangler, none even returning for dinner. Before leaving I had lunched at Los Lobos with its owner, and on reaching the wagon, Levering and I assisted the cook to harness in and start the commissary. The general course of the Nueces River was southeast by northwest, and as our route lay on the latter angle, the herd would follow up the valley for the first day. Once outside the boundaries of our camp of the past week, the grass matted the ground with its rank young growth. As far as the eye could see, the mesas, clothed in the verdure of spring, rolled in long swells away to the divides. Along the river and in the first bottom, the timber and mesquite thickets were in leaf and blossom, while on the outlying prairies the only objects which dotted this sea of green were range cattle and an occasional band of horses.

The start was made on the 27th of March. By easy drives and within a week, we crossed the "Sunset" Railway, about thirty miles to the westward of the ranch in Medina. On reaching the divide between the Leona and Frio rivers, we sighted our first herd of trail cattle, heading northward. We learned that some six herds had already passed upward on the main Frio, while a number of others were reported as having taken the east fork of that river. The latter stream almost paralleled the line between Medina and Uvalde counties, and as we expected some word from headquarters, we crossed over to the east fork.

When westward of and opposite the ranch, Runt Pickett was sent in for any necessary orders that might be waiting. By leaving us early in the evening he could reach headquarters that night and overtake us before noon the next day. We grazed leisurely forward the next morning, killing as much time as possible, and Pickett overtook us before the wagon had even gone into camp for dinner. Lovell had not stopped on his return from the west, but had left with the depot agent at the home station a letter for the ranch. From its contents we learned that the other two Buford herds had started from Uvalde, Sponsilier in the lead, one on the 24th and the other the following day. Local rumors were encouraging in regard to grass and water to the westward, and the intimation was clear that if favorable reports continued, the two Uvalde herds would intersect an old trail running from the head of Nueces Canon to the Llano River. Should they follow this route there was little hope of their coming into the main western trail before reaching the Colorado River. Sponsilier was a daring fellow, and if there was a possible chance to get through beyond the borders of any settlement, he was certain to risk it.

The letter contained no personal advice. Years of experience in trail matters had taught my employer that explicit orders were often harmful. The emergencies to be met were of such a varied nature that the best method was to trust to an outfit worming its way out of any situation which confronted it. From the information disclosed, it was evident that the other Buford herds were then somewhere to the northwest, and possibly over a hundred miles distant. Thus freed from any restraint, we held a due northward course for several days, or until we encountered some rocky country. Water was plentiful and grass fairly good, but those flinty hills must be avoided or sorefooted beeves would be the result. I had seen trails of blood left by cattle from sandy countries on encountering rock, and now the feet of ours were a second consideration to their stomachs. But long before the herd reached this menace, Morg Tussler and myself, scouting two full days in advance, located a safe route to the westward. Had we turned to the other hand, we should have been forced into the main trail below

Fredericksburg, and we preferred the sea-room of the boundless plain. From every indication and report, this promised to be the banner year in the exodus of cattle from the South to the then new Northwest. This latter section was affording the long-looked-for outlet, by absorbing the offerings of cattle which came up from Texas over the trail, and marking an epoch barely covering a single decade.

Turning on a western angle, a week's drive brought us out on a high tableland. Veering again to the north, we snailed along through a delightful country, rich in flora and the freshness of the season. From every possible elevation, we scanned the west in the hope of sighting some of the herd which had followed up the main Frio, but in vain. Sweeping northward at a leisurely gait, the third week out we sighted the Blue Mountains, the first familiar landmark on our course. As the main western trail skirted its base on the eastward, our position was easily established.

So far the cattle were well behaved, not a run, and only a single incident occurring worth mention. About half an hour before dawn one morning, the cook aroused the camp with the report that the herd was missing. The beeves had been bedded within two hundred yards of the wagon, and the last watch usually hailed the rekindling of the cook's fire as the first harbinger of day. But on this occasion the absence of the usual salutations from the bed-ground aroused Parent's suspicion. He rushed into camp, and laboring under the impression that the cattle had stampeded, trampled over our beds, yelling at the top of his lungs. Aroused in the darkness from heavy sleep, bewildered by a bright fire burning and a crazy man shouting, "The beeves have stampeded! the herd's gone! Get up, everybody!" we were almost thrown into a panic. Many of the boys ran for their night-horses, but Clay Zilligan and I fell on the cook and shook the statement out of him that the cattle had left their beds. This simplified the situation, but before I could recall the men, several of them had reached the bed-ground. As fast as horses could be secured, others dashed through the lighted circle and faded into the darkness. From the flickering of matches it was evident that the boys were dismounting and looking for some sign of trouble. Zilligan was swearing like a pirate, looking for his horse in the murky night; but instead of any alarm, oaths and derision greeted our ears as the men returned to camp. Halting their horses within the circle of the fire, Dorg Seay said to the cook:

"Neal, the next time you find a mare's nest, keep the secret to yourself. I don't begrudge losing thirty minutes' beauty sleep, but I hate to be scared out of a year's growth. Haven't you got cow-sense enough to know that if those beeves had run, they'd have shook the earth? If they had stampeded, that alarm clock of yours wouldn't be a circumstance to the barking of the boys' guns. Why, the cattle haven't been gone thirty minutes. You can see where they got up and then quietly walked away. The ground where they lay is still steaming and warm. They were watered a little too soon yesterday and naturally got up early this morning. The boys on guard didn't want to alarm the outfit, and just allowed the beeves to graze off on their course. When day breaks, you'll see they ain't far away, and in the right direction. Parent, if I didn't sabe cows better than you do, I'd confine my attention to a cotton patch."

Seay had read the sign aright. When day dawned the cattle were in plain view about a mile distant. On the return of the last guard to camp, Vick Wolf explained the situation in a few words. During their watch the herd had grown restless, many of the cattle arising; and knowing that dawn was near at hand, the boys had pushed the sleepy ones off their beds and started them feeding. The incident had little effect on the irrepressible Parent, who seemed born to blunder, yet gifted with a sunny disposition which atoned for his numerous mistakes.

With the Blue Mountains as our guiding star, we kept to the westward of that landmark, crossing the Llano River opposite some Indian mounds. On reaching the divide between this and the next water, we sighted two dust-clouds to the westward. They were ten to fifteen miles distant, but I was anxious to hear any word of Sponsilier or Forrest, and sent Jake Blair to make a social call. He did not return until the next day, and reported the first herd as from the mouth of the Pecos, and the more distant one as belonging to Jesse Presnall. Blair had stayed all night with the latter, and while its foreman was able to locate at least a dozen trail herds in close proximity, our two from Uvalde had neither been seen nor heard of. Baffled again, necessity compelled us to turn within touch of some outfitting point. The staples of life were running low in our commissary, no opportunity having presented itself to obtain a new supply since we left the ranch in Medina over a month before. Consequently, after crossing the San Saba, we made our first tack to the eastward.

Brady City was an outfitting point for herds on the old western trail. On coming opposite that frontier village, Parent and I took the wagon and went in after supplies, leaving the herd on its course, paralleling the former route. They had instructions to camp on Brady Creek that night. On reaching the supply point, there was a question if we could secure the simple staples needed. The drive that year had outstripped all calculations, some half-dozen chuck-wagons being in waiting for the arrival of a freight outfit which was due that morning. The nearest railroad was nearly a hundred miles to the eastward, and all supplies must be freighted in by mule and ox teams. While waiting for the freight wagons, which were in sight several miles distant, I made inquiry of the two outfitting stores if our Buford herds had passed. If they had, no dealings had taken place on the credit of Don Lovell, though both merchants knew him well. Before the freight outfit arrived, some one took Abb Blocker, a trail foreman for his brother John, to task for having an odd ox in his wheel team. The animal was a raw, unbroken "7L" bull, surly and chafing under the yoke, and attracted general attention. When several friends of Blocker, noticing the brand, began joking him, he made this explanation: "No, I don't claim him; but he came into my herd the other night and got to hossing my steers around. We couldn't keep him out, and I thought if he would just go along, why we'd put him under the yoke and let him hoss that chuck-wagon to amuse himself. One of my wheelers was getting a little tenderfooted, anyhow."

On the arrival of the freight outfit, short shift was made in transferring a portion of the cargo to the waiting chuck-wagons. As we expected to reach Abilene, a railroad point, within a week, we took on only a small stock of staple supplies. Having helped ourselves, the only delay was in getting a clerk to look over our appropriation, make out an itemized bill, and receive a draft on my employer. When finally the merchant in person climbed into our wagon and took a list of the articles, Parent started back to overtake the herd. I remained behind several hours, chatting with the other foremen.

None of the other trail bosses had seen anything of Lovell's other herds, though they all knew him personally or by reputation, and inquired if he was driving again in the same road brand. By general agreement, in case of trouble, we would pick up each other's cattle; and from half a cent to a cent a head was considered ample remuneration in buying water in Texas. Owing to the fact that many drovers had shipped to Red River, it was generally believed that there would be no congestion of cattle south of that point. All herds were then keeping well to the westward, some even declaring their intention to go through the Panhandle until the Canadian was reached.

Two days later we came into the main trail at the crossing of the Colorado River. Before we reached it, several ominous dust-clouds hung on our right for hours, while beyond the river were others, indicating the presence of herds. Summer weather had already set in, and during the middle of the day the glare of heat-waves and mirages obstructed our view of other wayfarers like ourselves, but morning and evening we were never out of sight of their signals. The banks of the river at the ford were trampled to the level of the water, while at both approach and exit the ground was cut into dust. On our arrival, the stage of water was favorable, and we crossed without a halt of herd, horses, or commissary. But there was little inducement to follow the old trail. Washed into ruts by the seasons, the grass on either side eaten away for miles, there was a look of desolation like that to be seen in the wake of an army. As we felt under obligations to touch at Abilene within a few days, there was a constant skirmish for grass within a reasonable distance of the trail; and we were early, fully two thirds of the drive being in our rear. One sultry morning south of Buffalo Gap, as we were grazing past the foot of Table Mountain, several of us rode to the summit of that butte. From a single point of observation we counted twelve herds within a space of thirty miles both south and north, all moving in the latter direction.

When about midway between the Gap and the railroad we were met at noon one day by Don Lovell. This was his first glimpse of my herd, and his experienced eye took in everything from a broken harness to the peeling and legibility of the road brand. With me the condition of the cattle was the first requisite, but the minor details as well as the more important claimed my employer's attention. When at last, after riding with the herd for an hour, he spoke a few words of approbation on the condition, weight, and uniformity of the beeves, I felt a load lifted from my shoulders. That the old man was in a bad humor on meeting us was evident; but as he rode along beside the cattle, lazy and large as oxen, the cockles of his heart warmed and he grew sociable. Near the middle of the afternoon, as we were in the rear, looking over the drag steers, he complimented me on having the fewest tender-footed animals of any herd that had passed Abilene since his arrival. Encouraged, I ventured the double question as to how this one would average with the other Buford herds, and did he know their whereabouts. As I recall his reply, it was that all Nueces Valley cattle were uniform, and if there was any difference it was due to carelessness in receiving. In regard to the locality of the other herds, it was easily to be seen that he was provoked about something.

"Yes, I know where they are," said he, snappishly, "but that's all the good it does me. They crossed the railroad, west, at Sweetwater, about a week ago. I don't blame Quince, for he's just trailing along, half a day behind Dave's herd. But Sponsilier, knowing that I wanted to see him, had the nerve to write me a postal card with just ten words on it, saying that all was well and to meet him in Dodge. Tom, you don't know what a satisfaction it is to me to spend a day or so with each of the herds. But those rascals didn't pay any more attention to me than if I was an old woman. There was some reason for it - sore-footed cattle, or else they have skinned up their remudas and didn't want me to see them. If I drive a hundred herds hereafter, Dave Sponsilier will stay at home as far as I'm concerned. He may think it's funny to slip past, but this court isn't indulging in any levity just at present. I fail to see the humor in having two outfits with sixty-seven hundred cattle somewhere between the Staked Plain and No-Man's-Land, and unable to communicate with them. And while my herds are all contracted, mature beeves have broke from three to five dollars a head in price since these started, and it won't do to shout before we're out of the woods. Those fool boys don't know that, and I can't get near enough to tell them."

I knew better than to ask further questions or offer any apologies for others. My employer was naturally irritable, and his abuse or praise of a foreman was to be expected. Previously and under the smile of prosperity, I had heard him laud Sponsilier, and under an imaginary shadow abuse Jim Flood, the most experienced man in his employ. Feeling it was useless to pour oil on the present troubled waters, I excused myself, rode back, and ordered the wagon to make camp ahead about four miles on Elm Creek. We watered late in the afternoon, grazing thence until time to bed the herd. When the first and second guards were relieved to go in and catch night-horses and get their supper, my employer remained behind with the cattle. While feeding during the evening, we allowed the herd to scatter over a thousand acres. Taking advantage of the loose order of the beeves, the old man rode back and forth through them until approaching darkness compelled us to throw them together on the bedground. Even after the first guard took charge, the drover loitered behind, reluctant to leave until the last steer had lain down; and all during the night, sharing my blankets, he awoke on every change of guards, inquiring of the returning watch how the cattle were sleeping.

As we should easily pass Abilene before noon, I asked him as a favor that he take the wagon in and get us sufficient supplies to last until Red River was reached. But he preferred to remain behind with the herd, and I went instead. This suited me, as his presence overawed my outfit, who were delirious to see the town. There was no telling how long he would have stayed with us, but my brother Bob's herd was expected at any time. Remaining with us a second night, something, possibly the placidness of the cattle, mellowed the old man and he grew amiable with the outfit, and myself in particular. At breakfast the next morning, when I asked him if he was in a position to recommend any special route, he replied:

"No, Tom, that rests with you. One thing's certain; herds are going to be dangerously close together on the regular trail which crosses Red River at Doan's. The season is early yet, but over fifty herds have already crossed the Texas Pacific Railway. Allowing one half the herds to start north of that line, it gives you a fair idea what to expect. When seven hundred thousand cattle left Texas two years ago, it was considered the banner year, yet it won't be a marker to this one. The way prices are tumbling shows that the Northwest was bluffing when they offered to mature all the cattle that Texas could breed for the next fifty years. That's the kind of talk that suits me, but last year there were some forty herds unsold, which were compelled to winter in the North. Not over half the saddle horses that came up the trail last summer were absorbed by these Northern cowmen. Talk's cheap, but it takes money to buy whiskey. Lots of these men are new ones at the business and may lose fortunes. The banks are getting afraid of cattle paper, and conditions are tightening. With the increased drive this year, if the summer passes without a slaughter in prices, the Texas drovers can thank their lucky stars. I'm not half as bright as I might be, but this is one year that I'm smooth enough not to have unsold cattle on the trail."

The herd had started an hour before, and when the wagon was ready to move, I rode a short distance with my employer. It was possible that he had something to say of a confidential nature, for it was seldom that he acted so discouraged when his every interest seemed protected by contracts. But at the final parting, when we both had dismounted and sat on the ground for an hour, he had disclosed nothing. On the contrary, he even admitted that possibly it was for the best that the other Buford herds had held a westward course and thus avoided the crush on the main routes. The only intimation which escaped him was when we had remounted and each started our way, he called me back and said, "Tom, no doubt but you've noticed that I'm worried. Well, I am. I'd tell you in a minute, but I may be wrong in the matter. But I'll know before you reach Dodge, and then, if it's necessary, you shall know all. It's nothing about the handling of the herds, for my foremen have always considered my interests first. Keep this to yourself, for it may prove a nightmare. But if it should prove true, then we must stand together. Now, that's all; mum's the word until we meet. Drop me a line if you get a chance, and don't let my troubles worry you."

While overtaking the herd, I mused over my employer's last words. But my brain was too muddy even to attempt to solve the riddle. The most plausible theory that I could advance was that some friendly cowmen were playing a joke on him, and that the old man had taken things too seriously. Within a week the matter was entirely forgotten, crowded out of mind by the demands of the hour. The next night, on the Clear Fork of the Brazos, a stranger, attracted by our camp-fire, rode up to the wagon. Returning from the herd shortly after his arrival, I recognized in our guest John Blocker, a prominent drover. He informed us that he and his associates had fifty-two thousand cattle on the trail, and that he was just returning from overtaking two of their five lead herds. Knowing that he was a well-posted cowman on routes and sustenance, having grown up on the trail, I gave him the best our camp afforded, and in return I received valuable information in regard to the country between our present location and Doan's Crossing. He reported the country for a hundred miles south of Red River as having had a dry, backward spring, scanty of grass, and with long dry drives; and further, that in many instances water for the herds would have to be bought from those in control.

The outlook was not to my liking. The next morning when I inquired of our guest what he would advise me to do, his answer clearly covered the ground. "Well, I'm not advising any one," said he, "but you can draw your own conclusions. The two herds of mine, which I overtook, have orders to turn northeast and cross into the Nations at Red River Station. My other cattle, still below, will all be routed by way of Fort Griffin. Once across Red River, you will have the Chisholm Trail, running through civilized tribes, and free from all annoyance of blanket Indians. South of the river the grass is bound to be better than on the western route, and if we have to buy water, we'll have the advantage of competition."

With this summary of the situation, a decision was easily reached. The Chisholm Trail was good enough for me. Following up the north side of the Clear Fork, we passed about twenty miles to the west of Fort Griffin. Constantly bearing east by north, a few days later we crossed the main Brazos at a low stage of water. But from there to Red River was a trial not to be repeated. Wire fences halted us at every turn. Owners of pastures refused permission to pass through. Lanes ran in the wrong direction, and open country for pasturage was scarce. What we dreaded most, lack of drink for the herd, was the least of our troubles, necessity requiring its purchase only three or four times. And like a climax to a week of sore trials, when we were in sight of Red River a sand and dust storm struck us, blinding both men and herd for hours. The beeves fared best, for with lowered heads they turned their backs to the howling gale, while the horsemen caught it on every side. The cattle drifted at will in an uncontrollable mass. The air was so filled with sifting sand and eddying dust that it was impossible to see a mounted man at a distance of fifty yards. The wind blew a hurricane, making it impossible to dismount in the face of it. Our horses trembled with fear, unsteady on their feet. The very sky overhead darkened as if night was falling. Two thirds of the men threw themselves in the lead of the beeves, firing six-shooters to check them, which could not even be heard by the ones on the flank and in the rear. Once the herd drifted against a wire fence, leveled it down and moved on, sullen but irresistible. Towards evening the storm abated, and half the outfit was sent out in search of the wagon, which was finally found about dark some four miles distant.

That night Owen Ubery, as he bathed his bloodshot eyes in a pail of water, said to the rest of us: "Fellows, if ever I have a boy, and tell him how his pa suffered this afternoon, and he don't cry, I'll cut a switch and whip him until he does."

CHAPTER V.

RED RIVER STATION

When the spirit of a man is once broken, he becomes useless. On the trail it is necessary to have some diversion from hard work, long hours, and exposure to the elements. With man and beast, from the Brazos to Red River was a fire test of physical endurance. But after crossing into the Chickasaw Nation, a comparatively new country would open before us. When the strain of the past week was sorest, in buoying up the spirits of my outfit, I had promised them rest and recreation at the first possible opportunity.

Fortunately we had an easy ford. There was not even an indication that there had been a freshet on the river that spring. This was tempering the wind, for we were crippled, three of the boys being unable to resume their places around the herd on account of inflamed eyes. The cook had weathered the sand-storm better than any of us. Sheltering his team, and fastening his wagon-sheet securely, he took refuge under it until the gale had passed. Pressing him into the service the next morning, and assigning him to the drag end of the herd, I left the blind to lead the blind in driving the wagon. On reaching the river about the middle of the forenoon, we trailed the cattle across in a long chain, not an animal being compelled to swim. The wagon was carried over on a ferryboat, as it was heavily loaded, a six weeks' supply of provisions having been taken on before crossing. Once the trail left the breaks, on the north side of the river, we drew off several miles to the left and went into camp for the remainder of the day. Still keeping clear of the trail, daily we moved forward the wagon from three to five miles, allowing the cattle to graze and rest to contentment. The herd recuperated rapidly, and by the evening of the fourth day after crossing, the inflammation was so reduced in those whose eyes were inflamed, that we decided to start in earnest the next morning.

The cook was ordered to set out the best the wagon afforded, several outside delicacies were added, and a feast was in sight. G - G Cederdall had recrossed the river that day to mail a letter, and on his return proudly carried a basket of eggs on his arm. Three of the others had joined a fishing party from the Texas side, and had come in earlier in the day with a fine string of fish. Parent won new laurels in the supper to which he invited us about sundown. The cattle came in to their beds groaning and satiated, and dropped down as if ordered. When the first watch had taken them, there was nothing to do but sit around and tell stories. Since crossing Red River, we had slept almost night and day, but in that balmy May evening sleep was banished. The fact that we were in the Indian country, civilized though the Indians were, called forth many an incident. The raids of the Comanches into the Panhandle country during the buffalo days was a favorite topic. Vick Wolf, however, had had an Indian experience in the North with which he regaled us at the first opportunity.

"There isn't any trouble nowadays," said he, lighting a cigarette, "with these blanket Indians on the reservations. I had an experience once on a reservation where the Indians could have got me easy enough if they had been on the war-path. It was the first winter I ever spent on a Northern range, having gone up to the Cherokee Strip to avoid - well, no matter. I got a job in the Strip, not riding, but as a kind of an all-round rustler. This was long before the country was fenced, and they rode lines to keep the cattle on their ranges. One evening about nightfall in December, the worst kind of a blizzard struck us that the country had ever seen. The next day it was just as bad, and BLOODY cold. A fellow could not see any distance, and to venture away from the dugout meant to get lost. The third day she broke and the sun came out clear in the early evening. The next day we managed to gather the saddle horses, as they had not drifted like the cattle.

"Well, we were three days overtaking the lead of that cattle drift, and then found them in the heart of the Cheyenne country, at least on that reservation. They had drifted a good hundred miles before the storm broke. Every outfit in the Strip had gone south after their cattle. Instead of drifting them back together, the different ranches rustled for their own. Some of the foremen paid the Indians so much per head to gather for them, but ours didn't. The braves weren't very much struck on us on that account. I was cooking for the outfit, which suited me in winter weather. We had a permanent camp on a small well-wooded creek, from which we worked all the country round.

"One afternoon when I was in camp all alone, I noticed an Indian approaching me from out of the timber. There was a Winchester standing against the wagon wheel, but as the bucks were making no trouble, I gave the matter no attention. Mr. Injun came up to the fire and professed to be very friendly, shook hands, and spoke quite a number of words in English. After he got good and warm, he looked all over the wagon, and noticing that I had no sixshooter on, he picked up the carbine and walked out about a hundred yards to a little knoll, threw his arms in the air, and made signs.

"Instantly, out of the cover of some timber on the creek a quarter above, came about twenty young bucks, mounted, and yelling like demons. When they came up, they began circling around the fire and wagon. I was sitting on an empty corn-crate by the fire. One young buck, seeing that I was not scaring to suit him, unslung a carbine as he rode, and shot into the fire before me. The bullet threw fire and ashes all over me, and I jumped about ten feet, which suited them better. They circled around for several minutes, every one uncovering a carbine, and they must have fired a hundred and fifty shots into the fire. In fact they almost shot it out, scattering the fire around so that it came near burning up the bedding of our outfit. I was scared thoroughly by this time. If it was possible for me to have had fits, I'd have had one sure. The air seemed full of coals of fire and ashes. I got good practical insight into what hell's like. I was rustling the rolls of bedding out of the circle of fire, expecting every moment would be my last. It's a wonder I wasn't killed. Were they throwing lead? Well, I should remark! You see the ground was not frozen around the fire, and the bullets buried themselves in the soft soil.

"After they had had as much fun as they wanted, the leader gave a yell and they all circled the other way once, and struck back into the timber. Some of them had brought up the decoy Indian's horse when they made the dash at first, and he suddenly turned as wild as a Cheyenne generally gets. When the others were several hundred yards away, he turned his horse, rode back some little distance, and attracted my attention by holding out the Winchester. From his horse he laid it carefully down on the ground, whirled his pony, and rode like a scared wolf after the others. I could hear their yells for miles, as they made for their encampment over on the North Fork. As soon as I got the fire under control, I went out and got the carbine. It was empty; the Indian had used its magazine in the general hilarity. That may be an Indian's style of fun, but I failed to see where there was any in it for me."

The cook threw a handful of oily fish-bones on the fire, causing it to flame up for a brief moment. With the exception of Wayne Outcault, who was lying prone on the ground, the men were smoking and sitting Indian fashion around the fire. After rolling awhile uneasily, Outcault sat up and remarked, "I feel about half sick. Eat too much? Don't you think it. Why, I only ate seven or eight of those fish, and that oughtn't to hurt a baby. There was only half a dozen hard-boiled eggs to the man, and I don't remember of any of you being so generous as to share yours with me. Those few plates of prunes that I ate for dessert wouldn't hurt nobody - they're medicine to some folks. Unroll our bed, pardner, and I'll thrash around on it awhile."

ANDY ADAMS

Several trail stories of more or less interest were told, when Runt Pickett, in order to avoid the smoke, came over and sat down between Burl Van Vedder and me. He had had an experience, and instantly opened on us at short range. "Speaking of stampedes," said Runt, "reminds me of a run I was in, and over which I was paid by my employer a very high compliment. My first trip over the trail, as far north as Dodge, was in '78. The herd sold next day after reaching there, and as I had an old uncle and aunt living in middle Kansas, I concluded to run down and pay them a short visit. So I threw away all my trail togs - well, they were worn out, anyway - and bought me a new outfit complete. Yes, I even bought button shoes. After visiting a couple of weeks with my folks, I drifted back to Dodge in the hope of getting in with some herd bound farther north - I was perfectly useless on a farm. On my return to Dodge, the only thing about me that indicated a cow-hand was my Texas saddle and outfit, but in toggery, in my visiting harness, I looked like a rank tenderfoot.

"Well, boys, the first day I struck town I met a through man looking for hands. His herd had just come in over the Chisholm Trail, crossing to the western somewhere above. He was disgusted with his outfit, and was discharging men right and left and hiring new ones to take their places. I apologized for my appearance, showed him my outfit, and got a job cow-punching with this through man. He expected to hold on sale a week or two, when if unsold he would drift north to the Platte. The first week that I worked, a wet stormy night struck us, and before ten o clock we lost every hoof of cattle. I was riding wild after little squads of cattle here and there, guided by flashes of lightning, when the storm finally broke. Well, there it was midnight, and I didn't have a HOOF OF CATTLE to hold and no one to help me if I had. The truth is, I was lost. Common horse-sense told me that; but where the outfit or wagon was was anybody's guess. The horses in my mount were as good as worthless; worn out, and if you gave one free rein he lacked the energy to carry you back to camp. I ploughed around in the darkness for over an hour, but finally came to a sudden stop on the banks of the muddy Arkansaw.

Right there I held a council of war with myself, the decision of which was that it was at least five miles to the wagon.

"After I'd prowled around some little time, a bright flash of lightning revealed to me an old deserted cabin a few rods below. To this shelter I turned without even a bid, unsaddled my horse and picketed him, and turned into the cabin for the night. Early the next morning I was out and saddled my horse, and the question was, Which way is camp? As soon as the sun rose clearly, I got my bearings. By my reasoning, if the river yesterday was south of camp, this morning the wagon must be north of the river, so I headed in that direction. Somehow or other I stopped my horse on the first little knoll, and looking back towards the bottom, I saw in a horseshoe which the river made a large bunch of cattle. Of course I knew that all herds near about were through cattle and under herd, and the absence of any men in sight aroused my curiosity. I concluded to investigate it, and riding back found over five hundred head of the cattle we had lost the night before. 'Here's a chance to make a record with my new boss,' I said to myself, and circling in behind, began drifting them out of the bottoms towards the uplands. By ten o'clock I had got them to the first divide, when who should ride up but the owner, the old cowman himself - the sure enough big auger.

"'Well, son,' said my boss, 'you held some of them, didn't you?' 'Yes,' I replied, surly as I could, giving him a mean look, 'I've nearly ridden this horse to death, holding this bunch all night. If I had only had a good man or two with me, we could have caught twice as many. What kind of an outfit are you working, anyhow, Captain?' And at dinner that day, the boss pointed me out to the others and said, 'That little fellow standing over there with the button shoes on is the only man in my outfit that is worth a --.'"

The cook had finished his work, and now joined the circle. Parent began regaling us with personal experiences, in which it was evident that he would prove the hero. Fortunately, however, we were spared listening to his self-laudation. Dorg

Seay and Tim Stanley, bunkies, engaged in a friendly scuffle, each trying to make the other get a firebrand for his pipe. In the tussle which followed, we were all compelled to give way or get trampled underfoot. When both had exhausted themselves in vain, we resumed our places around the fire. Parent, who was disgusted over the interruption, on resuming his seat refused to continue his story at the request of the offenders. replying, "The more I see of you two varmints the more you remind me of mule colts."

Once the cook refused to pick up the broken thread of his story, John Levering, our horse-wrangler, preempted the vacated post. "I was over in Louisiana a few winters ago with a horse herd," said John, "and had a few experiences. Of all the simple people that I ever met, the 'Cajin' takes the bakery. You'll meet darkies over there that can't speak a word of anything but French. It's nothing to see a cow and mule harnessed together to a cart. One day on the road, I met a man, old enough to be my father, and inquired of him how far it was to the parish centre, a large town. He didn't know, except it was a long, long ways. He had never been there, but his older brother, once when he was a young man, had been there as a witness at court. The brother was dead now, but if he was living and present, it was quite possible that he would remember the distance. The best information was that it was a very long ways off. I rode it in the mud in less than two hours; just about ten miles.

"But that wasn't a circumstance to other experiences. We had driven about three hundred horses and mules, and after disposing of over two thirds of them, my employer was compelled to return home, leaving me to dispose of the remainder. I was a fair salesman, and rather than carry the remnant of the herd with me, made headquarters with a man who owned a large cane-brake pasture. It was a convenient stopping-place, and the stock did well on the young cane. Every week I would drive to some distant town eighteen or twenty head, or as many as I could handle alone. Sometimes I would sell out in a few days, and then again it would take me longer. But when possible I always made it a rule to get back to my headquarters to spend Sunday. The owner of the cane-brake and his wife were a simple couple, and just a shade or two above the Arcadians. But they had a daughter who could pass muster, and she took quite a shine to the 'Texas-Hoss-Man,' as they called me. I reckon you understand now why I made that headquarters? - there were other reasons besides the good pasturage.

"Well, the girl and her mother both could read, but I have some doubt about the old man on that score. They took no papers, and the nearest approach to a book in the house was an almanac three years old. The women folks were ravenous for something to read, and each time on my return after selling out, I'd bring them a whole bundle of illustrated papers and magazines. About my fourth return after more horses, - I was mighty near one of the family by that time, - when we were all seated around the fire one night, the women poring over the papers and admiring the pictures, the old man inquired what the news was over in the parish where I had recently been. The only thing that I could remember was the suicide of a prominent man. After explaining the circumstances, I went on to say that some little bitterness arose over his burial. Owing to his prominence it was thought permission would be given to bury him in the churchyard. But it seems there was some superstition about permitting a self-murderer to be buried in the same field as decent folks. It was none of my funeral, and I didn't pay overmuch attention to the matter, but the authorities refused, and they buried him just outside the grounds, in the woods.

"My host and I discussed the matter at some length. He contended that if the man was not of sound mind, he should have been given his little six feet of earth among the others. A horse salesman has to be a good second-rate talker, and being anxious to show off before the girl, I differed with her father. The argument grew spirited yet friendly, and I appealed to the women in supporting my view. My hostess was absorbed at the time in reading a sensational account of a woman shooting her

ANDY ADAMS

betrayer. The illustrations covered a whole page, and the girl was simply burning, at short range, the shirt from off her seducer. The old lady was bogged to the saddle skirts in the story, when I interrupted her and inquired, 'Mother, what do you think ought to be done with a man who commits suicide?' She lowered the paper just for an instant, and looking over her spectacles at me replied, 'Well, I think any man who would do THAT ought to be made to support the child.'"

No comment was offered. Our wrangler arose and strolled away from the fire under the pretense of repicketing his horse. It was nearly time for the guards to change, and giving the last watch orders to point the herd, as they left the bed-ground in the morning, back on an angle towards the trail, I prepared to turn in. While I was pulling off my boots in the act of retiring, Clay Zilligan rode in from the herd to call the relief. The second guard were bridling their horses, and as Zilligan dismounted, he said to the circle of listeners, "Didn't I tell you fellows that there was another herd just ahead of us? I don't care if they didn't pass up the trail since we've been laying over, they are there just the same. Of course you can't see their camp-fire from here, but it's in plain view from the bed-ground, and not over four or five miles away. If I remember rightly, there's a local trail comes in from the south of the Wichita River, and joins the Chisholm just ahead. And what's more, that herd was there at nine o'clock this morning, and they haven't moved a peg since. Well, there's two lads out there waiting to be relieved, and you second guard know where the cattle are bedded."

CHAPTER VI.

CAMP SUPPLY

In gala spirits we broke camp the next morning. The herd had left the bed-ground at dawn, and as the outfit rode away to relieve the last guard, every mother's son was singing. The cattle were a refreshing sight as they grazed forward, their ragged front covering half a mile in width. The rest of the past few days had been a boon to the few tender-footed ones. The lay-over had rejuvenated both man and beast. From maps in our possession we knew we were somewhere near the western border of the Chickasaw Nation, while on our left was the reservation of three blanket tribes of Indians. But as far as signs of occupancy were concerned, the country was unmarked by any evidence of civilization. The Chisholm Cattle Trail, which ran from Red River to the Kansas line, had almost fallen into disuse, owing to encroachments of settlements south of the former and westward on the latter. With the advancement of immigration, Abilene and Ellsworth as trail terminals yielded to the tide, and the leading cattle trace of the '70's was relegated to local use in '84.

The first guard was on the qui vive for the outfit whose camp-fire they had sighted the night before. I was riding with Clay Zilligan on the left point, when he sighted what we supposed was a small bunch of cattle lying down several miles distant. When we reached the first rise of ground, a band of saddle horses came in view, and while we were trying to locate their camp, Jack Splann from the opposite point attracted our attention and pointed straight ahead. There a large band of cattle under herd greeted our view, compelling us to veer to the right and intersect the trail sooner than we intended. Keeping a clear half-mile between us, we passed them within an hour and exchanged the compliments of the trail. They proved to be "Laurel Leaf" and "Running W" cattle, the very ones for which the International Railway agent at the meeting in February had so boastfully shown my employer the application for cars. The foreman was cursing like a stranded pirate over the predicament in which he found himself. He had left Santo Gertrudo Ranch over a month before with a herd of three thousand straight two-year-old steers. But in the shipment of some thirty-three thousand cattle from the two ranches to Wichita Falls, six trains had been wrecked, two of which were his own. Instead of being hundreds of miles ahead in the lead of the year's drive, as he expected, he now found himself in charge of a camp of cripples. What few trains belonging to his herd had escaped the ditch were used in filling up other unfortunate ones, the injured cattle from the other wrecks forming his present holdings.

"Our people were anxious to get their cattle on to the market early this year," said he, "and put their foot into it up to the knee. Shipping to Red River was an experiment with them, and I hope they've got their belly full. We've got dead and dying cattle in every pasture from the falls to the river, while these in sight aren't able to keep out of the stench of those that croaked between here and the ford. Oh, this shipping is a fine thing - for the railroads. Here I've got to rot all summer with these cattle, just because two of my trains went into the ditch while no other foreman had over one wrecked. And mind you, they paid the freight in advance, and now King and Kennedy have brought suit for damages amounting to double the shipping expense. They'll get it all right - in pork. I'd rather have a claim against a nigger than a railroad company. Look at your beeves, slick as weasels, and from the Nueces River. Have to hold them in, I reckon, to keep from making twenty miles a day. And here I am - Oh, hell, I'd rather be on a rock-pile with a ball and chain to my foot! Do you see those objects across yonder about two miles - in that old grass? That's where we bedded night before last and forty odd died. We only lost twenty-two last night. Oh, we're getting in shape fast. If you think you can hold your breakfast down, just take a ride through mine. No, excuse me - I've seen them too often already."

Several of the boys and myself rode into the herd some little distance, but the sight was enough to turn a copper-lined stomach. Scarcely an animal had escaped without more or less injury. Fully one half were minus one or both horns, leaving instead bloody stumps. Broken bones and open sores greeted us on every hand; myriads of flies added to the misery of the cattle, while in many instances there was evidence of maggots at work on the living animal. Turning from the herd in disgust, we went back to our own, thankful that the rate offered us had been prohibitory. The trials and vexations of the road were mere nothings to be endured, compared to the sights we were then leaving. Even what we first supposed were cattle lying down, were only bed-grounds, the occupants having been humanely relieved by unwaking sleep. Powerless to render any assistance, we trailed away, glad to blot from our sight and memory such scenes of misery and death.

Until reaching the Washita River, we passed through a delightful country. There were numerous local trails coming into the main one, all of which showed recent use. Abandoned campfires and bed-grounds were to be seen on every hand, silent witnesses of an exodus which was to mark the maximum year in the history of the cattle movement from Texas. Several times we saw some evidence of settlement by the natives, but as to the freedom of the country, we were monarchs of all we surveyed. On arriving at the Washita, we encountered a number of herds, laboring under the impression that they were water-bound. Immediate entrance at the ford was held by a large herd of young cattle in charge of a negro outfit. Their stock were scattered over several thousand acres, and when I asked for the boss, a middle-aged darky of herculean figure was pointed out as in charge. To my inquiry why he was holding the ford, his answer was that until to-day the river had been swimming, and now he was waiting for the banks to dry.

Ridiculing his flimsy excuse, I kindly yet firmly asked him either to cross or vacate the ford by three o'clock that afternoon. Receiving no definite reply, I returned to our herd, which was some five miles in the rear. Beyond the river's steep, slippery banks and cold water, there was nothing to check a herd.

After the noonday halt, the wrangler and myself took our remuda and went on ahead to the river. Crossing and recrossing our saddle stock a number of times, we trampled the banks down to a firm footing. While we were doing this work, the negro foreman and a number of his men rode up and sullenly watched us. Leaving our horses on the north bank, Levering and I returned, and ignoring the presence of the darky spectators, started back to meet the herd, which was just then looming up in sight. But before we had ridden any distance, the dusky foreman overtook us and politely said, "Look-ee here, Cap'n; ain't you-all afraid of losin' some of your cattle among ours?" Never halting, I replied, "Not a particle; if we lose any, you eat them, and we'll do the same if our herd absorbs any of yours. But it strikes me that you had better have those lazy niggers throw your cattle to one side," I called back, as he halted his horse. We did not look backward until we reached the herd; then as we turned, one on each side to support the points, it was evident that a clear field would await us on reaching the river. Every horseman in the black outfit was pushing cattle with might and main, to give us a clean cloth at the crossing.

The herd forded the Washita without incident. I remained on the south bank while the cattle were crossing, and when they were about half over some half-dozen of the darkies rode up and stopped apart, conversing among themselves. When the drag cattle passed safely out on the farther bank, I turned to the dusky group, only to find their foreman absent. Making a few inquiries as to the ownership of their herd, its destination, and other matters of interest, I asked the group to express my thanks to their foreman for moving his cattle aside. Our commissary crossed shortly afterward, and the Washita was in our rear. But that night, as some of my outfit returned from the river, where they had been fishing, they reported the negro outfit as having crossed and encamped several miles in our rear.

"All they needed was a good example," said Dorg Seay. "Under a white foreman, I'll bet that's a good lot of darkies. They were just about the right shade - old shiny black. As good cowhands as ever I saw were nigs, but they need a white man to blow and brag on them. But it always ruins one to give him any authority."

Without effort we traveled fifteen miles a day. In the absence of any wet weather to gall their backs, there was not a horse in our remuda unfit for the saddle. In fact, after reaching the Indian Territory, they took on flesh and played like lambs. With the exception of long hours and night-herding, the days passed in seeming indolence as we swept northward, crossing rivers without a halt which in previous years had defied the moving herds. On arriving at the Cimarron River, in reply to a letter written to my employer on leaving Texas behind us, an answer was found awaiting me at Red Fork. The latter was an Indian trading-post, located on the mail route to Fort Reno, and only a few miles north of the Chisholm Crossing. The letter was characteristic of my employer. It contained but one imperative order, - that I should touch, either with or without the herd, at Camp Supply. For some unexplained reason he would make that post his headquarters until after the Buford herds had passed that point. The letter concluded with the injunction, in case we met any one, to conceal the ownership of the herd and its destination.

The mystery was thickening. But having previously declined to borrow trouble, I brushed this aside as unimportant, though I gave my outfit instructions to report the herd to every one as belonging to Omaha men, and on its way to Nebraska to be corn-fed. Fortunately I had ridden ahead of the herd after crossing the Cimarron, and had posted the outfit before they reached the trading-station. I did not allow one of my boys near the store, and the herd passed by as in contempt of such a wayside place. As the Dodge cut-off left the Chisholm Trail some ten miles above the Indian trading-post, the next morning we waved good-bye to the old cattle trace and turned on a northwest angle. Our route now lay up the Cimarron, which we crossed and recrossed at our pleasure, for the sake of grazing or to avoid several large alkali flats. There was evidence of herds in our advance, and had we not hurried past Red Fork, I might have learned something to our advantage. But disdaining all inquiry of the cut-off, fearful lest our identity be discovered, we deliberately walked into the first real danger of the trip.

At low water the Cimarron was a brackish stream. But numerous tributaries put in from either side, and by keeping above the river's ebb, an abundance of fresh water was daily secured from the river's affluents. The fifth day out from Red Rock was an excessively sultry one, and suffering would have resulted to the herd had we not been following a divide where we caught an occasional breeze. The river lay some ten miles to our right, while before us a tributary could be distinctly outlined by the cottonwoods which grew along it. Since early morning we had been paralleling the creek, having nooned within sight of its confluence with the mother stream, and consequently I had considered it unnecessary to ride ahead and look up the water. When possible, we always preferred watering the herd between three and four o'clock in the afternoon. But by holding our course, we were certain to intersect the creek at about the usual hour for the cattle's daily drink, and besides, as the creek neared the river, it ran through an alkali flat for some distance. But before the time arrived to intersect the creek on our course, the herd turned out of the trail, determined to go to the creek and quench their thirst. The entire outfit, however, massed on the right flank, and against their will we held them on their course. As their thirst increased with travel, they made repeated attempts to break through our cordon, requiring every man to keep on the alert. But we held them true to the divide, and as we came to the brow of a small hill within a quarter-mile of the water, a stench struck us until we turned in our saddles, gasping for breath. I was riding third man in the swing from the point, and noticing something wrong in front, galloped to the brow of the hill. The smell was sickening and almost unendurable, and there before us in plain view lay hundreds of dead cattle, bloated and decaying in the summer sun.

I was dazed by the awful scene. A pretty, greenswarded little valley lay before me, groups of cottonwoods fringed the stream here and there, around the roots of which were both shade and water. The reeking stench that filled the air stupefied me for the instant, and I turned my horse from the view, gasping for a mouthful of God's pure ozone. But our beeves had been scenting the creek for hours, and now a few of the leaders started forward in a trot for it. Like a flash it came to me that death lurked in that water, and summoning every man within hearing, I dashed to the lead of our cattle to turn them back over the hill. Jack Splann was on the point, and we turned the leaders when within two hundred yards of the creek, frequently jumping our horses over the putrid carcasses of dead cattle. The main body of the herd were trailing for three quarters of a mile in our rear, and none of the men dared leave their places. Untying our slickers, Splann and I fell upon the leaders and beat them back to the brow of the hill, when an unfortunate breeze was wafted through that polluted atmosphere from the creek to the cattle's nostrils. Turning upon us and now augmented to several hundred head, they sullenly started forward. But in the few minutes' interim, two other lads had come to our support, and dismounting we rushed them, whipping our slickers into ribbons over their heads. The mastery of man again triumphed over brutes in their thirst, for we drove them in a rout back over the divide.

Our success, however, was only temporary. Recovering our horses we beat the cattle back, seemingly inch by inch, until the rear came up, when we rounded them into a compact body. They quieted down for a short while, affording us a breathing spell, for the suddenness of this danger had not only unnerved me but every one of the outfit who had caught a glimpse of that field of death. The wagon came up, and those who needed them secured a change of horses. Leaving the outfit holding the herd, Splann and I took fresh mounts, and circling around, came in on the windward side of the creek. As we crossed it half a mile above the scene of disaster, each of us dipped a hand in the water and tasted it. The alkali was strong as concentrated lye, blistering our mouths in the experiment. The creek was not even running, but stood in long, deep pools, clear as crystal and as inviting to the thirsty as a mountain spring. As we neared the dead cattle, Splann called my attention to the attitude of the animals when death relieved them, the heads of fully two thirds being thrown back on their sides. Many, when stricken, were unable to reach the bank, and died in the bed of the stream. Making a complete circle of the ghastly scene, we returned to our own, agreeing that between five and six hundred cattle had met their fate in those death-dealing pools.

We were not yet out of the woods. On our return, many of the cattle were lying down, while in the west thunder-clouds were appearing. The North Fork of the Canadian lay on our left, which was now our only hope for water, yet beyond our reach for the day. Keeping the slight divide between us and the creek, we started the herd forward. Since it was impossible to graze them in their thirsty condition, I was determined to move them as far as possible before darkness overtook us. But within an hour we crossed a country trail over which herds had passed on their way northwest, having left the Chisholm after crossing the North Fork. At the first elevation which would give me a view of the creek, another scene of death and desolation greeted my vision, only a few miles above the first one. Yet from this same hill I could easily trace the meanderings of the creek for miles as it made a half circle in our front, both inviting and defying us. Turning the herd due south, we traveled until darkness fell, going into camp on a high, flat mesa of several thousand acres. But those evening breezes wafted an invitation to come and drink, and our thirsty herd refused to bed down. To add to our predicament, a storm thickened in the west. Realizing that we were confronting the most dangerous night in all my cattle experience, I ordered every man into the saddle. The remuda and team were taken in charge by the wrangler and cook, and going from man to man, I warned them what the consequences would be if we lost the herd during the night, and the cattle reached the creek.

The cattle surged and drifted almost at will, for we were compelled to hold them loose to avoid milling. Before ten o'clock the lightning was flickering overhead and around us, revealing acres of big beeves, which in an instant might take fright, and then, God help us. But in that night of trial a mercy was extended to the dumb brutes in charge. A warm rain began falling, first in a drizzle, increasing after the first hour, and by midnight we could hear the water slushing under our horses' feet. By the almost constant flashes of lightning we could see the cattle standing as if asleep, in grateful enjoyment of the sheeting downpour. As the night wore on, our fears of a stampede abated, for the buffalo wallows on the mesa filled, and water was on every hand. The rain ceased before dawn, but owing to the saturated condition underfoot, not a hoof lay down during the night, and when the gray of morning streaked the east, what a sense of relief it brought us. The danger had passed.

Near noon that day, and within a few miles of the North Fork, we rounded an alkaline plain in which this deadly creek had its source. Under the influence of the season, alkali had oozed up out of the soil until it looked like an immense lake under snow. The presence of range cattle in close proximity to this creek, for we were in the Cherokee Strip, baffled my reasoning; but the next day we met a range-rider who explained that the present condition of the stream was unheard of before, and that native cattle had instinct enough to avoid it. He accounted for its condition as due to the dry season, there being no general rains sufficient to flood the alkaline plain and thoroughly flush the creek. In reply to an inquiry as to the ownership of the unfortunate herds, he informed me that there were three, one belonging to Bob Houston, another to Major Corouthers, and the third to a man named Murphy, the total loss amounting to about two thousand cattle.

From this same range-man we also learned our location. Camp Supply lay up the North Fork some sixty miles, while a plain trail followed up the first bottom of the river. Wishing to avoid, if possible, intersecting the western trail south of Dodge, the next morning I left the herd to follow up, and rode into Camp Supply before noon. Lovell had sighted me a mile distant, and after a drink at the sutler's bar, we strolled aside for a few minutes' chat. Once I had informed him of the locality of the herd and their condition, he cautioned me not to let my business be known while in the post. After refreshing the inner man, my employer secured a horse and started with me on my return. As soon as the flag over Supply faded out of sight in our rear, we turned to the friendly shade of the timber on the North Fork and dismounted. I felt that the precaution exercised by the drover was premonitory of some revelation, and before we arose from the cottonwood log on which we took seats, the scales had fallen from my eyes and the atmosphere of mystery cleared.

"Tom," said my employer, "I am up against a bad proposition. I am driving these Buford cattle, you understand, on a sub-contract. I was the second lowest bidder with the government, and no sooner was the award made to The Western Supply Company than they sent an agent who gave me no peace until they sublet their contract. Unfortunately for me, when the papers were drawn, my regular attorney was out of town, and I was compelled to depend on a stranger. After the articles were executed, I submitted the matter to my old lawyer; he shook his head, arguing that a loophole had been left open, and that I should have secured an assignment of the original contract. After studying the matter over, we opened negotiations to secure a complete relinquishment of the award. But when I offered the company a thousand dollars over and above what they admitted was their margin, and they refused it, I opened my eyes to the true situation. If cattle went up, I was responsible and would have to fill my contract; if they went down, the company would buy in the cattle and I could go to hell in a hand-basket for all they cared. Their bond to the government does me no good, and beyond that they are irresponsible. Beeves have broken from four to five dollars a head, and unless I can deliver these Buford herds on my contract, they will lose me fifty thousand dollars."

"Have you any intimation that they expect to buy in other cattle?" I inquired.

"Yes. I have had a detective in my employ ever since my suspicions were aroused. There are two parties in Dodge this very minute with the original contract, properly assigned, and they are looking for cattle to fill it. That's why I'm stopping here and lying low. I couldn't explain it to you sooner, but you understand now why I drove those Buford herds in different road brands. Tom, we're up against it, and we've got to fight the devil with fire. Henceforth your name will be Tom McIndoo, your herd will be the property of the Marshall estate, and their agent, my detective, will be known as Charles Siringo. Any money or supplies you may need in Dodge, get in the usual form through the firm of Wright, Beverly & Co. - they understand. Hold your herd out south on Mulberry, and Siringo will have notice and be looking for you, or you can find him at the Dodge House. I've sent a courier to Fort Elliott to meet Dave and Quince, and once I see them, I'll run up to Ogalalla and wait for you. Now, until further orders, remember you never knew a man by the name of Don Lovell, and by all means don't forget to use what wits Nature gave you."

CHAPTER VII.

WHEN GREEK MEETS GREEK

It was late that night when I reached the herd. Before I parted with my employer we had carefully reviewed the situation in its minutest details. Since the future could not be foreseen, we could only watch and wait. The Texan may have his shortcomings, but lack of fidelity to a trust is not one of them, and relying on the metal of my outfit, I at once put them in possession of the facts. At first their simple minds could hardly grasp the enormity of the injustice to our employer, but once the land lay clear, they would gladly have led a forlorn hope in Don Lovell's interests. Agitation over the matter was maintained at white heat for several days, as we again angled back towards the Cimarron. Around the camp-fires at night, the chicanery of The Western Supply Company gave place to the best stories at our command. "There ought to be a law." said Runt Pickett, in wrathy indignation, "making it legal to kill some people, same as rattlesnakes. Now, you take a square gambler and I don't think anything of losing my money against his game, but one of these sneaking, under-dealing, top-and-bottom-business pimps, I do despise. You can find them in every honest calling, same as vultures hover round when cattle are dying. Honest, fellows, I'd just dearly love to pull on a rope and watch one of the varmints make his last kick."

Several days of showery weather followed. Crossing the Cimarron, we followed up its north slope to within thirty miles of the regular western trail. Not wishing to intercept it until necessity compelled us, when near the Kansas line we made our last tack for Dodge. The rains had freshened the country and flushed the creeks, making our work easy, and early in the month of June we reached the Mulberry. Traveling at random, we struck that creek about twenty miles below the trail, and moved up the stream to within a short distance of the old crossing. The presence of a dozen other herds holding along it forced us into a permanent camp a short half-day's ride from the town. The horse-wrangler was pressed into service in making up the first guard that night, and taking Morg Tussler with me, I struck out for Dodge in the falling darkness. On reaching the first divide, we halted long enough to locate the camp-fires along the Mulberry to our rear, while above and below and beyond the river, fires flickered like an Indian encampment. The lights of Dodge were inviting us, and after making a rough estimate of the camps in sight, we rode for town, arriving there between ten and eleven o'clock. The Dodge House was a popular hostelry for trail men and cattle buyers, and on our making inquiry of the night clerk if a Mr. Siringo was stopping there, we were informed that he was, but had retired. I put up a trivial excuse for seeing him, the clerk gave me the number of his room, and Tussler and I were soon closeted with him. The detective was a medium-sized, ordinary man, badly pock-marked, with a soft, musical voice, and apparently as innocent as a boy. In a brief preliminary conversation, he proved to be a Texan, knowing every in and out of cattle, having been bred to the occupation. Our relations to each other were easily established. Reviewing the situation thoroughly, he informed me that he had cultivated the acquaintance of the parties holding the assignment of the Buford award. He had represented to them that he was the fiscal agent of some six herds on the trail that year, three of which were heavy beeves, and they had agreed to look them over, provided they arrived before the 15th of the month. He further assured me that the parties were mere figureheads of The Supply Company; that they were exceedingly bearish on the market, gloating over the recent depreciation in prices, and perfectly willing to fatten on the wreck and ruin of others.

It was long after midnight when the consultation ended.

Appointing an hour for showing the herd the next day, or that one rather, Tussler and I withdrew, agreeing to be out of town before daybreak. But the blaze of gambling and the blare of dance-halls held us as in a siren's embrace until the lights dimmed with the breaking of dawn. Mounting our horses, we forded the river east of town and avoided the herds, which were just arising from their bed-grounds. On the divide we halted. Within the horizon before us, it is safe to assert that one hundred thousand cattle grazed in lazy contentment, all feeding against the morning breeze. Save for the freshness of early summer, with its background of green and the rarified atmosphere of the elevated plain, the scene before us might be compared to a winter drift of buffalo, ten years previous. Riding down the farther slope, we reached our camp in time for a late breakfast, the fifteen-mile ride having whetted our appetites. Three men were on herd, and sending two more with instructions to water the cattle an hour before noon, Tussler and I sought the shade of the wagon and fell asleep. It was some time after midday when, on sighting the expected conveyance approaching our camp, the cook aroused us. Performing a rather hasty ablution, I met the vehicle, freshened, and with my wits on tap. I nearly dragged the detective from the livery rig, addressing him as "Charley," and we made a rough ado over each other. Several of the other boys came forward and, shaking hands, greeted him with equal familiarity. As two strangers alighted on the opposite side, the detective took me around and they were introduced as Mr. Field and Mr. Radcliff, prospective beef buyers. The boys had stretched a tarpaulin, affording ample shade, and Parent invited every one to dinner. The two strangers were rather testy, but Siringo ate ravenously, repeatedly asking for things which were usually kept in a well-stocked chuck-wagon, meanwhile talking with great familiarity with Tussler and me.

The strangers said little, but were amused at the lightness of our dinner chat. I could see at a glance that they were not cowmen. They were impatient to see the cattle; and when dinner was over, I explained to them that the men on herd would be relieved for dinner by those in camp, and orders would be given, if it was their wish, to throw the cattle compactly together. To this Siringo objected. "No, Mac," said he, "that isn't the right way to show beeves. Here, Morg, listen to me; I'm foreman for the time being. When you relieve the other lads, edge in your cattle from an ordinary loose herd until you have them on two or three hundred acres. Then we can slowly drive through them for an hour or so, or until these gentlemen are satisfied. They're not wild, are they, Mac?"

I assured every one that the cattle were unusually gentle; that we had not had a run so far, but urged caution in approaching them with a conveyance. As soon as the relief started, I brought in the livery team off picket, watered, and harnessed them into the vehicle. It was my intention to accompany them on horseback, but Siringo hooted at the idea, and Mr. Radcliff and I occupied the back seat, puffing splendid cigars. We met the relieved men coming in, who informed us that the herd was just over the hill on the south side of the creek. On reaching the gentle rise, there below us grazed the logy, lazy beeves, while the boys quietly rode round, silently moving them together as instructed. Siringo drove to their lead, and halting, we allowed the cattle to loiter past us on either side of the conveyance. It was an easy herd to show, for the pounds avoirdupois were there. Numerous big steers, out of pure curiosity, came up near the vehicle and innocently looked at us as if expecting a dole or sweetmeat. A snap of the finger would turn them, showing their rounded buttocks, and they would rejoin the guard of honor. If eyes could speak, the invitation was timidly extended, "Look at me, Mr. Buyer." We allowed the herd to pass by us, then slowly circled entirely around them, and finally drove back and forth through them for nearly two hours, when the prospective buyers expressed themselves as satisfied.

But the fiscal agent was not. Calling two of the boys, he asked for the loan of their horses and insisted that the buyers ride the cattle over and thoroughly satisfy themselves on the brands. The boys gladly yielded, and as Mr. Field and Mr. Radcliff mounted to ride away, the detective halted them long enough to say: "Now, gentlemen, I wish to call your attention to the fact that over one half the herd are in the single Marshall ranch brand. There are also some five hundred head in the '8=8,' that being an outside ranch, but belonging to the estate. I am informed that the remainder of nearly a thousand were turned in by neighboring ranchmen in making up the herd, and you'll find those in various mixed brands. If there's a hoof among them not in the 'Open A' road, we'll cut them out for fear of trouble to the buyer. I never sold a man cattle in my life who wasn't my customer ever afterward. You gentlemen are strangers to me; and for that reason I conceal nothing. Now look them over carefully, and keep a sharp lookout for strays - cattle not in the road brand."

I knew there were about twenty strays in the herd, and informed Siringo to that effect, but the cattle buyers noticed only two, a red and a roan, which again classed them as inexperienced men among cattle. We returned to camp, not a word being said about trading, when the buyers suggested returning to town. Siringo looked at his watch, asked if there was anything further they wished to see or know, and expressed himself like a true Texan, "that there was ample time." I was the only one who had alighted, and as they started to drive away, I said to Siringo: "Charley, let me talk to you a minute first. You see how I'm situated here - too many neighbors. I'm going to ride north of town to-morrow, and if I can find a good camp on Saw Log, why I'll move over. We are nearly out of supplies, anyhow, and the wagon can go by town and load up. There's liable to be a mix-up here some night on the Mulberry, and I'd rather be excused than present."

"That's all right, Mac; that's just what I want you to do. If we trade, we'll make the deal within a day or two, and if not you can start right on for Ogalalla. I've been selling cattle the last few years to the biggest feeders in Nebraska, and I'm not a little bit afraid of placing those 'Open A's.' About four months full feed on corn will fit those steers to go to any market. Drop into town on your way back from the Saw Log to-morrow."

That evening my brother Bob rode into camp. He had seen our employer at Supply, and accordingly understood the situation. The courier had returned from Fort Elliott and reported his mission successful; he had met both Forrest and Sponsilier. The latter had had a slight run in the Panhandle during a storm, losing a few cattle, which he recovered the next day. For fear of a repetition, Forrest had taken the lead thereafter, and was due at Supply within a day or two. Flood and Priest had passed Abilene, Texas, in safety, but no word had reached our employer since, and it was believed that they had turned eastward and would come up the Chisholm Trail. Bob reported the country between Abilene and Doan's Crossing as cut into dust and barren of sustenance, many weak cattle having died in crossing the dry belt. But the most startling news, seriously disturbing us both, was that Archie Tolleston was stationed at Doan's Crossing on Red River as a trail-cutter. He had come up from the south to Wichita Falls by train with trail cattle, and finding no opening as a foreman, had accepted the position of inspector for some Panhandle cattle companies. He and Bob had had a friendly chat, and Archie admitted that it was purely his own hot-headedness which prevented his being one of Lovell's foremen on the present drive. The disturbing feature was, that after leaving headquarters in Medina County, he had gone into San Antonio, where he met a couple of strangers who partially promised him a job as trail boss, in case he presented himself in Dodge about June 15. They had intimated to him that it was possible they would need a foreman or two who knew the trail from the Arkansaw to the Yellowstone and Missouri River country. Putting this and that together, the presence of Archie Tolleston in Dodge was not at all favorable to the working out of our plans. "And Arch isn't the man to forget a humiliation," concluded Bob, to which I agreed.

The next morning I rode across to the Saw Log, and up that creek beyond all the herds. The best prospect for a camp was nearly due north opposite us, as the outfit lowest down the stream expected to start for the Platte the next morning. Having fully made up my mind to move camp, I rode for town, taking dinner on Duck Creek, which was also littered with cattle and outfits. I reached town early in the afternoon, and after searching all the hotels, located the fiscal agent in company with the buyers at the Lone Star saloon. They were seated around a table, and Mr. Field, noticing my entrance, beckoned me over and offered a chair. As I took the proffered seat, both strangers turned on me, and Mr. Radcliff said: "McIndoo, this agent of yours is the hardest man I ever tried to trade with. Here we've wasted the whole morning dickering, and are no nearer together than when we started. The only concession which Mr. Siringo seems willing to admit is that cattle are off from three to five dollars a head, while we contend that heavy beeves are off seven dollars."

"Excuse me for interrupting," said the fiscal agent, "but since you have used the words HEAVY BEEVES, either one of you ask Mac, here, what those 'Open A's' will dress to-day, and what they ought to gain in the next three months on good grass and water. There he sits; ask him."

Mr. Field explained that they had also differed as to what the herd would dress out, and invited my opinion. "Those beeves will dress off from forty-five to fifty per cent.," I replied. "The Texan being a gaunt animal does not shrink like a domestic beef. Take that 'Open A' herd straight through and they will dress from four fifty to six hundred pounds, or average better than five hundred all round. In three months, under favorable conditions, those steers ought to easily put on a hundred pounds of tallow apiece. Mr. Radcliff, do you remember pointing out a black muley yesterday and saying that he looked like a native animal? I'll just bet either one of you a hundred dollars that he'll dress out over five hundred pounds; and I'll kill him in your presence and you can weigh his quarters with a steelyard."

They laughed at me, Siringo joining in, and Mr. Field ordered the drinks. "Mac," said the detective, "these gentlemen are all right, and you shouldn't take any offense, for I don't blame them for driving a hard bargain. I'd probably do the same thing if I was the buyer instead of the seller. And remember, Mac, if the deal goes through, you are to drive the herd at the seller's risk, and deliver it at any point the buyer designates, they accepting without expense or reserve the cattle only. It means over three months' further expense, with a remuda thrown back on your hands; and all these incidentals run into money fast. Gentlemen, unless you increase the advance cash payment, I don't see how you can expect me to shade my offer. What's your hurry, Mac?"

As it was growing late, I had arisen, and saying that I expected to move camp to-morrow, invited the party to join me at the bar. I informed the buyers, during the few minutes' interim, that if they wished to look the cattle over again, the herd would cross the river below old Fort Dodge about noon the next day. They thanked me for the information, saying it was quite possible that they might drive down, and discussing the matter we all passed into the street. With the understanding that the prospect of making a deal was not hopeless, Siringo excused himself, and we strolled away together. No sooner was the coast clear than I informed the detective of the arrival of my brother, putting him in possession of every fact regarding Archie Tolleston. He readily agreed with me that the recent break between the latter and his former employer was a dangerous factor, and even went so far as to say that Tolleston's posing as a trail-cutter at Doan's Crossing was more than likely a ruse. I was giving the detective a detailed description of Archie, when he stopped me and asked what his special weaknesses were, if he had any. "Whiskey and women," I replied. "That's good," said he, "and I want you to send me in one of your best men in the morning - I mean one who will drink and carouse. He can watch the trains, and if this fellow shows up, we'll keep him soaked and let him enjoy himself. Send me one that's good for a ten days' protracted drunk. You think the other herds will be here within a few days? That's all I want to know."

I reached camp a little before dark, and learned that Bob's herd had dropped in just below us on the Mulberry. He expected to lie over a few days in passing Dodge, and I lost no time in preparing to visit his camp. While riding out that evening, I had made up my mind to send in Dorg Seay, as he was a heady fellow, and in drinking had an oak-tan stomach. Taking him with me, I rode down the Mulberry and reached the lower camp just as my brother and his outfit were returning from bedding-down the cattle. Bob readily agreed that the detective's plans were perfectly feasible, and offered to play a close second to Seay if it was necessary. And if his own brother does say so, Bob Quirk never met the man who could drink him under the table.

My herd started early for the Saw Log, and the wagon for town. Bob had agreed to go into Dodge in the morning, so Dorg stayed with our outfit and was to go in with me after crossing the river. We threaded our way through the other herds, and shortly before noon made an easy ford about a mile below old Fort Dodge. As we came down to the river, a carriage was seen on the farther bank, and I dropped from the point back to the drag end. Sure enough, as we trailed out, the fiscal agent and the buyers were awaiting me. "Well, Mac, I sold your herd last night after you left," said Siringo, dejectedly. "It was a kind of compromise trade; they raised the cash payment to thirty thousand dollars, and I split the difference in price. The herd goes at $29 a head all round. So from now on, Mac, you're subject to these gentlemen's orders."

Mr. Field, the elder of the two buyers, suggested that if a convenient camp could be found, we should lie over a few days, when final instructions would be given me. He made a memorandum of the number of head that I claimed in our road brand, and asked me if we could hold up the herd for a closer inspection. The lead cattle were then nearly a mile away, and galloping off to overtake the point, I left the party watching the saddle horses, which were then fording in our rear. But no sooner had I reached the lead and held up the herd, than I noticed Siringo on the wrangler's horse, coming up on the opposite side of the column of cattle from the vehicle. Supposing he had something of a private nature to communicate, I leisurely rode down the line and met him.

"Did you send that man in this morning?" he sternly demanded. I explained that my brother had done, properly coached, and that Seay would go in with me in the course of an hour.

"Give him any money you have and send him at once," commanded the detective. "Tolleston was due on the ten o'clock train, but it was an hour late. Those buyers wanted me to wait for it, so he could come along, but I urged the importance of catching you at the ford. Now, send your man Seay at once, get Tolleston beastly drunk, and quarter him in some crib until night."

Unobserved by the buyers, I signaled Seay, and gave him the particulars and what money I had. He rode back through the saddle stock, recrossed the river, and after rounding the bend, galloped away. Siringo continued: "You see, after we traded, they inquired if you were a safe man, saying if you didn't know the Yellowstone country, they had a man in sight who did. That was last night, and it seems that this morning they got a letter from Tolleston, saying he would be there on the next train. They're either struck on him, or else he's in their employ. Mark my words."

When we had showed the herd to the satisfaction of the purchasers, they expressed themselves as anxious to return to town; but the fiscal agent of the Marshall estate wished to look over the saddle horses first. Since they were unsold, and amounted to quite an item, he begged for just a few minutes' time to look them over carefully. Who could refuse such a reasonable request? The herd had started on for the Saw Log, while the remuda had wandered down the river about half a mile, and it took us nearly an hour to give them a thorough inspection. Once by ourselves, the detective said, with a chuckle: "All I was playing for was to get as large a cash payment as possible. Those mixed brands were my excuse for the money; the Marshall estate might wait for theirs, but the small ranchmen would insist on an immediate settlement the moment the cattle were reported sold. If it wasn't for this fellow Tolleston, I'd sell the other two Buford herds the day they arrive, and then we could give The Western Supply Company the laugh. And say, when they drew me a draft for thirty thousand dollars on a Washington City bank, I never let the ink dry on it until I took it around to Wright, Beverly & Co., and had them wire its acceptance. We'll give Seay plenty of time, and I think there'll be an answer on the check when we get back to town."

CHAPTER VIII.

EN PASSANT

It was intentionally late in the day when we reached Dodge. My horse, which I was leading, gave considerable trouble while returning, compelling us to drive slow. The buyers repeatedly complained that dinner would be over at their hotel, but the detective knew of a good restaurant and promised all of us a feast. On reaching town, we drove to the stable where the rig belonged, and once free of the horses, Siringo led the way to a well-known night-and-day eating-house on a back street. No sooner had we entered the place than I remembered having my wagon in town, and the necessity of its reaching camp before darkness made my excuse imperative. I hurried around to the outfitting house and found the order filled and all ready to load into the wagon. But Parent was missing, and in skirmishing about to locate him, I met my brother Bob. Tolleston had arrived, but his presence had not been discovered until after Seay reached town. Archie was fairly well "organized" and had visited the hotel where the buyers were stopping, leaving word for them of his arrival. My brother and Seay had told him that they had met, down the trail that morning, two cattle buyers by the name of Field and Radcliff; that they were inquiring for a herd belonging to Tom Coleman, which was believed to be somewhere between Dodge and the Cimarron River. The two had assured Tolleston that the buyers might not be back for a week, and suggested a few drinks in memory of old times. As Archie was then three sheets in the wind, his effacement, in the hands of two rounders like Dorg Seay and Bob Quirk, was an easy matter.

ANDY ADAMS

Once the wagon was loaded and started for camp, I returned to the restaurant. The dinner was in progress, and taking the vacant seat, I lifted my glass with great regularity as toast after toast was drunk. Cigars were ordered, and with our feet on the table, the fiscal agent said: "Gentlemen, this is a mere luncheon and don't count. But if I'm able to sell you my other two beef herds, why, I'll give you a blow-out right. We'll make it six-handed - the three trail foremen and ourselves - and damn the expense so long as the cattle are sold. Champagne will flow like water, and when our teeth float, we'll wash our feet in what's left."

At a late hour the dinner ended. We were all rather unsteady on our feet, but the pock-marked detective and myself formed a guard of honor in escorting the buyers to their hotel, when an officious clerk attempted to deliver Tolleston's message. But anticipating it, I interrupted his highness and informed him that we had met the party; I was a thousand times obliged to him for his kindness, and forced on him a fine cigar, which had been given me by Bob Wright of the outfitting store. While Siringo and the buyers passed upstairs, I entertained the office force below with an account of the sale of my herd, constantly referring to my new employers. The fiscal agent returned shortly, bought some cigars at the counter, asked if he could get a room for the night, in case he was detained in town, and then we passed out of the hotel. This afforded me the first opportunity to notify Siringo of the presence of Tolleston, and I withheld nothing which was to his interest to know. But he was impatient to learn if the draft had been accepted, and asking me to bring my brother to his room within half an hour, he left me.

It was growing late in the day. The sun had already set when I found my brother, who was anxious to return to his camp for the night. But I urged his seeing Siringo first, and after waiting in the latter's room some time, he burst in upon us with a merry chuckle. "Well, the draft was paid all right," said he; "and this is Bob Quirk. Boys, things are coming nicely. This fellow Tolleston is the only cloud in the sky. If we can keep him down for a week, and the other herds come in shortly, I see nothing to thwart our plans. Where have you picketed Tolleston?" "Around in Dutch Jake's crib," replied Bob.

"That's good," continued the fiscal agent, "and I'll just drop in to-night and see the madam. A little money will go a long way with her, and in a case like this, the devil himself would be a welcome ally. You boys stay in town as much as you can and keep Tolleston snowed deep, and I'll take the buyers down the trail in the morning and meet the herds coming up."

My brother returned to his camp, and Siringo and I separated for the time being. In '84 Dodge, the Port Said of the plains, was in the full flower of her wickedness. Literally speaking, night was turned into day in the old trail town, for with the falling of darkness, the streets filled with people. Restaurants were crowded with women of the half-world, bar-rooms thronged with the wayfaring man, while in gambling and dance halls the range men congregated as if on special invitation. The familiar bark of the six-shooter was a matter of almost nightly occurrence; a dispute at the gaming table, a discourteous word spoken, or the rivalry for the smile of a wanton was provocation for the sacrifice of human life. Here the man of the plains reverted to and gave utterance to the savagery of his nature, or, on the other hand, was as chivalrous as in the days of heraldry.

I knew the town well, this being my third trip over the trail, and mingled with the gathering throng. Near midnight, and when in the Lady Gay dance-hall, I was accosted by Dorg Seay and the detective. They had just left Dutch Jake's, and reported all quiet on the Potomac. Seay had not only proved himself artful, but a good fellow, and had unearthed the fact that Tolleston had been in the employ of Field and Radcliff for the past three months. "You see," said Dorg, "Archie never knew me except the few days that I was about headquarters in Medina before we started. He fully believes that I've been discharged - and with three months' pay in my hip-pocket. The play now is that he's to first help me spend my wages, and then I'm to have a job under him with beeves which he expects to drive to the Yellowstone. He has intimated that he might be able to give me a herd. So, Tom, if I come out there and take possession of your cattle, don't be surprised. There's only one thing to beat our game - I can't get him so full but what he's over-anxious to see his employers. But if you fellows furnish the money, I'll try and pickle him until he forgets them."

The next morning Siringo and the buyers started south on the trail, and I rode for my camp on the Saw Log. Before riding many miles I sighted my outfit coming in a long lope for town. They reported everything serene at camp, and as many of the boys were moneyless, I turned back with them. An enjoyable day was before us; some drank to their hearts' content, while all gambled with more or less success. I was anxious that the outfit should have a good carouse, and showed the lights and shadows of the town with a pride worthy of one of its founders. Acting the host, I paid for our dinners; and as we sauntered into the street, puffing vile cigars, we nearly ran amuck of Dorg Seay and Archie Tolleston, trundling a child's wagon between them up the street. We watched them, keeping a judicious distance, as they visited saloon after saloon, the toy wagon always in possession of one or the other.

While we were amusing ourselves at the antics of these two, my attention was attracted by a four-mule wagon pulling across the bridge from the south. On reaching the railroad tracks, I recognized the team, and also the driver, as Quince Forrest's. Here was news, and accordingly I accosted him. Fortunately he was looking for me or my brother, as his foreman could not come in with the wagon, and some one was wanted to vouch for him in getting the needed supplies. They had reached the Mulberry the evening before, but several herds had mixed in a run during the night, though their cattle had escaped. Forrest was determined not to risk a second night on that stream, and had started his herd with the dawn, expecting to camp with his cattle that night west on Duck Creek. The herd was then somewhere between the latter and the main Arkansaw, and the cook was anxious to secure the supplies and reach the outfit before darkness overtook him. Sponsilier was reported as two days behind Forrest when the latter crossed the Cimarron, since when there had been no word from his cattle. They had met the buyers near the middle of the forenoon, and when Forrest admitted having the widow Timberlake's beef herd, they turned back and were spending the day with the cattle.

The situation demanded instant action. Taking Forrest's cook around to our outfitting store, I introduced and vouched for him. Hurrying back, I sent Wayne Outcault, as he was a stranger to Tolleston, to mix with the two rascals and send Seay to me at once. Some little time was consumed in engaging Archie in a game of pool, but when Dorg presented himself I lost no time in explaining the situation. He declared that it was no longer possible to interest Tolleston at Dutch Jake's crib during the day, and that other means of amusement must be resorted to, as Archie was getting clamorous to find his employers. To my suggestion to get a livery rig and take him for a ride, Dorg agreed. "Take him down the river to Spearville," I urged, "and try and break into the calaboose if you can. Paint the town red while you're about it, and if you both land in the lock-up, all the better. If the rascal insists on coming back to Dodge, start after night, get lost, and land somewhere farther down the river. Keep him away from this town for a week, and I'll gamble that you boss a herd for old man Don next year."

The afternoon was waning. The buyers might return at any moment, as Forrest's herd had no doubt crossed the river but a few miles above town.

I was impatiently watching the boys, as Dorg and Wayne cautiously herded Tolleston around to a livery stable, when my brother Bob rode up. He informed me that he had moved his camp that day across to the Saw Log; that he had done so to accommodate Jim Flood and The Rebel with a camp; their herds were due on the Mulberry that evening. The former had stayed all night at Bob's wagon, and reported his cattle, considering the dry season, in good condition. As my brother expected to remain in town overnight, I proposed starting for my camp as soon as Seay and his ward drove out of sight. They parleyed enough before going to unnerve a saint, but finally, with the little toy wagon on Tolleston's knee and the other driving, they started. Hurrahing my lads to saddle up, we rode past the stable where Seay had secured the conveyance; and while I was posting the stable-keeper not to be uneasy if the rig was gone a week, Siringo and the buyers drove past the barn with a flourish. Taking a back street, we avoided meeting them, and just as darkness was falling, rode into our camp some twelve miles distant.

My brother Bob's camp was just above us on the creek, and a few miles nearer town. As his wagon expected to go in after supplies the next morning, a cavalcade of fifteen men from the two outfits preceded it. My horse-wrangler had made arrangements with the cook to look after his charges, and in anticipation of the day before him, had our mounts corralled before sun-up. Bob's wrangler was also with us, and he and Levering quarreled all the way in about the respective merits of each one's remuda. A match was arranged between the two horses which they were riding, and on reaching a straight piece of road, my man won it and alsoconsiderable money. But no matter how much we differed among ourselves, when the interests of our employer were at stake, we were a unit. On reaching town, our numbers were augmented by fully twenty more from the other Lovell outfits, including the three foremen. My old bunkie, The Rebel, nearly dragged me from my horse, while Forrest and I forgot past differences over a social glass. And then there was Flood, my first foreman, under whom I served my apprenticeship on the trail, the same quiet, languid old Jim. The various foremen and their outfits were aware of the impending trouble over the Buford delivery, and quietly expressed their contempt for such underhand dealings. Quince Forrest had spent the evening before in town, and about midnight his herd of "Drooping T's" were sold at about the same figures as mine, except five thousand more earnest-money, and the privilege of the buyers placing their own foreman in charge thereafter. Forrest further reported that the fiscal agent and the strangers had started to meet Sponsilier early that morning, and that the probability of all the herds moving out in a few days was good.

Seay and his charge were still absent, and the programme, as outlined, was working out nicely. With the exception of Forrest and myself, the other foremen were busy looking after their outfits, while Bob Quirk had his wagon to load and start on its return. Quince confided to me that though he had stayed on Duck Creek the night before, his herd would noon that day on Saw Log, and camp that evening on the next creek north. When pressed for his reasons, he shrugged his shoulders, and with a quiet wink, said: "If this new outfit put a man over me, just the minute we get out of the jurisdiction of this county, off his horse he goes and walks back. If it's Tolleston, the moment he sees me and recognizes my outfit as belonging to Lovell, he'll raise the long yell and let the cat out. When that happens, I want to be in an unorganized country where a six-shooter is the highest authority." The idea was a new one to me, and I saw the advantage of it, but could not move without Siringo's permission, which Forrest had. Accordingly about noon, Quince summoned his men together, and they rode out of town. Looking up a map of Ford County, I was delighted to find that my camp on Saw Log was but a few miles below the north line.

Among the boys the day passed in riotousness. The carousing was a necessary stimulant after the long, monotonous drive and exposure to the elements. Near the middle of the forenoon, Flood and The Rebel rounded up their outfits and started south for the Mulberry, while Bob Quirk gathered his own and my lads preparatory to leaving for the Saw Log. I had agreed to remain on guard for that night, for with the erratic turn on Tolleston's part, we were doubly cautious. But when my outfit was ready to start, Runt Pickett, the feisty little rascal, had about twenty dollars in his possession which he insisted on gambling away before leaving town. Runt was comfortably drunk, and as Bob urged humoring him, I gave my consent, provided he would place it all at one bet, to which Pickett agreed. Leaving the greater part of the boys holding the horses, some half-dozen of us entered the nearest gambling-house, and Runt bet nineteen dollars "Alce" on the first card which fell in a monte lay-out. To my chagrin, he won. My brother was delighted over the little rascal's luck, and urged him to double his bet, but Pickett refused and invited us all to have a drink. Leaving this place, we entered the next gaming-hall, when our man again bet nineteen dollars alce on the first card. Again he won, and we went the length of the street, Runt wagering nineteen dollars alce on the first card for ten consecutive times without losing a bet. In his groggy condi-tion, the prospect of losing Pickett's money was hopeless, and my brother and I promised him that he might come back the next morning and try to get rid of his winnings.

Two whole days passed with no report from either Seay or the buyers. Meanwhile Flood and The Rebel threaded their way through the other herds, crossing the Arkansaw above town, their wagons touching at Dodge for new supplies, never halting except temporarily until they reached the creek on which Forrest was encamped. The absence of Siringo and the buyers, to my thinking, was favorable, for no doubt when they came in, a deal would have been effected on the last of the Buford herds. They returned some time during the night of the third day out, and I failed to see the detective before sunrise the next morning. When I did meet him, everything seemed so serene that I felt jubilant over the outlook. Sponsilier's beeves had firmly caught the fancy of the buyers, and the delay in closing the trade was only temporary. "I can close the deal any minute I want to," said Siringo to me, "but we mustn't appear too anxious. Old man Don's idea was to get about one hundred thousand dollars earnest-money in hand, but if I can get five or ten more, it might help tide us all over a hard winter. My last proposition to the buyers was that if they would advance forty-five thousand dollars on the 'Apple' beeves - Sponsilier's cattle - they might appoint, at the seller's expense, their own foreman from Dodge to the point of delivery. They have agreed to give me an answer this morning, and after sleeping over it, I look for no trouble in closing the trade."

The buyers were also astir early. I met Mr. Field in the post-office, where he was waiting for it to open. To his general inquiries I reported everything quiet, but suggested we move camp soon or the cattle would become restless. He listened very attentively, and promised that within a few days permission would be given to move out for our final destination. The morning were the quiet hours of the town, and when the buyers had received and gone over their large and accumulated mail, the partners came over to the Dodge House, looking for the fiscal agent, as I supposed, to close the trade on Sponsilier's cattle. Siringo was the acme of indifference, but listened to a different tale. A trusted man, in whom they had placed a great deal of confidence, had failed to materialize. He was then overdue some four or five days, and foul play was suspected. The wily detective poured oil on the troubled waters, assuring them if their man failed to appear within a day or two, he would gladly render every assistance in looking him up. Another matter of considerable moment would be the arrival that morning of a silent partner, the financial man of the firm from Washington, D.C. He was due to arrive on the "Cannon Ball" at eight o'clock, and we all sauntered down to meet the train from the East. On its arrival, Siringo and I stood back among the crowd, but the buyers pushed forward, looking for their friend. The first man to alight from the day coach, coatless and with both eyes blackened, was Archie Tolleston; he almost fell into the arms of our cattle buyers. I recognized Archie at a glance, and dragging the detective inside the waiting-room, posted him as to the arrival with the wild look and blood-shot optics. Siringo cautioned me to go to his room and stay there, promising to report as the day advanced.

Sponsilier had camped the night before on the main river, and as I crossed to the hotel, his commissary pulled up in front of Wright, Beverly & Co.'s outfitting store. Taking the chances of being seen, I interviewed Dave's cook, and learned that his foreman had given him an order for the supplies, and that Sponsilier would not come in until after the herd had passed the Saw Log. As I turned away, my attention was attracted by the deference being shown the financial man of the cattle firm, as the party wended their way around to the Wright House. The silent member of the firm was a portly fellow, and there was no one in the group but did him honor, even the detective carrying a light grip, while Tolleston lumbered along with a heavy one.

My effacement was only temporary, as Siringo appeared at his room shortly afterward. "Well, Quirk," said he, with a smile. "I reckon my work is all done. Field and Radcliff didn't feel like talking business this morning, at least until they had shown the financial member their purchases, both real and prospective. Yes, they took the fat Colonel and Tolleston with them and started for your camp with a two-seated rig. From yours they expect to drive to Forrest's camp, and then meet Sponsilier on the way coming back. No; I declined a very pressing invitation to go along - you see my mixed herds might come in any minute. And say, that man Tolleston was there in a hundred places with the big conversation; he claims to have been kidnapped, and was locked up for the last four days. He says he whipped your man Seay, but couldn't convince the authorities of his innocence until last night, when they set him free. According to his report, Seay's in jail yet at a little town down the road called Kinsley. Now, I'm going to take a conveyance to Spearville, and catch the first train out of there East. Settle my bill with this hotel, and say that I may be out of town for a few days, meeting a herd which I'm expecting. When Tolleston recognizes all three of those outfits as belonging to Don Lovell - well, won't there be hell to pay? Yes, my work is all done."

I fully agreed with the detective that Archie would recognize the remudas and outfits as Lovell's, even though the cattle were road-branded out of the usual "Circle Dot." Siringo further informed me that north of Ford County was all an unorganized country until the Platte River was reached at

Ogalalla, and advised me to ignore any legal process served outside those bounds. He was impatient to get away, and when he had put me in possession of everything to our advantage, we wrung each other's hands in farewell. As the drive outlined by the cattle buyers would absorb the day, I felt no necessity of being in a hurry. The absence of Dorg Seay was annoying, and the fellow had done us such valiant service, I felt in honor bound to secure his release. Accordingly I wired the city marshal at Kinsley, and received a reply that Seay had been released early that morning, and had started overland for Dodge. This was fortunate, and after settling all bills, I offered to pay the liveryman in advance for the rig in Seay's possession, assuring him by the telegram that it would return that evening. He refused to make any settlement until the condition of both the animal and the conveyance had been passed upon, and fearful lest Dorg should come back moneyless, I had nothing to do but await his return. I was growing impatient to reach camp, there being no opportunity to send word to my outfit, and the passing hours seemed days, when late in the afternoon Dorg Seay drove down the main street of Dodge as big as a government beef buyer. The liveryman was pleased and accepted the regular rate, and Dorg and I were soon galloping out of town. As we neared the first divide, we dropped our horses into a walk to afford them a breathing spell, and in reply to my fund of information, Seay said:

"So Tolleston's telling that he licked me. Well, that's a good one on this one of old man Seay's boys. Archie must have been crazy with the heat. The fact is that he had been trying to quit me for several days. We had exhausted every line of dissipation, and when I decided that it was no longer possible to hold him, I insulted and provoked him into a quarrel, and we were both arrested. Licked me, did he? He couldn't lick his upper lip."

CHAPTER IX.

AT SHERIFF'S CREEK

The sun had nearly set when we galloped into Bob Quirk's camp. Halting only long enough to advise my brother of the escape of Tolleston and his joining the common enemy, I asked him to throw any pursuit off our trail, as I proposed breaking camp that evening. Seay and myself put behind us the few miles between the two wagons, and dashed up to mine just as the outfit were corralling the remuda for night-horses. Orders rang out, and instead of catching our regular guard mounts, the boys picked the best horses in their strings. The cattle were then nearly a mile north of camp, coming in slowly towards the bed-ground, but a half-dozen of us rushed away to relieve the men on herd and turn the beeves back. The work-mules were harnessed in, and as soon as the relieved herders secured mounts, our camp of the past few days was abandoned. The twilight of evening was upon us, and to the rattling of the heavily loaded wagon and the shouting of the wrangler in our rear were added the old herd songs. The cattle, without trail or trace to follow, and fit ransom for a dozen kings in pagan ages, moved north as if imbued with the spirit of the occasion.

A fair moon favored us. The night was an ideal one for work, and about twelve o'clock we bedded down the herd and waited for dawn. As we expected to move again with the first sign of day, no one cared to sleep; our nerves were under a high tension with expectation of what the coming day might bring forth. Our location was an unknown quantity. All agreed that we were fully ten miles north of the Saw Log, and, with the best reasoning at my command, outside the jurisdiction of Ford County. The regular trail leading north was some six or eight miles to the west, and fearful that we had not reached unorganized territory, I was determined to push farther on our course before veering to the left. The night halt, however, afforded us an opportunity to compare notes and arrive at some definite understanding as to the programme of the forthcoming day. "Quirk, you missed the sight of your life," said Jake Blair, as we dismounted around the wagon, after bedding the cattle, "by not being there when the discovery was made that these 'Open A's' were Don Lovell's cattle. Tolleston, of course, made the discovery; but I think he must have smelt the rat in advance. Archie and the buyers arrived for a late dinner, and several times Tolleston ran his eye over one of the boys and asked, 'Haven't I met you somewhere?' but none of them could recall the meeting. Then he got to nosing around the wagon and noticing every horse about camp. The road-brand on the cattle threw him off the scent just for a second, but when he began reading the ranch-brands, he took a new hold. As he looked over the remuda, the scent seemed to get stronger, and when he noticed the 'Circle Dot' on those work-mules, he opened up and bayed as if he had treed something. And sure enough he had; for you know, Tom, those calico lead mules belonged in his team last year, and he swore he'd know them in hell, brand or no brand. When Archie announced the outfit, lock, stock, and barrel, as belonging to Don Lovell, the old buyers turned pale as ghosts, and the fat one took off his hat and fanned himself. That act alone was worth the price of admission. But when we boys were appealed to, we were innocent and likewise ignorant, claiming that we always understood that the herd belonged to the Marshall estate, but then we were just common hands and not supposed to know the facts in the case. Tolleston argued one way, and we all pulled the other, so they drove away, looking as if they hoped it wasn't true. But it was the sight of your life to see that fat fellow fan himself as he kept repeating, 'I thought you boys hurried too much in buying these cattle.'

The guards changed hourly. No fire was allowed, but Parent

set out all the cold food available, and supplementing this with canned goods, we had a midnight lunch. Dorg Seay regaled the outfit with his recent experience, concealing nothing, and regretfully admitting that his charge had escaped before the work was finished. A programme was outlined for the morrow, the main feature of which was that, in case of pursuit, we would all tell the same story. Dawn came between three and four on those June mornings, and with the first streak of gray in the east we divided the outfit and mounted our horses, part riding to push the cattle off their beds and the others to round in the remuda. Before the herd had grazed out a half-mile, we were overtaken by half the outfit on fresh mounts, who at once took charge of the herd. When the relieved men had secured horses, I remained behind and assisted in harnessing in the team and gathering the saddle stock, a number of which were missed for lack of proper light. With the wagon once started, Levering and myself soon had the full remuda in hand and were bringing up the rear in a long, swinging trot. Before the sun peeped over the eastern horizon, we passed the herd and overtook the wagon, which was bumping along over the uneven prairie. Ordering the cook to have breakfast awaiting us beyond a divide which crossed our front, I turned back to the herd, now strung out in regular trailing form. The halt ahead would put us full fifteen miles north of our camp on the Saw Log. An hour later, as we were scaling the divide, one of the point-men sighted a posse in our rear, coming after us like fiends. I was riding in the swing at the time, the herd being strung out fully a mile, and on catching first sight of the pursuers, turned and hurried to the rear. To my agreeable surprise, instead of a sheriff's posse, my brother and five of his men galloped up and overtook us.

"Well, Tom, it's a good thing you moved last night," said Bob, as he reined in his reeking horse. "A deputy sheriff and posse of six men had me under arrest all night, thinking I was the Quirk who had charge of Don Lovell's 'Open A' herd. Yes, they came to my camp about midnight, and I admitted that my name was Quirk and that we were holding Lovell's cattle. They guarded me until morning, - I slept like an innocent babe myself, - when the discovery was made that my herd was in a 'Circle Dot' road-brand instead of an 'Open A,' which their warrant called for. Besides, I proved by fourteen competent witnesses, who had known me for years, that my name was Robert Burns Quirk. My outfit told the posse that the herd they were looking for were camped three miles below, but had left during the afternoon before, and no doubt were then beyond their bailiwick. I gave the posse the horse-laugh, but they all went down the creek, swearing they would trail down that herd of Lovell's. My cattle are going to follow up this morning, so I thought I'd ride on ahead and be your guest in case there is any fun to-day."

The auxiliary was welcomed. The beeves moved on up the divide like veterans assaulting an intrenchment. On reaching a narrow mesa on the summit, a northwest breeze met the leaders, and facing it full in the eye, the herd was allowed to tack westward as they went down the farther slope. This watershed afforded a fine view of the surrounding country, and from its apex I scanned our rear for miles without detecting any sign of animate life. From our elevation, the plain dipped away in every direction. Far to the east, the depression seemed as real as a trough in the ocean when seen from the deck of a ship. The meanderings of this divide were as crooked as a river, and as we surveyed its course one of Bob's men sighted with the naked eye two specks fully five miles distant to the northwest, and evidently in the vicinity of the old trail. The wagon was in plain view, and leaving three of my boys to drift the cattle forward, we rode away with ravenous appetites to interview the cook. Parent maintained his reputation as host, and with a lofty conversation reviewed the legal aspect of the situation confronting us. A hasty breakfast over, my brother asked for mounts for himself and men; and as we were corralling our remuda, one of the three lads on herd signaled to us from the mesa's summit. Catching the nearest horses at hand, and taking our wrangler with us, we cantered up the slope to our waiting sentinel.

"You can't see them now," said Burl Van Vedder, our outlook;

"but wait a few minutes and they'll come up on higher ground. Here, here, you are looking a mile too far to the right - they're not following the cattle, but the wagon's trail. Keep your eyes to the left of that shale outcropping, and on a line with that lone tree on the Saw Log. Hold your horses a minute; I've been watching them for half an hour before I called you; be patient, and they'll rise like a trout. There! there comes one on a gray horse. See those two others just behind him. Now, there come the others - six all told." Sure enough, there came the sleuths of deputy sheriffs, trailing up our wagon. They were not over three miles away, and after patiently waiting nearly an hour, we rode to the brink of the slope, and I ordered one of the boys to fire his pistol to attract their attention. On hearing the report, they halted, and taking off my hat I waved them forward. Feeling that we were on safe territory, I was determined to get in the first bluff, and as they rode up, I saluted the leader and said:

"Good-morning, Mr. Sheriff. What are you fooling along on our wagon track for, when you could have trailed the herd in a long lope? Here we've wasted a whole hour waiting for you to come up, just because the sheriff's office of Ford County employs as deputies 'nesters' instead of plainsmen. But now since you are here, let us proceed to business, or would you like to breakfast first? Our wagon is just over the other slope, and you-all look pale around the gills this morning after your long ride and sleepless night. Which shall it be, business or breakfast?"

Haughtily ignoring my irony, the leader of the posse drew from his pocket several papers, and first clearing his throat, said in an imperious tone, "I have a warrant here for the arrest of Tom Quirk, alias McIndoo, and a distress warrant for a herd of 'Open A' - "

"Old sport, you're in the right church, but the wrong pew," I interrupted. "This may be the state of Kansas, but at present we are outside the bailiwick of Ford County, and those papers of yours are useless. Let me take those warrants and I'll indorse them for you, so as to dazzle your superiors on their return without the man or property. I was deputized once by a constable in Texas to assist in recovering some cattle, but just like the present case they got out of our jurisdiction before we overtook them. The constable was a lofty, arrogant fellow like yourself, but had sense enough to keep within his rights. But when it came to indorsing the warrant for return, we were all up a stump, and rode twenty miles out of our way so as to pass Squire Little's ranch and get his advice on the matter. The squire had been a justice in Tennessee before coming to our state, and knew just what to say. Now let me take those papers, and I'll indorse them 'Non est inventus,' which is Latin for SCOOTED, BY GOSH! Ain't you going to let me have them?"

"Now, look here, young man," scornfully replied the chief deputy, "I'll -"

"No, you won't," I again interrupted. "Let me read you a warrant from a higher court. In the name of law, you are willing to prostitute your office to assist a gang of thieves who have taken advantage of an opportunity to ruin my employer, an honest trail drover. The warrant I'm serving was issued by Judge Colt, and it says he is supreme in unorganized territory; that your official authority ceases the moment you step outside your jurisdiction, and you know the Ford County line is behind us. Now, as a citizen, I'll treat you right, but as an official, I won't even listen to you. And what's more, you can't arrest me or any man in my outfit; not that your hair's the wrong color, but because you lack authority. I'm the man you're looking for, and these are Don Lovell's cattle, but you can't touch a hoof of them, not even a stray. Now, if you want to dispute the authority which I've sighted, all you need to do is pull your guns and open your game."

"Mr. Quirk," said the deputy, "you are a fugitive from justice, and I can legally take you wherever I find you. If you resist arrest, all the worse, as it classes you an outlaw. Now, my advice is -"

But the sentence was never finished, for coming down the divide like a hurricane was a band of horsemen, who, on sighting us, raised the long yell, and the next minute Dave Sponsilier and seven of his men dashed up. The boys opened out to avoid the momentum of the onslaught, but the deputies sat firm; and as Sponsilier and his lads threw their horses back on their haunches in halting, Dave stood in his stirrups, and waving his hat shouted, "Hurrah for Don Lovell, and to hell with the sheriff and deputies of Ford County!" Sponsilier and I were great friends, as were likewise our outfits, and we nearly unhorsed each other in our rough but hearty greetings. When quiet was once more restored, Dave continued: "I was in Dodge last night, and Bob Wright put me next that the sheriff was going to take possession of two of old man Don's herds this morning. You can bet your moccasins that the grass didn t grow very much while I was getting back to camp. Flood and The Rebel took fifteen men and went to Quince's support, and I have been scouting since dawn trying to locate you. Yes, the sheriff himself and five deputies passed up the trail before daybreak to arrest Forrest and take possession of his herd - I don't think. I suppose these strangers are deputy sheriffs? If it was me, do you know what I'd do with them?"

The query was half a command. It required no order, for in an instant the deputies were surrounded, and had it not been for the cool judgment of Bob Quirk, violence would have resulted. The primitive mind is slow to resent an affront, and while the chief deputy had couched his last remarks in well-chosen language, his intimation that I was a fugitive from justice, and an outlaw in resisting arrest, was tinder to stubble. Knowing the metal of my outfit, I curbed the tempest within me, and relying on a brother whom I would gladly follow to death if need be, I waved hands off to my boys. "Now, men," said Bob to the deputies, "the easiest way out of this matter is the best. No one here has committed any crime subjecting him to arrest, neither can you take possession of any cattle belonging to Don Lovell. I'll renew the invitation for you to go down to the wagon and breakfast, or I'll give you the best directions at my command to reach Dodge. Instead of trying to attempt to accomplish your object you had better go back to the chaparral - you're spelled down. Take your choice, men."

Bob's words had a soothing effect. He was thirty-three years old and a natural born leader among rough men. His advice carried the steely ring of sincerity, and for the first time since the meeting, the deputies wilted. The chief one called his men aside, and after a brief consultation my brother was invited to join them, which he did. I afterwards learned that Bob went into detail in defining our position in the premises, and the posse, once they heard the other side of the question, took an entirely different view of the matter. While the consultation was in progress, we all dismounted; cigarettes were rolled, and while the smoke arose in clouds, we reviewed the interim since we parted in March in old Medina. The sheriff's posse accompanied my brother to the wagon, and after refreshing themselves, remounted their horses. Bob escorted them back across the summit of the mesa, and the olive branch waved in peace on the divide.

The morning was not far advanced. After a brief consultation, the two older foremen urged that we ride to the relief of Forrest. A hint was sufficient, and including five of my best-mounted men, a posse of twenty of us rode away. We held the divide for some distance on our course, and before we left it, a dust-cloud, indicating the presence of Bob's herd, was sighted on the southern slope, while on the opposite one my cattle were beginning to move forward. Sponsilier knew the probable whereabouts of Forrest, and under his lead we swung into a free gallop as we dropped down the northern slope from the mesa. The pace was carrying us across country at a rate of ten miles an hour, scarcely a word being spoken, as we shook out kink after kink in our horses or reined them in to recover their wind. Our objective point was a slight elevation on the plain, from which we expected to sight the trail if not the herds of Flood, Forrest, and The Rebel. On reaching this gentle swell, we reined in and halted our horses, which were then fuming with healthy sweat. Both creek and trail were clearly outlined before us, but with the heat-waves and mirages beyond, our view was naturally restricted. Sponsilier felt confident that Forrest was north of the creek and beyond the trail, and again shaking out our horses, we silently put the intervening miles behind us. Our mounts were all fresh and strong, and in crossing the creek we allowed them a few swallows of water before continuing our ride. We halted again in crossing the trail, but it was so worn by recent use that it afforded no clue to guide us in our quest. But from the next vantage-point which afforded us a view, a sea of cattle greeted our vision, all of which seemed under herd. Wagon sheets were next sighted, and finally a horseman loomed up and signaled to us. He proved to be one of Flood's men, and under his direction Forrest's camp and cattle were soon located. The lad assured us that a pow-wow had been in session since daybreak, and we hurried away to add our numbers to its council. When we sighted Forrest's wagon among some cottonwoods, a number of men were just mounting to ride away, and before we reached camp, they crossed the creek heading south. A moment later, Forrest walked out, and greeting us, said:

"Hello, fellows. Get down and let your horses blow and enjoy yourselves. You're just a minute late to meet some very nice people. Yes, we had the sheriff from Dodge and a posse of men for breakfast. No - no particular trouble, except John Johns, the d - fool, threw the loop of his rope over the neck of the sheriff's horse, and one of the party offered to unsling a carbine. But about a dozen six-shooters clicked within hearing, and he acted on my advice and cut gun-plays out. No trouble at all except a big medicine talk, and a heap of legal phrases that I don't sabe very clear. Turn your horses loose, I tell you, for I'm going to kill a nice fat stray, and towards evening, when the other herds come up, we'll have a round-up of Don Lovell's outfits. I'll make a little speech, and on account of the bloodless battle this morning, this stream will be rechristened Sheriff's Creek."

CHAPTER X.

A FAMILY REUNION

The hospitality of a trail wagon was aptly expressed in the invitation to enjoy ourselves. Some one had exercised good judgment in selecting a camp, for every convenience was at hand, including running water and ample shade from a clump of cottonwoods. Turning our steaming horses free, we threw ourselves, in complete abandonment and relaxation, down in the nearest shade. Unmistakable hints were given our host of certain refreshments which would be acceptable, and in reply Forrest pointed to a bucket of creek water near the wagon wheel, and urged us not to be at all backward.

Every one was well fortified with brown cigarette papers and smoking tobacco, and singly and in groups we were soon smoking like hired hands and reviewing the incidents of the morning. Forrest's cook, a tall, red-headed fellow, in anticipation of the number of guests his wagon would entertain for the day, put on the little and the big pot. As it only lacked an hour of noon on our arrival, the promised fresh beef would not be available in time for dinner; but we were not like guests who had to hurry home - we would be right there when supper was ready.

The loss of a night's sleep on my outfit was a good excuse for an after-dinner siesta. Untying our slickers, we strolled out of hearing of the camp, and for several hours obliterated time. About three o'clock Bob Quirk aroused and informed us that he had ordered our horses, and that the signal of Sponsilier's cattle had been seen south on the trail. Dave was impatient to intercept his herd and camp them well down the creek, at least below the regular crossing. This would throw Bob's and my cattle still farther down the stream; and we were all determined to honor Forrest with our presence for supper and the evening hours. Quince's wrangler rustled in the horses, and as we rejoined the camp the quarters of a beef hung low on a cottonwood, while a smudge beneath them warned away all insect life. Leaving word that we would return during the evening, the eleventh-hour guests rode away in the rough, uneven order in which we had arrived. Sponsilier and his men veered off to the south, Bob Quirk and his lads soon following, while the rest of us continued on down the creek. My cattle were watering when we overtook them, occupying fully a mile of the stream, and nearly an hour's ride below the trail crossing. It takes a long time to water a big herd thoroughly, and we repeatedly turned them back and forth across the creek, but finally allowed them to graze away with a broad, fan-like front. As ours left the stream, Bob's cattle were coming in over a mile above, and in anticipation of a dry camp that night, Parent had been advised to fill his kegs and supply himself with wood.

Detailing the third and fourth guard to wrangle the remuda, I sent Levering up the creek with my brother's horses and to recover our loaned saddle stock; even Bob Quirk was just thoughtless enough to construe a neighborly act into a horse trade. About two miles out from the creek and an equal distance from the trail, I found the best bed-ground of the trip. It sloped to the northwest, was covered with old dry grass, and would catch any vagrant breeze except an eastern one. The wagon was ordered into camp, and the first and second guards were relieved just long enough to secure their night-horses. Nearly all of these two watches had been with me during the day, and on the return of Levering with the horses, we borrowed a number of empty flour-sacks for beef, and cantered away, leaving behind only the cook and the first two guards.

What an evening and night that was! As we passed up the creek, we sighted in the gathering twilight the camp-fires of

Sponsilier and my brother, several miles apart and south of the stream. When we reached Forrest's wagon the clans were gathering, The Rebel and his crowd being the last to come in from above. Groups of saddle horses were tied among the trees, while around two fires were circles of men broiling beef over live coals. The red-headed cook had anticipated forty guests outside of his own outfit, and was pouring coffee into tin cups and shying biscuit right and left on request. The supper was a success, not on account of the spread or our superior table manners, but we graced the occasion with appetites which required the staples of life to satisfy. Then we smoked, falling into groups when the yarning began. All the fresh-beef stories of our lives, and they were legion, were told, no one group paying any attention to another.

"Every time I run a-foul of fresh beef," said The Rebel, as he settled back comfortably between the roots of a cottonwood, with his back to its trunk, "it reminds me of the time I was a prisoner among the Yankees. It was the last year of the war, and I had got over my first desire to personally whip the whole North. There were about five thousand of us held as prisoners of war for eleven months on a peninsula in the Chesapeake Bay. The fighting spirit of the soldier was broken in the majority of us, especially among the older men and those who had families. But we youngsters accepted the fortunes of war and were glad that we were alive, even if we were prisoners. In my mess in prison there were fifteen, all having been captured at the same time, and many of us comrades of three years' standing.

"I remember the day we were taken off the train and marched through the town for the prison, a Yankee band in our front playing national airs and favorites of their army, and the people along the route jeering us and asking how we liked the music. Our mess held together during the march, and some of the boys answered them back as well as they could. Once inside the prison stockade, we went into quarters and our mess still held together. Before we had been there long, one day there was a call among the prisoners for volunteers to form a roustabout crew. Well, I enlisted as a roustabout. We had to report to an officer twice a day, and then were put under guard and set to work. The kind of labor I liked best was unloading the supplies for the prison, which were landed on a near-by wharf. This roustabout crew had all the unloading to do, and the reason I liked it was it gave us some chance to steal. Whenever there was anything extra, intended for the officers, to be unloaded, look out for accidents. Broken crates were common, and some of the contents was certain to reach our pockets or stomachs, in spite of the guard.

"I was a willing worker and stood well with the guards. They never searched me, and when they took us outside the stockade, the captain of the guard gave me permission, after our work was over, to patronize the sutler's store and buy knick-knacks from the booths. There was always some little money amongst soldiers, even in prison, and I was occasionally furnished money by my messmates to buy bread from a baker's wagon which was outside the walls. Well, after I had traded a few times with the baker's boy, I succeeded in corrupting him. Yes, had him stealing from his employer and selling to me at a discount. I was a good customer, and being a prisoner, there was no danger of my meeting his employer. You see the loaves were counted out to him, and he had to return the equivalent or the bread. At first the bread cost me ten cents for a small loaf, but when I got my scheme working, it didn't cost me five cents for the largest loaves the boy could steal from the bakery. I worked that racket for several months, and if we hadn't been exchanged, I'd have broke that baker, sure.

"But the most successful scheme I worked was stealing the kidneys out of beef while we were handling it. It was some distance from the wharf to the warehouse, and when I'd get a hind quarter of beef on my shoulder, it was an easy trick to burrow my hand through the tallow and get a good grip on the kidney. Then when I'd throw the quarter down in the warehouse, it would be minus a kidney, which secretly found lodgment in a large pocket in the inside of my shirt. I was satisfied with one or two kidneys a day when I first worked the trick, but my mess caught on, and then I had to steal by wholesale to satisfy them. Some days, when the guards were too watchful, I couldn't get very many, and then again when things were lax, 'Elijah's Raven' would get a kidney for each man in our mess. With the regular allowance of rations and what I could steal, when the Texas troops were exchanged, our mess was ragged enough, but pig-fat, and slick as weasels. Lord love you, but we were a great mess of thieves."

Nearly all of Flood's old men were with him again, several of whom were then in Forrest's camp. A fight occurred among a group of saddle horses tied to the front wheel of the wagon, among them being the mount of John Officer. After the belligerents had been quieted, and Officer had removed and tied his horse to a convenient tree, he came over and joined our group, among which were the six trail bosses. Throwing himself down among us, and using Sponsilier for a pillow and myself for footstool, he observed:

"All you foremen who have been over the Chisholm Trail remember the stage-stand called Bull Foot, but possibly some of the boys haven't. Well, no matter, it's just about midway between Little Turkey Creek and Buffalo Springs on that trail, where it runs through the Cherokee Strip. I worked one year in that northern country - lots of Texas boys there too. It was just about the time they began to stock that country with Texas steers, and we rode lines to keep our cattle on their range. You bet, there was riding to do in that country then. The first few months that these Southern steers are turned loose on a new range, Lord! but they do love to drift against a breeze. In any kind of a rain-storm, they'll travel farther in a night than a whole outfit can turn them back in a day.

"Our camp was on the Salt Fork of the Cimarron, and late in the fall when all the beeves had been shipped, the outfit were riding lines and loose-herding a lot of Texas yearlings, and mixed cattle, natives to that range. Up in that country they have Indian summer and Squaw winter, both occurring in the fall. They have lots of funny weather up there. Well, late one evening that fall there came an early squall of Squaw winter, sleeted and spit snow wickedly. The next morning there wasn't a hoof in sight, and shortly after daybreak we were riding deep in our saddles to catch the lead drift of our cattle. After a hard day's ride, we found that we were out several hundred head, principally yearlings of the through Texas stock. You all know how locoed a bunch of dogies can get - we hunted for three days and for fifty miles in every direction, and neither hide, hair, nor hoof could we find. It was while we were hunting these cattle that my yarn commences.

"The big augers of the outfit lived in Wichita, Kansas. Their foreman, Bibleback Hunt, and myself were returning from hunting this missing bunch of yearlings when night overtook us, fully twenty-five miles from camp. Then this Bull Foot stage came to mind, and we turned our horses and rode to it. It was nearly dark when we reached it, and Bibleback said for me to go in and make the talk. I'll never forget that nice little woman who met me at the door of that sod shack. I told her our situation, and she seemed awfully gracious in granting us food and shelter for the night. She told us we could either picket our horses or put them in the corral and feed them hay and grain from the stage-company's supply. Now, old Bibleback was what you might call shy of women, and steered clear of the house until she sent her little boy out and asked us to come in. Well, we sat around in the room, owly-like, and to save my soul from the wrath to come, I couldn't think of a word that was proper to say to the little woman, busy getting supper. Bibleback was worse off than I was; he couldn't do anything but look at the pictures on the wall. What was worrying me was, had she a husband? Or what was she doing away out there in that lonesome country? Then a man old enough to be her grandfather put in an appearance. He was friendly and quite talkative, and I built right up to him. And then we had a supper that I distinctly remember yet. Well, I should say I do - it takes a woman to get a good supper, and cheer it with her presence, sitting at the head of the table and pouring the coffee.

"This old man was a retired stage-driver, and was doing the wrangling act for the stage-horses. After supper I went out to the corral and wormed the information out of him that the woman was a widow; that her husband had died before she came there, and that she was from Michigan. Amongst other things that I learned from the old man was that she had only been there a few months, and was a poor but deserving woman. I told Bibleback all this after we had gone to bed, and we found that our finances amounted to only four dollars, which she was more than welcome to. So the next morning after breakfast, when I asked her what I owed her for our trouble, she replied so graciously: 'Why, gentlemen, I couldn't think of taking advantage of your necessity to charge you for a favor that I'm only too happy to grant.' 'Oh,' said I, 'take this, anyhow,' laying the silver on the corner of the table and starting for the door, when she stopped me. 'One moment, sir; I can't think of accepting this. Be kind enough to grant my request,' and returned the money. We mumbled out some thanks, bade her good-day, and started for the corral, feeling like two sheep thieves. While we were saddling up - will you believe it? - her little boy came out to the corral and gave each one of us as fine a cigar as ever I buttoned my lip over. Well, fellows, we had had it put all over us by this little Michigan woman, till we couldn't look each other in the face. We were accustomed to hardship and neglect, but here was genuine kindness enough to kill a cat.

"Until we got within five miles of our camp that morning, old Bibleback wouldn't speak to me as we rode along. Then he turned halfway in his saddle and said: 'What kind of folks are those?' 'I don't know,' I replied, 'what kind of people they are, but I know they are good ones.' 'Well, I'll get even with that little woman if it takes every sou in my war-bags,' said Hunt.

"When within a mile of camp, Bibleback turned again in his saddle and asked, 'When is Christmas?' 'In about five weeks,' I answered. 'Do you know where that big Wyoming stray ranges?' he next asked. I trailed onto his game in a second. 'Of course I do.' 'Well,' says he, 'let's kill him for Christmas and give that little widow every ounce of the meat. It'll be a good one on her, won't it? We'll fool her a plenty. Say nothing to the others,' he added; and giving our horses the rein we rode into camp on a gallop.

"Three days before Christmas we drove up this Wyoming stray and beefed him. We hung the beef up overnight to harden in the frost, and the next morning bright and early, we started for the stage-stand with a good pair of ponies to a light wagon. We reached the widow's place about eleven o'clock, and against her protests that she had no use for so much, we hung up eight hundred pounds of as fine beef as you ever set your peepers on. We wished her a merry Christmas, jumped into the wagon, clucked to the ponies, and merely hit the high places getting away. When we got well out of sight of the house - well, I've seen mule colts play and kid goats cut up their antics; I've seen children that was frolicsome; but for a man with gray hair on his head, old Bibleback Hunt that day was the happiest mortal I ever saw. He talked to the horses; he sang songs; he played Injun; and that Christmas was a merry one, for the debt was paid and our little widow had beef to throw to the dogs. I never saw her again, but wherever she is to-night, if my prayer counts, may God bless her!"

Early in the evening I had warned my boys that we would start on our return at ten o'clock. The hour was nearly at hand, and in reply to my inquiry if our portion of the beef had been secured, Jack Splann said that he had cut off half a loin, a side of ribs, and enough steak for breakfast. Splann and I tied the beef to our cantle-strings, and when we returned to the group, Sponsilier was telling of the stampede of his herd in the Panhandle about a month before. "But that run wasn't a circumstance to one in which I figured once, and in broad daylight," concluded Dave. It required no encouragement to get the story; all we had to do was to give him time to collect his thoughts.

"Yes, it was in the summer of '73," he finally continued. 'It was my first trip over the trail, and I naturally fell into position at the drag end of the herd. I was a green boy of about eighteen at the time, having never before been fifty miles from the ranch where I was born. The herd belonged to Major Hood, and our destination was Ellsworth, Kansas. In those days they generally worked oxen to the chuck-wagons, as they were ready sale in the upper country, and in good demand for breaking prairie. I reckon there must have been a dozen yoke of work-steers in our herd that year, and they were more trouble to me than all the balance of the cattle, for they were slothful and sinfully lazy. My vocabulary of profanity was worn to a frazzle before we were out a week, and those oxen didn't pay any more attention to a rope or myself than to the buzzing of a gnat.

"There was one big roan ox, called Turk, which we worked to the wagon occasionally, but in crossing the Arbuckle Mountains in the Indian Territory, he got tender-footed. Another yoke was substituted, and in a few days Turk was on his feet again. But he was a cunning rascal and had learned to soldier, and while his feet were sore, I favored him with sandy trails and gave him his own time. In fact, most of my duties were driving that one ox, while the other boys handled the herd. When his feet got well - I had toadied and babied him so - he was plum ruined. I begged the foreman to put him back in the chuck team, but the cook kicked on account of his well-known laziness, so Turk and I continued to adorn the rear of the column. I reckon the foreman thought it better to have Turk and me late than no dinner. I tried a hundred different schemes to instill ambition and self-respect into that ox, but he was an old dog and contented with his evil ways.

"Several weeks passed, and Turk and I became a standing joke with the outfit. One morning I made the discovery that he was afraid of a slicker. For just about a full half day, I had the best of him, and several times he was out of sight in the main body of the herd. But he always dropped to the rear, and finally the slicker lost its charm to move him. In fact he rather enjoyed having me fan him with it - it seemed to cool him. It was the middle of the afternoon, and Turk had dropped about a quarter-mile to the rear, while I was riding along beside and throwing the slicker over him like a blanket. I was letting him carry it, and he seemed to be enjoying himself, switching his tail in appreciation, when the matted brush of his tail noosed itself over one of the riveted buttons on the slicker. The next switch brought the yellow 'fish' bumping on his heels, and emitting a blood-curdling bellow, he curved his tail and started for the herd. Just for a minute it tickled me to see old Turk getting such a wiggle on him, but the next moment my mirth turned to seriousness, and I tried to cut him off from the other cattle, but he beat me, bellowing bloody murder. The slicker was sailing like a kite, and the rear cattle took fright and began bawling as if they had struck a fresh scent of blood. The scare flashed through the herd from rear to point, and hell began popping right then and there. The air filled with dust and the earth trembled with the running cattle. Not knowing which way to turn, I stayed right where I was - in the rear. As the dust lifted, I followed up, and about a mile ahead picked up my slicker, and shortly afterward found old Turk, grazing contentedly. With every man in the saddle, that herd ran seven miles and was only turned by the Cimarron River. It was nearly dark when I and the roan ox overtook the cattle. Fortunately none of the swing-men had seen the cause of the stampede, and I attributed it to fresh blood, which the outfit believed. My verdant innocence saved my scalp that time, but years afterward I nearly lost it when I admitted to my old foreman what had caused the stampede that afternoon. But I was a trail boss then and had learned my lesson."

The Rebel, who was encamped several miles up the creek, summoned his men, and we all arose and scattered after our horses. There was quite a cavalcade going our way, and as we halted within the light of the fires for the different outfits to gather, Flood rode up, and calling Forrest, said: "In the absence of any word from old man Don, we might as well all pull out in the morning. More than likely we'll hear from him at Grinnell, and until we reach the railroad, the Buford herds had better take the lead. I'll drag along in the rear, and if there's another move made from Dodge, you will have warning. Now, that's about all, except to give your cattle plenty of time; don't hurry. S'long, fellows."

CHAPTER XI.

ALL IN THE DAY'S WORK

The next morning the herds moved out like brigades of an army on dress-parade. Our front covered some six or seven miles, the Buford cattle in the lead, while those intended for Indian delivery naturally fell into position on flank and rear. My beeves had enjoyed a splendid rest during the past week, and now easily took the lead in a steady walk, every herd avoiding the trail until necessity compelled us to reenter it. The old pathway was dusty and merely pointed the way, and until rain fell to settle it, our intention was to give it a wide berth. As the morning wore on and the herds drew farther and farther apart, except for the dim dust-clouds of ten thousand trampling feet on a raw prairie, it would have been difficult for us to establish each other's location. Several times during the forenoon, when a swell of the plain afforded us a temporary westward view, we caught glimpses of Forrest's cattle as they snailed forward, fully five miles distant and barely noticeable under the low sky-line. The Indian herds had given us a good start in the morning, and towards evening as the mirages lifted, not a dust-signal was in sight, save one far in our lead.

The month of June, so far, had been exceedingly droughty. The scarcity of water on the plains between Dodge and Ogalalla was the dread of every trail drover. The grass, on the other hand, had matured from the first rank growth of early spring into a forage, rich in sustenance, from which our beeves took on flesh and rounded into beauties. Lack of water being the one drawback, long drives, not in miles but hours, became the order of the day; from four in the morning to eight at night, even at an ox's pace, leaves every landmark of the day far in the rear at nightfall. Thus for the next few days we moved forward, the monotony of existence broken only by the great variety of mirage, the glare of heat-waves, and the silent signal in the sky of other voyageurs like ourselves. On reaching Pig Boggy, nothing but pools greeted us, while the regular crossing was dry and dusty and paved with cattle bones. My curiosity was strong enough to cause me to revisit the old bridge which I had helped to build two seasons before; though unused, it was still intact, a credit to the crude engineering of Pete Slaughter. After leaving the valley of the Solomon, the next running water was Pawnee Fork, where we overtook and passed six thousand yearling heifers in two herds, sold the winter before by John Blocker for delivery in Montana. The Northwest had not yet learned that Texas was the natural breeding-ground for cattle, yet under favorable conditions in both sections, the ranchman of the South could raise one third more calves from an equal number of cows.

The weather continued hot and sultry. Several times storms hung on our left for hours which we hoped would reach us, and at night the lightning flickered in sheets, yet with the exception of cooling the air, availed us nothing. But as we encamped one night on the divide before reaching the Smoky River, a storm struck us that sent terror to our hearts. There were men in my outfit, and others in Lovell's employ, who were from ten to twenty years my senior, having spent almost their lifetime in the open, who had never before witnessed such a night. The atmosphere seemed to be overcharged with electricity, which played its pranks among us, neither man nor beast being exempt. The storm struck the divide about two hours after the cattle had been bedded, and from then until dawn every man was in the saddle, the herd drifting fully three miles during the night. Such keen flashes of lightning accompanied by instant thunder I had never before witnessed, though the rainfall, after the first dash, was light in quantity. Several times the rain ceased entirely, when the phosphorus, like a prairie fire, appeared on every hand. Great sheets of it flickered about, the cattle and saddle stock were soon covered, while every bit of metal on our accoutrements was coated and twinkling with phosphorescent light. My gauntlets were covered, and wherever I touched myself, it seemed to smear and spread and refuse to wipe out. Several times we were able to hold up and quiet the cattle, but along their backs flickered the ghostly light, while across the herd, which occupied acres, it reminded one of the burning lake in the regions infernal. As the night wore on, several showers fell, accompanied by almost incessant bolts of lightning, but the rainfall only added moisture to the ground and this acted like fuel in reviving the phosphor. Several hours before dawn, great sheets of the fiery elements chased each other across the northern sky, lighting up our surroundings until one could have read ordinary print. The cattle stood humped or took an occasional step forward; the men sat their horses, sullen and morose, forming new resolutions for the future, in which trail work was not included. But morning came at last, cool and cloudy, a slight recompense for the heat which we had endured since leaving Dodge.

With the breaking of day, the herd was turned back on its course. For an hour or more the cattle grazed freely, and as the sun broke through the clouds, they dropped down like tired infantry on a march, and we allowed them an hour's rest. We were still some three or four miles eastward of the trail, and after breakfasting and changing mounts we roused the cattle and started on an angle for the trail, expecting to intercept it before noon. There was some settlement in the Smoky River Valley which must be avoided, as in years past serious enmity had been engendered between settlers and drovers in consequence of the ravages of Texas fever among native cattle. I was riding on the left point, and when within a short distance of the trail, one of the boys called my attention to a loose herd of cattle, drifting south and fully two miles to the west of us. It was certainly something unusual, and as every man of us scanned them, a lone horseman was seen to ride across their front, and, turning them, continue on for our herd. The situation was bewildering, as the natural course of every herd was northward, but here was one apparently abandoned like a water-logged ship at sea.

The messenger was a picture of despair. He proved to be the owner of the abandoned cattle, and had come to us with an appeal for help. According to his story, he was a Northern cowman and had purchased the cattle a few days before in Dodge. He had bought the outfit complete, with the understanding that the through help would continue in his service until his range in Wyoming was reached. But it was a Mexican outfit, foreman and all, and during the storm of the night before, one of the men had been killed by lightning. The accident must have occurred near dawn, as the man was not missed until daybreak, and like ours, his cattle had drifted with the storm. Some time was lost in finding the body, and to add to the panic that had already stricken the outfit, the shirt of the unfortunate vaquero was burnt from the corpse. The horse had escaped scathless, though his rider met death, while the housings were stripped from the saddle so that it fell from the animal. The Mexican foreman and vaqueros had thrown their hands in the air; steeped in superstition, they considered the loss of their comrade a bad omen, and refused to go farther. The herd was as good as abandoned unless we could lend a hand.

The appeal was not in vain. Detailing four of my men, and leaving Jack Splann as segundo in charge of our cattle, I galloped away with the stranger. As we rode the short distance between the two herds and I mentally reviewed the situation, I could not help but think it was fortunate for the alien outfit that their employer was a Northern cowman instead of a Texan. Had the present owner been of the latter school, there would have been more than one dead Mexican before a valuable herd would have been abandoned over an unavoidable accident. I kept my thoughts to myself, however, for the man had troubles enough, and on reaching his drifting herd, we turned them back on their course. It was high noon when we reached his wagon and found the Mexican outfit still keening over their dead comrade. We pushed the cattle, a mixed herd of about twenty-five hundred, well past the camp, and riding back, dismounted among the howling vaqueros. There was not the semblance of sanity among them. The foreman, who could speak some little English, at least his employer declared he could, was carrying on like a madman, while a majority of the vaqueros were playing a close second. The dead man had been carried in and was lying under a tarpaulin in the shade of the wagon. Feeling that my boys would stand behind me, and never offering to look at the corpse, I inquired in Spanish of the vaqueros which one of the men was their corporal. A heavy-set, bearded man was pointed out, and walking up to him, with one hand I slapped him in the face and with the other relieved him of a six-shooter. He staggered back, turned ashen pale, and before he could recover from the surprise, in his own tongue I berated him as a worthless cur for deserting his employer over an accident. Following up the temporary advantage, I inquired for the cook and horse-wrangler, and intimated clearly that there would be other dead Mexicans if the men were not fed and the herd and saddle stock looked after; that they were not worthy of the name of vaqueros if they were lax in a duty with which they had been intrusted.

"But Pablo is dead," piped one of the vaqueros in defense.

"Yes, he is," said G - G Cederdall in Spanish, bristling up to the vaquero who had volunteered the reply; "and we'll bury him and a half-dozen more of you if necessary, but the cattle will not be abandoned - not for a single hour. Pablo is dead, but he was no better than a hundred other men who have lost their lives on this trail. If you are a lot of locoed sheep-herders instead of vaqueros, why didn't you stay at home with the children instead of starting out to do a man's work. Desert your employer, will you? Not in a country where there is no chance to pick up other men. Yes, Pablo is dead, and we ll bury him."

The aliens were disconcerted, and wilted. The owner picked up courage and ordered the cook to prepare dinner. We loaned our horses to the wrangler and another man, the remuda was brought in, and before we sat down to the midday meal, every vaquero had a horse under saddle, while two of them had ridden away to look after the grazing cattle. With order restored, we set about systematically to lay away the unfortunate man. A detail of vaqueros under Cederdall prepared a grave on the nearest knoll, and wrapping the corpse in a tarpaulin, we buried him like a sailor at sea. Several vaqueros were visibly affected at the graveside, and in order to pacify them, I suggested that we unload the wagon of supplies and haul up a load of rock from a near-by outcropping ledge. Pablo had fallen like a good soldier at his post, I urged, and it was befitting that his comrades should mark his last resting-place. To our agreeable surprise the corporal hurrahed his men and the wagon was unloaded in a jiffy and dispatched after a load of rock. On its return, we spent an hour in decorating the mound, during which time lament was expressed for the future of Pablo's soul. Knowing the almost universal faith of this alien race, as we stood around the finished mound, Cederdall, who was Catholic born, called for contributions to procure the absolution of the Church. The owner of the cattle was the first to respond, and with the aid of my boys and myself, augmented later by the vaqueros, a purse of over fifty dollars was raised and placed in charge of the corporal, to be expended in a private mass on their return to San Antonio. Meanwhile the herd and saddle stock had started, and reloading the wagon, we cast a last glance at the little mound which made a new landmark on the old trail.

The owner of the cattle was elated over the restoration of order. My contempt for him, however, had not decreased; the old maxim of fools rushing in where angels feared to tread had only been again exemplified. The inferior races may lack in courage and leadership, but never in cunning and craftiness. This alien outfit had detected some weakness in the armor of their new employer, and when the emergency arose, were ready to take advantage of the situation. Yet under an old patron, these same men would never dare to mutiny or assert themselves. That there were possible breakers ahead for this cowman there was no doubt; for every day that those Mexicans traveled into a strange country, their Aztec blood would yearn for their Southern home. And since the unforeseen could not be guarded against, at the first opportunity I warned the stranger that it was altogether too soon to shout. To his anxious inquiries I replied that his very presence with the herd was a menace to its successful handling by the Mexican outfit He should throw all responsibility on the foreman, or take charge himself, which was impossible now; for an outfit which will sulk and mutiny once will do so again under less provocation. When my curtain lecture was ended, the owner authorized me to call his outfit together and give them such instructions as I saw fit.

We sighted our cattle but once during the afternoon. On locating the herd, two of my boys left us to return, hearing the message that the rest of us might not put in an appearance before morning. All during the evening, I made it a point to cultivate the acquaintance of several vaqueros, and learned the names of their master and rancho. Taking my cue from the general information gathered, when we encamped for the night and all hands, with the exception of those on herd, had finished catching horses, I attracted their attention by returning the six-shooter taken from their corporal at noontime. Commanding attention, in their mother tongue I addressed myself to the Mexican foreman.

"Felipe Esquibil," said I, looking him boldly in the face, "you were foreman of this herd from Zavalla County, Texas, to the Arkansaw River, and brought your cattle through without loss or accident.

"The herd changed owners at Dodge, but with the understanding that you and your vaqueros were to accompany the cattle to this gentleman's ranch in the upper country. An accident happens, and because you are not in full control, you shift the responsibility and play the baby act by wanting to go home. Had the death of one of your men occurred below the river, and while the herd was still the property of Don Dionisio of Rancho Los Olmus, you would have lost your own life before abandoning your cattle. Now, with the consent and approval of the new owner, you are again invested with full charge of this herd until you arrive at the Platte River. A new outfit will relieve you on reaching Ogalalla, and then you will be paid your reckoning and all go home. In your immediate rear are five herds belonging to my employer, and I have already sent warning to them of your attempted desertion. A fortnight or less will find you relieved, and the only safety in store for you is to go forward. Now your employer is going to my camp for the night, and may not see you again before this herd reaches the Platte. Remember, Don Felipe, that the opportunity is yours to regain your prestige as a corporal - and you need it after to-day's actions. What would Don Dionisio say if he knew the truth? And do you ever expect to face your friends again at Los Olmus? From a trusted corporal back to a sheep-shearer would be your reward - and justly."

Cederdall, Wolf, and myself shook hands with several vaqueros, and mounting our horses we started for my camp, taking the stranger with us. Only once did he offer any protest to going. "Very well, then," replied G - G, unable to suppress his contempt, "go right back. I'll gamble that you sheathe a knife before morning if you do. It strikes me you don't sabe Mexicans very much."

Around the camp-fire that night, the day's work was reviewed. My rather drastic treatment of the corporal was fully commented upon and approved by the outfit, yet provoked an inquiry from the irrepressible Parent. Turning to the questioner, Burl Van Vedder said in dove-like tones: "Yes, dear, slapped him just to remind the varmint that his feet were on the earth, and that pawing the air and keening didn't do any good. Remember, love, there was the living to be fed, the dead to bury, and the work in hand required every man to do his duty. Now was there anything else you'd like to know?"

CHAPTER XII.

MARSHALING THE FORCES

Both herds had watered in the Smoky during the afternoon. The stranger's cattle were not compelled to go down to the crossing, but found an easy passage several miles above the regular ford. After leaving the river, both herds were grazed out during the evening, and when darkness fell we were not over three miles apart, one on either side of the trail. The Wyoming cowman spent a restless night, and early the next morning rode to the nearest elevation which would give him a view of his cattle. Within an hour after sun-up he returned, elated over the fact that his herd was far in the lead of ours, camp being already broken, while we were only breakfasting. Matters were working out just as I expected. The mixed herd under the Mexican corporal, by moving early and late, could keep the lead of our beeves, and with the abundance of time at my disposal we were in no hurry. The Kansas Pacific Railroad was but a few days' drive ahead, and I advised our guest to take the train around to Ogalalla and have a new outfit all ready to relieve the aliens immediately on their arrival. Promising to take the matter under consideration, he said nothing further for several days, his cattle in the mean time keeping a lead of from five to ten miles.

The trail crossed the railroad at a switch east of Grinnell. I was naturally expecting some word from Don Lovell, and it was my intention to send one of the boys into that station to inquire for mail. There was a hostelry at Grinnell, several stores and a livery stable, all dying an easy death from the blight of the arid plain, the town profiting little or nothing from the cattle trade. But when within a half-day's drive of the railway, on overtaking the herd after dinner, there was old man Don talking to the boys on herd. The cattle were lying down, and rather than disturb them, he patiently bided his time until they had rested and arose to resume their journey. The old man was feeling in fine spirits, something unusual, and declined my urgent invitation to go back to the wagon and have dinner. I noticed that he was using his own saddle, though riding a livery horse, and in the mutual inquiries which were exchanged, learned that he had arrived at Grinnell but a few days before. He had left Camp Supply immediately after Forrest and Sponsilier passed that point, and until Siringo came in with his report, he had spent the time about detective headquarters in Kansas City. From intimate friends in Dodge, he had obtained the full particulars of the attempted but unsuccessful move of The Western Supply Company to take possession of his two herds. In fact there was very little that I could enlighten him on, except the condition of the cattle, and they spoke for themselves, their glossy coats shining with the richness of silk. On the other hand, my employer opened like a book.

"Tom, I think we're past the worst of it," said he. "Those Dodge people are just a trifle too officious to suit me, but Ogalalla is a cow-town after my own heart. They're a law unto themselves up there, and a cowman stands some show - a good one against thieves. Ogalalla is the seat of an organized county, and the town has officers, it's true, but they've got sense enough to know which side their bread's buttered on; and a cowman who's on the square has nothing to fear in that town. Yes, the whole gang, Tolleston and all, are right up here at Ogalalla now; bought a herd this week, so I hear, and expect to take two of these away from us the moment we enter Keith County. Well, they may; I've seen bad men before take a town, but it was only a question of time until the plain citizens retook it. They may try to bluff us, but if they do, we'll meet them a little over halfway. Which one of your boys was it that licked Archie? I want to thank him until such a time as I can reward him better."

The herd was moving out, and as Seay was working in the swing on the opposite side, we allowed the cattle to trail past, and then rode round and overtook him. The two had never met before, but old man Don warmed towards Dorg, who recited his experience in such an inimitable manner that our employer rocked in his saddle in spasms of laughter. Leaving the two together, I rode on ahead to look out the water, and when the herd came up near the middle of the afternoon, they were still inseparable. The watering over, we camped for the night several miles south of the railroad, the mixed herd having crossed it about noon. My guest of the past few days had come to a point requiring a decision and was in a quandary to know what to do. But when the situation had been thoroughly reviewed between Mr. Lovell and the Wyoming man, my advice was indorsed, - to trust implicitly to his corporal, and be ready to relieve the outfit at the Platte. Saddles were accordingly shifted, and the stranger, after professing a profusion of thanks, rode away on the livery horse by which my employer had arrived. Once the man was well out of hearing, the old trail drover turned to my outfit and said:

"Boys, there goes a warning that the days of the trail are numbered. To make a success of any business, a little common sense is necessary. Nine tenths of the investing in cattle to-day in the Northwest is being done by inexperienced men. No other line of business could prosper in such incompetent hands, and it's foolish to think that cattle companies and individuals, nearly all tenderfeet at the business, can succeed. They may for a time, - there are accidents in every calling, - but when the tide turns, there won't be one man or company in ten survive. I only wish they would, as it means life and expansion for the cattle interests in Texas. As long as the boom continues, and foreigners and tenderfeet pour their money in, the business will look prosperous. Why, even the business men are selling out their stores and going into cattle. But there's a day of reckoning ahead, and there's many a cowman in this Northwest country who will never see his money again. Now the government demand is a healthy one: it needs the cattle for Indian and military purposes; but this crazy investment, especially in she stuff, I wouldn't risk a dollar in it."

During the conversation that evening, I was delighted to learn that my employer expected to accompany the herds overland to Ogalalla. There was nothing pressing elsewhere, and as all the other outfits were within a short day's ride in the rear, he could choose his abode. He was too good a cowman to interfere with the management of cattle, and the pleasure of his company, when in good humor, was to be desired. The next morning a horse was furnished him from our extras, and after seeing us safely across the railroad track, he turned back to meet Forrest or Sponsilier. This was the last we saw of him until after crossing into Nebraska. In the mean time my boys kept an eye on the Mexican outfit in our front, scarcely a day passing but what we sighted them either in person or by signal. Once they dropped back opposite us on the western side of the trail, when Cedardall, under the pretense of hunting lost horses, visited their camp, finding them contented and enjoying a lay-over. They were impatient to know the distance to the Rio Platte, and G - G assured them that within a week they would see its muddy waters and be relieved. Thus encouraged they held the lead, but several times vaqueros dropped back to make inquiries of drives and the water. The route was passable, with a short dry drive from the head of Stinking Water across to the Platte River, of which they were fully advised. Keeping them in sight, we trailed along leisurely, and as we went down the northern slope of the divide approaching the Republican River, we were overtaken at noon by Don Lovell and Dave Sponsilier.

"Quirk," said the old man, as the two dismounted, "I was just telling Dave that twenty years ago this summer I carried a musket with Sherman in his march to the sea. And here we are to-day, driving beef to feed the army in the West. But that's neither here nor there under the present programme. Jim Flood and I have talked matters over pretty thoroughly, and have decided to switch the foremen on the 'Open A' and 'Drooping T' cattle until after Ogalalla is passed. From their actions at Dodge, it is probable that they will try and arrest the foreman of those two herds as accessory under some charge or other. By shifting the foremen, even if the ones in charge are detained, we will gain time and be able to push the Buford cattle across the North Platte. The chances are that they will prefer some charges against me, and if they do, if necessary, we will all go to the lock-up together. They may have spotters ahead here on the Republican; Dave will take charge of your 'Open A's' at once, and you will drop back and follow up with his cattle. For the time being and to every stranger, you two will exchange names. The Rebel is in charge of Forrest's cattle now, and Quince will drop back with Paul's herd. Dave, here, gave me the slip on crossing the Texas Pacific in the lower country, but when we reach the Union Pacific, I want to know where he is, even if in jail. And I may be right there with him, but we'll live high, for I've got a lot of their money."

Sponsilier reported his herd on the same side of the trail and about ten miles to our rear. I had no objection to the change, for those arid plains were still to be preferred to the lock-up in Ogalalla. My only regret was in temporarily losing my mount; but as Dave's horses were nearly as good, no objection was urged, and promising, in case either landed in jail, to send flowers, I turned back, leaving my employer with the lead herd. Before starting, I learned that the "Drooping T" cattle were in advance of Sponsilier's, and as I soldiered along on my way back, rode several miles out of my way to console my old bunkie, The Rebel. He took my chaffing good-naturedly and assured me that his gray hairs were a badge of innocence which would excuse him on any charge. Turning, I rode back with him over a mile, this being my first opportunity of seeing Forrest's beeves. The steers were large and rangy, extremely uniform in ages and weight, and in general relieved me of considerable conceit that I had the best herd among the Buford cattle. With my vanity eased, I continued my journey and reached Sponsilier's beeves while they were watering. Again a surprise was in store for me, as the latter herd had, if any, the edge over the other two, while "The Apple" was by all odds the prettiest road brand I had ever seen. I asked the acting segundo, a lad named Tupps, who cut the cattle when receiving; light was thrown on the situation by his reply.

"Old man Don joined the outfit the day we reached Uvalde," said he, "and until we began receiving, he poured it into our foreman that this year the cattle had to be something extra – muy escogido, as the Mexicans say. Well, the result was that Sponsilier went to work with ideas pitched rather high. But in the first bunch received, the old man cut a pretty little four-year-old, fully a hundred pounds too light. Dave and Mr. Lovell had a set-to over the beef, the old man refusing to cut him back, but he rode out of the herd and never again offered to interfere. Forrest was present, and at dinner that day old man Don admitted that he was too easy when receiving. Sponsilier and Forrest did the trimming afterward, and that is the secret of these two herds being so uniform."

A general halt was called at the head of Stinking Water. We were then within forty miles of Ogalalla, and a day's drive would put us within the jurisdiction of Keith County. Some time was lost at this last water, waiting for the rear herds to arrive, as it was the intention to place the "Open A" and "Drooping T" cattle at the rear in crossing this dry belt. At the ford on the Republican, a number of strangers were noticed, two of whom rode a mile or more with me, and innocently asked numerous but leading questions. I frankly answered every inquiry, and truthfully, with the exception of the names of the lead foreman and my own. Direct, it was only sixty miles from the crossing on the Republican to Ogalalla, an easy night's ride, and I was conscious that our whereabouts would be known at the latter place the next morning. For several days before starting across this arid stretch, we had watered at ten o'clock in the morning, so when Flood and Forrest came up, mine being the third herd to reach the last water, I was all ready to pull out. But old man Don counseled another day's lie-over, as it would be a sore trial for the herds under a July sun, and for a full day twenty thousand beeves grazed in sight of each other on the mesas surrounding the head of Stinking Water. All the herds were aroused with the dawn, and after a few hours' sun on the cattle, the Indian beeves were turned onto the water and held until the middle of the forenoon, when the start was made for the Platte and Ogalalla.

I led out with "The Apple" cattle, throwing onto the trail for the first ten miles, which put me well in advance of Bob Quirk and Forrest, who were in my immediate rear. A well-known divide marked the halfway between the two waters, and I was determined to camp on it that night. It was fully nine o'clock when we reached it, Don Lovell in the mean time having overtaken us. This watershed was also recognized as the line of Keith County, an organized community, and the next morning expectation ran high as to what the day would bring forth. Lovell insisted on staying with the lead herd, and pressing him in as horse-wrangler, I sent him in the lead with the remuda and wagon, while Levering fell into the swing with the trailing cattle. A breakfast halt was made fully seven miles from the bed-ground, a change of mounts, and then up divide, across mesa, and down slope at the foot of which ran the Platte. Meanwhile several wayfaring men were met, but in order to avoid our dust, they took the right or unbranded side of our herd on meeting, and passed on their way without inquiry. Near noon a party of six men, driving a number of loose mounts and a pack-horse, were met, who also took the windward side. Our dragmen learned that they were on their way to Dodge to receive a herd of range horses. But when about halfway down the slope towards the river, two mounted men were seen to halt the remuda and wagon for a minute, and then continue on southward. Billy Tupps was on the left point, myself next in the swing; and as the two horsemen turned out on the branded side, their identity was suspected. In reply to some inquiry, Tupps jerked his thumb over his shoulder as much as to say, "Next man." I turned out and met the strangers, who had already noted the road brand, and politely answered every question. One of the two offered me a cigar, and after lighting it, I did remember hearing one of my boys say that among the herds lying over on the head of Stinking Water was an "Open A" and "Drooping T," but I was unable to recall the owner's or foremen's names. Complimenting me on the condition of my beeves, and assuring me that I would have time to water my herd and reach the mesa beyond Ogalalla, they passed on down the column of cattle.

I had given the cook an order on an outfitting house for new supplies, saying I would call or send a draft in the morning. A new bridge had been built across the Platte opposite the town, and when nearing the river, the commissary turned off the trail for it, but the horse-wrangler for the day gave the bridge a wide berth and crossed the stream a mile below the village. The width of the river was a decided advantage in watering a thirsty herd, as it gave the cattle room to thrash around, filling its broad bed for fully a half mile. Fortunately there were few spectators, but I kept my eye on the lookout for a certain faction, being well disguised with dust and dirt and a month's growth of beard. As we pushed out of the river and were crossing the tracks below the railroad yards, two other herds were sighted coming down to the water, their remudas having forded above and below our cattle. On scaling the bluffs, we could see the trail south of the Platte on which arose a great column of dust. Lovell was waiting with the saddle stock in the hills beyond the town, and on striking the first good grass, the cattle fell to grazing while we halted to await the arrival of the wagon. The sun was still several hours high, and while waiting for our commissary to come up, my employer and myself rode to the nearest point of observation to reconnoitre the rear. Beneath us lay the hamlet; but our eyes were concentrated beyond the narrow Platte valley on a dust-cloud which hung midway down the farther slope. As we watched, an occasional breeze wafted the dust aside, and the sinuous outline of a herd creeping forward greeted our vision. Below the town were two other herds, distinctly separate and filling the river for over a mile with a surging mass of animals, while in every direction cattle dotted the plain and valley. Turning aside from the panorama before us, my employer said:

"Tom, you will have time to graze out a few miles and camp to the left of the trail. I'll stay here and hurry your wagon forward, and wait for Bob and Quince. That lead herd beyond

ANDY ADAMS

the river is bound to be Jim's, and he's due to camp on this mesa to-night, so these outfits must give him room. If Dave and Paul are still free to act, they'll know enough to water and camp on the south side of the Platte. I'll stay at Flood's wagon to-night, and you had better send a couple of your boys into town and let them nose around. They'll meet lads from the 'Open A' and 'Drooping T' outfits; and I'll send Jim and Bob in, and by midnight we'll have a report of what's been done. If any one but an officer takes possession of those two herds, it'll put us to the trouble of retaking them. And I think I've got men enough here to do it."

CHAPTER XIII.

JUSTICE IN THE SADDLE

It was an hour after the usual time when we bedded down the cattle. The wagon had overtaken us about sunset, and the cook's fire piloted us into a camp fully two miles to the right of the trail. A change of horses was awaiting us, and after a hasty supper Tupps detailed two young fellows to visit Ogalalla. It required no urging; I outlined clearly what was expected of their mission, requesting them to return by the way of Flood's wagon, and to receive any orders which my employer might see fit to send. The horse-wrangler was pressed in to stand the guard of one of the absent lads on the second watch, and I agreed to take the other, which fell in the third. The boys had not yet returned when our guard was called, but did so shortly afterward, one of them hunting me up on night-herd.

"Well," said he, turning his horse and circling with me, "we caught onto everything that was adrift. The Rebel and Sponsilier were both in town, in charge of two deputies. Flood and your brother went in with us, and with the lads from the other outfits, including those across the river, there must have been twenty-five of Lovell's men in town. I noticed that Dave and The Rebel were still wearing their six-shooters, while among the boys the arrests were looked upon as quite a joke. The two deputies had all kinds of money, and wouldn't allow no one but themselves to spend a cent. The biggest one of the two - the one who gave you the cigar - would say to my boss: 'Sponsilier, you're a trail foreman from Texas - one of Don Lovell's boss men - but you're under arrest; your cattle are in my possession this very minute. You understand that, don't you? Very well, then; everybody come up and have a drink on the sheriff's office.' That was about the talk in every saloon and dance-hall visited. But when we proposed starting back to camp, about midnight, the big deputy said to Flood: 'I want you to tell Colonel Lovell that I hold a warrant for his arrest: urge him not to put me to the trouble of coming out after him. If he had identified himself to me this afternoon, he could have slept on a goose-hair bed to-night instead of out there on the mesa, on the cold ground. His reputation in this town would entitle him to three meals a day, even if he was under arrest. Now, we'll have one more, and tell the damned old rascal that I'll expect him in the morning.'"

We rode out the watch together. On returning to Flood's camp, they had found Don Lovell awake. The old man was pleased with the report, but sent me no special word except to exercise my own judgment. The cattle were tired after their long tramp of the day before, the outfit were saddle weary, and the first rays of the rising sun flooded the mesa before men or animals offered to arise. But the duties of another day commanded us anew, and with the cook calling us, we rose to meet them. I was favorably impressed with Tupps as a segundo, and after breakfast suggested that he graze the cattle over to the North Platte, cross it, and make a permanent camp. This was agreed to, half the men were excused for the day, and after designating, beyond the river, a clump of cottonwoods where the wagon would be found, seven of us turned and rode back for Ogalalla. With picked mounts under us, we avoided the other cattle which could be seen grazing northward, and when fully halfway to town, there before us on the brink of the mesa loomed up the lead of a herd. I soon recognized Jack Splann on the point, and taking a wide circle, dropped in behind him, the column stretching back a mile and coming up the bluffs, forty abreast like an army in loose marching order. I was proud of those "Open A's;" they were my first herd, and though in a hurry to reach town, I turned and rode back with them for fully a mile.

Splann was acting under orders from Flood, who had met him

at the ford that morning. If the cattle were in the possession of any deputy sheriff, they had failed to notify Jack, and the latter had already started for the North Platte of his own accord. The "Drooping T" cattle were in the immediate rear under Forrest's segundo, and Splann urged me to accompany him that forenoon, saying: "From what the boys said this morning, Dave and Paul will not be given a hearing until two o'clock this afternoon. I can graze beyond the North Fork by that time, and then we'll all go back together. Flood's right behind here with the 'Drooping T's,' and I think it's his intention to go all the way to the river. Drop back and see him."

The boys who were with me never halted, but had ridden on towards town. When the second herd began the ascent of the mesa, I left Splann and turned back, waiting on the brink for its arrival. As it would take the lead cattle some time to reach me, I dismounted, resting in the shade of my horse. But my rest was brief, for the clattering hoofs of a cavalcade of horsemen were approaching, and as I arose, Quince Forrest and Bob Quirk with a dozen or more men dashed up and halted. As their herds were intended for the Crow and Fort Washakie agencies, they would naturally follow up the south side of the North Platte, and an hour or two of grazing would put them in camp. The Buford cattle, as well as Flood's herd, were due to cross this North Fork of the mother Platte within ten miles of Ogalalla, their respective routes thenceforth being north and northeast. Forrest, like myself, was somewhat leary of entering the town, and my brother and the boys passed on shortly, leaving Quince behind. We discussed every possible phase of what might happen in case we were recognized, which was almost certain if Tolleston or the Dodge buyers were encountered. But an overweening hunger to get into Ogalalla was dominant in us, and under the excuse of settling for our supplies, after the herd passed, we remounted our horses, Flood joining us, and rode for the hamlet.

There was little external and no moral change in the town. Several new saloons had opened, and in anticipation of the large drive that year, the Dew-Drop-In dance-hall had been enlarged, and employed three shifts of bartenders. A stage had been added with the new addition, and a special importation of ladies had been brought out from Omaha for the season. I use the term LADIES advisedly, for in my presence one of the proprietors, with marked courtesy, said to an Eastern stranger, "Oh, no, you need no introduction. My wife is the only woman in town; all the balance are ladies." Beyond a shave and a hair-cut, Forrest and I fought shy of public places. But after the supplies were settled for, and some new clothing was secured, we chambered a few drinks and swaggered about with considerable ado. My bill of supplies amounted to one hundred and twenty-six dollars, and when, without a word, I drew a draft for the amount, the proprietor of the outfitting store, as a pelon, made me a present of two fine silk handkerchiefs.

Forrest was treated likewise, and having invested ourselves in white shirts, with flaming red ties, we used the new handkerchiefs to otherwise decorate our persons. We had both chosen the brightest colors, and with these knotted about our necks, dangling from pistol-pockets, or protruding from ruffled shirt fronts, our own mothers would scarcely have known us. Jim Flood, whom we met casually on a back street, stopped, and after circling us once, said, "Now if you fellows just keep perfectly sober, your disguise will be complete."

Meanwhile Don Lovell had reported at an early hour to the sheriff's office. The legal profession was represented in Ogalalla by several firms, criminal practice being their specialty; but fortunately Mike Sutton, an attorney of Dodge, had arrived in town the day before on a legal errand for another trail drover. Sutton was a frontier advocate, alike popular with the Texas element and the gambling fraternity, having achieved laurels in his home town as a criminal lawyer. Mike was born on the little green isle beyond the sea, and, gifted with the Celtic wit, was also in logic clear as the tones of a bell, while his insight into human motives was almost superhuman. Lovell had had occasion in other years to rely on Sutton's counsel, and now would listen to no refusal of his services. As it turned out, the lawyer's mission in Ogalalla was so closely in sympathy with Lovell's trouble that they naturally strengthened each other. The highest tribunal of justice in Ogalalla was the county court, the judge of which also ran the stock-yards during the shipping season, and was banker for two monte games at the Lone Star saloon. He enjoyed the reputation of being an honest, fearless jurist, and supported by a growing civic pride, his decisions gave satisfaction. A sense of crude equity governed his rulings, and as one of the citizens remarked, "Whatever the judge said, went." It should be remembered that this was in '84, but had a similar trouble occurred five years earlier, it is likely that Judge Colt would have figured in the preliminaries, and the coroner might have been called on to impanel a jury. But the rudiments of civilization were sweeping westward, and Ogalalla was nerved to the importance of the occasion; for that very afternoon a hearing was to be given for the possession of two herds of cattle, valued at over a quarter-million dollars.

The representatives of The Western Supply Company were quartered in the largest hotel in town, but seldom appeared on the streets. They had employed a firm of local attorneys, consisting of an old and a young man, both of whom evidently believed in the justice of their client's cause. All the cattle-hands in Lovell's employ were anxious to get a glimpse of Tolleston, many of them patronizing the bar and table of the same hostelry, but their efforts were futile until the hour arrived for the hearing. They probably have a new court-house in Ogalalla now, but at the date of this chronicle the building which served as a temple of justice was poorly proportioned, its height being entirely out of relation to its width. It was a two-story affair, the lower floor being used for county offices, the upper one as the court-room. A long stairway ran up the outside of the building, landing on a gallery in front, from which the sheriff announced the sitting of the honorable court of Keith County. At home in Texas, lawsuits were so rare that though I was a grown man, the novelty of this one absorbed me. Quite a large crowd had gathered in advance of the hour, and while awaiting the arrival of Judge Mulqueen, a contingent of fifteen men from the two herds in question rode up and halted in front of the court-house. Forrest and I were lying low, not caring to be seen, when the three plaintiffs, the two local attorneys, and Tolleston put in an appearance. The cavalcade had not yet dismounted, and when Dorg Seay caught sight of Tolleston, he stood up in his stirrups and sang out, "Hello there, Archibald! my old college chum, how goes it?"

Judge Mulqueen had evidently dressed for the occasion, for with the exception of the plaintiffs, he was the only man in the court-room who wore a coat. The afternoon was a sultry one; in that first bottom of the Platte there was scarcely a breath of air, and collars wilted limp as rags. Neither map nor chart graced the unplastered walls, the unpainted furniture of the room was sadly in need of repair, while a musty odor permeated the room. Outside the railing the seating capacity of the court-room was rather small, rough, bare planks serving for seats, but the spectators gladly stood along the sides and rear, eager to catch every word, as they silently mopped the sweat which oozed alike from citizen and cattleman. Forrest and I were concealed in the rear, which was packed with Lovell's boys, when the judge walked in and court opened for the hearing. Judge Mulqueen requested counsel on either side to be as brief and direct as possible, both in their pleadings and testimony, adding: "If they reach the stock-yards in time, I may have to load out a train of feeders this evening. We'll bed the cars, anyhow." Turning to the sheriff, he continued: "Frank, if you happen outside, keep an eye up the river; those Lincoln feeders made a deal yesterday for five hundred three-year-olds. - Read your complaint."

The legal document was read with great fervor and energy by the younger of the two local lawyers. In the main it reviewed the situation correctly, every point, however, being made subservient to their object, - the possession of the cattle. The plaintiffs contended that they were the innocent holders of the original contract between the government and The Western Supply Company, properly assigned; that they had purchased these two herds in question, had paid earnest-money to the amount of sixty-five thousand dollars on the same, and concluded by petitioning the court for possession. Sutton arose, counseled a moment with Lovell, and borrowing a chew of tobacco from Sponsilier, leisurely addressed the court.

"I shall not trouble your honor by reading our reply in full, but briefly state its contents," said he, in substance. "We admit that the herds in question, which have been correctly described by road brands and ages, are the property of my client. We further admit that the two trail foremen here under arrest as accessories were acting under the orders of their employer, who assumes all responsibility for their acts, and in our pleadings we ask this honorable court to discharge them from further detention. The earnest-money, said to have been paid on these herds, is correct to a cent, and we admit having the amount in our possession. But," and the little advocate's voice rose, rich in its Irish brogue, "we deny any assignment of the original contract. The Western Supply Company is a corporation name, a shield and fence of thieves. The plaintiffs here can claim no assignment, because they themselves constitute the company. It has been decided that a man cannot steal his own money, neither can he assign from himself to himself. We shall prove by a credible witness that The Western Supply Company is but another name for John C. Fields, Oliver Radcliff, and the portly gentleman who was known a year ago as 'Honest' John Griscom, one of his many aliases. If to these names you add a few moneyed confederates, you have The Western Supply Company, one and the same. We shall also prove that for years past these same gentlemen have belonged to a ring, all brokers in government contracts, and frequently finding it necessary to use assumed names, generally that of a corporation."

Scanning the document in his hand, Sutton continued: "Our motive in selling and accepting money on these herds in Dodge demands a word of explanation. The original contract calls for five million pounds of beef on foot to be delivered at Fort Buford. My client is a sub-contractor under that award.

There are times, your honor, when it becomes necessary to resort to questionable means to attain an end. This is one of them. Within a week after my client had given bonds for the fulfillment of his contract, he made the discovery that he was dealing with a double-faced set of scoundrels. From that day until the present moment, secret-service men have shadowed every action of the plaintiffs. My client has anticipated their every move. When beeves broke in price from five to seven dollars a head, Honest John, here, made his boasts in Washington City over a champagne supper that he and his associates would clear one hundred thousand dollars on their Buford contract. Let us reason together how this could be done. The Western Supply Company refused, even when offered a bonus, to assign their contract to my client. But they were perfectly willing to transfer it, from themselves as a corporation, to themselves as individuals, even though they had previously given Don Lovell a subcontract for the delivery of the beees. The original award was made seven months ago, and the depreciation in cattle since is the secret of why the frog eat the cabbage. My client is under the necessity of tendering his cattle on the day of delivery, and proposes to hold this earnest-money to indemnify himself in case of an adverse decision at Fort Buford. It is the only thing he can do, as The Western Supply Company is execution proof, its assets consisting of some stud-horse office furniture and a corporate seal. On the other hand, Don Lovell is rated at half a million, mostly in pasture lands; is a citizen of Medina County, Texas, and if these gentlemen have any grievance, let them go there and sue him. A judgment against my client is good. Now, your honor, you have our side of the question. To be brief, shall these old Wisinsteins come out here from Washington City and dispossess any man of his property? There is but one answer - not in the Republic of Keith."

All three of the plaintiffs took the stand, their testimony supporting the complaint, Lovell's attorney refusing even to cross-examine any one of them. When they rested their case Sutton arose, and scanning the audience for some time, inquired, "Is Jim Reed there?" In response, a tall, one-armed man worked his way from the outer gallery through the crowd and advanced to the rail. I knew Reed by sight only, my middle brother having made several trips with his trail cattle, but he was known to every one by reputation. He had lost an arm in the Confederate service, and was recognized by the gambling fraternity as the gamest man among all the trail drovers, while every cowman from the Rio Grande to the Yellowstone knew him as a poker-player. Reed was asked to take the stand, and when questioned if he knew either of the plaintiffs, said:

"Yes, I know that fat gentleman, and I'm powerful glad to meet up with him again," replied the witness, designating Honest John. "That man is so crooked that he can't sleep in a bed, and it's one of the wonders of this country that he hasn't stretched hemp before this. I made his acquaintance as manager of The Federal Supply Company, and delivered three thousand cows to him at the Washita Indian Agency last fall. In the final settlement, he drew on three different banks, and one draft of twenty-eight thousand dollars came back, indorsed, DRAWEE UNKNOWN. I had other herds on the trail to look after, and it was a month before I found out that the check was bogus, by which time Honest John had sailed for Europe. There was nothing could be done but put my claim into a judgment and lay for him. But I've got a grapevine twist on him now, for no sooner did he buy a herd here last week than Mr. Sutton transferred the judgment to this jurisdiction, and his cattle will be attached this afternoon. I've been on his trail for nearly a year, but he'll come to me now, and before he can move his beeves out of this county, the last cent must come, with interest, attorney's fees, detective bills, and remuneration for my own time and trouble. That's the reason that I'm so glad to meet him. Judge, I've gone to the trouble and expense to get his record for the last ten years. He's so snaky he sheds his name yearly, shifting for a nickname from Honest John to The Quaker. In '80 he and his associates did business under the name of The Army & Sutler Supply Company, and I know of two judgments that can be bought very reasonable against that corporation. His record would convince any one that he despises to make an honest dollar."

The older of the two attorneys for the plaintiffs asked a few questions, but the replies were so unsatisfactory to their side, that they soon passed the witness. During the cross-questioning, however, the sheriff had approached the judge and whispered something to his honor. As there were no further witnesses to be examined, the local attorneys insisted on arguing the case, but Judge Mulqueen frowned them down, saying:

"This court sees no occasion for any argument in the present case. You might spout until you were black in the face and it wouldn't change my opinion any; besides I've got twenty cars to send and a train of cattle to load out this evening. This court refuses to interfere with the herds in question, at present the property of and in possession of Don Lovell, who, together with his men, are discharged from custody. If you're in town to-night, Mr. Reed, drop into the Lone Star. Couple of nice monte games running there; hundred-dollar limit, and if you feel lucky, there's a nice bank roll behind them. Adjourn court, Mr. Sheriff."

CHAPTER XIV.

TURNING THE TABLES

"Keep away from me, you common cow-hands," said Sponsilier, as a group of us waited for him at the foot of the court-house stairs. But Dave's gravity soon turned to a smile as he continued: "Did you fellows notice The Rebel and me sitting inside the rail among all the big augers? Paul, was it a dream, or did we sleep in a bed last night and have a sure-enough pillow under our heads? My memory is kind of hazy to-day, but I remember the drinks and the cigars all right, and saying to some one that this luck was too good to last. And here we are turned out in the cold world again, our fun all over, and now must go back to those measly cattle. But it's just what I expected."

The crowd dispersed quietly, though the sheriff took the precaution to accompany the plaintiffs and Tolleston back to their hotel. The absence of the two deputies whom we had met the day before was explained by the testimony of the one-armed cowman. When the two drovers came downstairs, they were talking very confidentially together, and on my employer noticing the large number of his men present, he gave orders for them to meet him at once at the White Elephant saloon. Those who had horses at hand mounted and dashed down the street, while the rest of us took it leisurely around to the appointed rendezvous, some three blocks distant. While on the way, I learned from The Rebel that the cattle on which the attachment was to be made that afternoon were then being held well up the North Fork. Sheriff Phillips joined us shortly after we entered the saloon, and informed my employer and

Mr. Reed that the firm of Field, Radcliff & Co. had declared war. They had even denounced him and the sheriff's office as being in collusion against them, and had dispatched Tolleston with orders to refuse service.

"Let them get on the prod all they want to," said Don Lovell to Reed and the sheriff. "I've got ninety men here, and you fellows are welcome to half of them, even if I have to go out and stand a watch on night-herd myself. Reed, we can't afford to have our business ruined by such a set of scoundrels, and we might as well fight it out here and now. Look at the situation I'm in. A hundred thousand dollars wouldn't indemnify me in having my cattle refused as late as the middle of September at Fort Buford. And believing that I will be turned down, under my contract, so Sutton says, I must tender my beeves on the appointed day of delivery, which will absolve my bondsmen and me from all liability. A man can't trifle with the government - the cattle must be there. Now in my case, Jim, what would you do?"

"That's a hard question, Don. You see we're strangers up in this Northwest country. Now, if it was home in Texas, there would be only one thing to do. Of course I'm no longer hardy with a shotgun, but you've got two good arms."

"Well, gentlemen," said the sheriff, "you must excuse me for interrupting, but if my deputies are to take possession of that herd this afternoon, I must saddle up and go to the front. If Honest John and associates try to stand up any bluffs on my office, they'll only run on the rope once. I'm much obliged to you, Mr. Lovell for the assurance of any help I may need, for it's quite likely that I may have to call upon you. If a ring of government speculators can come out here and refuse service, or dictate to my office, then old Keith County is certainly on the verge of decadence. Now, I'll be all ready to start for the North Fork in fifteen minutes, and I'd admire to have you all go along."

Lovell and Reed both expressed a willingness to accompany the sheriff. Phillips thanked them and nodded to the force behind the mahogany, who dexterously slid the glasses up and down the bar, and politely inquired of the double row confronting them as to their tastes. As this was the third round since entering the place, I was anxious to get away, and summoning Forrest, we started for our horses. We had left them at a barn on a back street, but before reaching the livery, Quince concluded that he needed a few more cartridges. I had ordered a hundred the day before for my own personal use, but they had been sent out with the supplies and were then in camp. My own belt was filled with ammunition, but on Forrest buying fifty, I took an equal number, and after starting out of the store, both turned back and doubled our purchases. On arriving at the stable, whom should I meet but the Wyoming cowman who had left us at Grinnell. During the few minutes in which I was compelled to listen to his troubles, he informed me that on his arrival at Ogalalla, all the surplus cow-hands had been engaged by a man named Tolleston for the Yellowstone country. He had sent to his ranch, however, for an outfit who would arrive that evening, and he expected to start his herd the next morning. But without wasting any words, Forrest and I swung into our saddles, waved a farewell to the wayfaring acquaintance, and rode around to the White Elephant. The sheriff and quite a cavalcade of our boys had already started, and on reaching the street which terminated in the only road leading to the North Fork, we were halted by Flood to await the arrival of the others. Jim Reed and my employer were still behind, and some little time was lost before they came up, sufficient to give the sheriff a full half-mile start. But under the leadership of the two drovers, we shook out our horses, and the advance cavalcade were soon overtaken.

"Well, Mr. Sheriff," said old man Don, as he reined in beside Phillips, "how do you like the looks of this for a posse? I'll vouch that they're all good cow-hands, and if you want to deputize the whole works, why, just work your rabbit's foot. You might leave Reed and me out, but I think there's some forty odd without us. Jim and I are getting a little too old, but we'll hang around and run errands and do the clerking. I'm perfectly willing to waste a week, and remember that we've got the chuck and nearly a thousand saddle horses right over here on the North Fork. You can move your office out to one of my wagons if you wish, and whatever's mine is yours, just so long as Honest John and his friends pay the fiddler. If he and his associates are going to make one hundred thousand dollars on the Buford contract, one thing is certain - I'll lose plenty of money on this year's drive. If he refuses service and you take possession, your office will be perfectly justified in putting a good force of men with the herd. And at ten dollars a day for a man and horse, they'll soon get sick and Reed will get his pay. If I have to hold the sack in the end, I don't want any company."

The location of the beeves was about twelve miles from town and but a short distance above the herds of The Rebel and Bob Quirk. It was nearly four o'clock when we left the hamlet, and by striking a free gait, we covered the intervening distance in less than an hour and a half. The mesa between the two rivers was covered with through cattle, and as we neared the herd in question, we were met by the larger one of the two chief deputies. The undersheriff was on his way to town, but on sighting his superior among us, he halted and a conference ensued. Sponsilier and Priest made a great ado over the big deputy on meeting, and after a few inquiries were exchanged, the latter turned to Sheriff Phillips and said:

"Well, we served the papers and I left the other two boys in temporary possession of the cattle. It's a badly mixed-up affair. The Texas foreman is still in charge, and he seems like a reasonable fellow. The terms of the sale were to be half cash here and the balance at the point of delivery. But the buyers only paid forty thousand down, and the trail boss refuses to start until they make good their agreement. From what I could gather from the foreman, the buyers simply buffaloed the young fellow out of his beeves, and are now hanging back for more favorable terms. He accepted service all right and assured me that our men would be welcome at his wagon until further notice, so I left matters just as I found them. But as I was on the point of leaving, that segundo of the buyers arrived and tried to stir up a little trouble. We all sat down on him rather hard, and as I left he and the Texas foreman were holding quite a big pow-wow."

"That's Tolleston all right," said old man Don, "and you can depend on him stirring up a muss if there's any show. It's a mystery to me how I tolerated that fellow as long as I did. If some of you boys will corner and hold him for me, I'd enjoy reading his title to him in a few plain words. It's due him, and I want to pay everything I owe. What's the programme, Mr. Sheriff?"

"The only safe thing to do is to get full possession of the cattle," replied Phillips. "My deputies are all right, but they don't thoroughly understand the situation. Mr. Lovell, if you can lend me ten men, I'll take charge of the herd at once and move them back down the river about seven miles. They're entirely too near the west line of the county to suit me, and once they're in our custody the money will be forthcoming, or the expenses will mount up rapidly. Let's ride."

The under-sheriff turned back with us. A swell of the mesa cut off a view of the herd, but under the leadership of the deputy we rode to its summit, and there before and under us were both camp and cattle. Arriving at the wagon, Phillips very politely informed the Texas foreman that he would have to take full possession of his beeves for a few days, or until the present difficulties were adjusted. The trail boss was a young fellow of possibly thirty, and met the sheriff's demand with several questions, but, on being assured that his employer's equity in the herd would be fully protected without expense, he offered no serious objection. It developed that Reed had some slight acquaintance with the seller of the cattle, and lost no time in informing the trail boss of the record of the parties with whom his employer was dealing. The one-armed drover's language was plain, the foreman knew Reed by reputation, and when Lovell assured the young man that he would be welcome at any of his wagons, and would be perfectly at liberty to see that his herd was properly cared for, he yielded without a word. My sympathies were with the foreman, for he seemed an honest fellow, and deliberately to take his herd from him, to my impulsive reasoning looked like an injustice. But the sheriff and those two old cowmen were determined, and the young fellow probably acted for the best in making a graceful surrender.

Meanwhile the two deputies in charge failed to materialize, and on inquiry they were reported as out at the herd with Tolleston. The foreman accompanied us to the cattle, and while on the way he informed the sheriff that he wished to count the beeves over to him and take a receipt for the same. Phillips hesitated, as he was no cowman, but Reed spoke up and insisted that it was fair and just, saying: "Of course, you'll count the cattle and give him a receipt in numbers, ages, and brands. It's not this young man's fault that his herd must undergo all this trouble, and when he turns them over to an officer of the law he ought to have something to show for it. Any of Lovell's foremen here will count them to a hair for you, and Don and I will witness the receipt, which will make it good among cowmen."

Without loss of time the herd was started east. Tolleston kept well out of reach of my employer, and besought every one to know what this movement meant. But when the trail boss and Jim Flood rode out to a swell of ground ahead, and the point-men began filing the column through between the two foremen, Archie was sagacious enough to know that the count meant something serious. In the mean time Bob Quirk had favored Tolleston with his company, and when the count was nearly half over, my brother quietly informed him that the sheriff was taking possession. Once the atmosphere cleared, Archie grew uneasy and restless, and as the last few hundred beeves were passing the counters, he suddenly concluded to return to Ogalalla. But my brother urged him not to think of going until he had met his former employer, assuring Tolleston that the old man had made inquiry about and was anxious to meet him. The latter, however, could not remember anything of urgent importance between them, and pleaded the lateness of the hour and the necessity of his immediate return to town. The more urgent Bob Quirk became, the more fidgety grew Archie. The last of the cattle were passing the count as Tolleston turned away from my brother's entreaty, and giving his horse the rowel, started off on a gallop. But there was a scattering field of horsemen to pass, and before the parting guest could clear it, a half-dozen ropes circled in the air and deftly settled over his horse's neck and himself, one of which pinioned his arms. The boys were expecting something of this nature, and fully half the men in Lovell's employ galloped up and formed a circle around the captive, now livid with rage. Archie was cursing by both note and rhyme, and had managed to unearth a knife and was trying to cut the lassos which fettered himself and horse, when Dorg Seay rode in and rapped him over the knuckles with a six-shooter, saying, "Don't do that, sweetheart; those ropes cost thirty-five cents apiece."

Fortunately the knife was knocked from Tolleston's hand and his six-shooter secured, rendering him powerless to inflict injury to any one. The cattle count had ended, and escorted by a cordon of mounted men, both horse and captive were led over to where a contingent had gathered around to hear the result of the count. I was merely a delighted spectator, and as the other men turned from the cattle and met us, Lovell languidly threw one leg over his horse's neck, and, suppressing a smile, greeted his old foreman.

"Hello, Archie," said he; "it's been some little time since last we met. I've been hearing some bad reports about you, and was anxious to meet up and talk matters over. Boys, take those ropes off his horse and give him back his irons; I raised this man and made him the cow-hand he is, and there's nothing so serious between us that we should remain strangers. Now, Archie, I want you to know that you are in the employ of my enemies, who are as big a set of scoundrels as ever missed a halter. You and Flood, here, were the only two men in my employ who knew all the facts in regard to the Buford contract. And just because I wouldn't favor you over a blind horse, you must hunt up the very men who are trying to undermine me on this drive. No wonder they gave you employment, for you're a valuable man to them; but it's at a serious loss, - the loss of your honor. You can't go home to Texas and again be respected among men. This outfit you are with will promise you the earth, but the moment that they're through with you, you won't cut any more figure than a last year's bird's nest. They'll throw you aside like an old boot, and you'll fall so hard that you'll hear the clock tick in China. Now, Archie, it hurts me to see a young fellow like you go wrong, and I'm willing to forgive the past and stretch out a hand to save you. If you'll quit those people, you can have Flood's cattle from here to the Rosebud Agency, or I'll buy you a ticket home and you can help with the fall work at the ranch. You may have a day or two to think this matter over, and whatever you decide on will be final. You have shown little gratitude for the opportunities that I've given you, but we'll break the old slate and start all over with a new one. Now, that's all I wanted to say to you, except to do your own thinking. If you're going back to town, I'll ride a short distance with you."

The two rode away together, but halted within sight for a short conference, after which Lovell returned. The cattle were being drifted east by the deputies and several of our boys, the trail boss having called off his men on an agreement of the count. The herd had tallied out thirty-six hundred and ten head, but in making out the receipt, the fact was developed that there were some six hundred beeves not in the regular road brand. These had been purchased extra from another source, and had been paid for in full by the buyers, the seller of the main herd agreeing to deliver them along with his own. This was fortunate, as it increased the equity of the buyers in the cattle, and more than established a sufficient interest to satisfy the judgment and all expenses.

Darkness was approaching, which hastened our actions. Two men from each outfit present were detailed to hold the cattle that night, and were sent on ahead to Priest's camp to secure their suppers and a change of mounts. The deposed trail boss accepted an invitation to accompany us and spend the night at one of our wagons, and we rode away to overtake the drifting herd. The different outfits one by one dropped out and rode for their camps; but as mine lay east and across the river, the course of the herd was carrying me home. After passing The Rebel's wagon fully a half mile, we rounded in the herd, which soon lay down to rest on the bedground. In the gathering twilight, the camp-fires of nearly a dozen trail wagons were gleaming up and down the river, and while we speculated with Sponsilier's boys which one was ours, the guard arrived and took the bedded herd. The two old cowmen and the trail boss had dropped out opposite my brother's camp, leaving something like ten men with the attached beeves; but on being relieved by the first watch, Flood invited Sheriff Phillips and his deputies across the river to spend the night with him.

"Like to, mighty well, but can't do it," replied Phillips. "The sheriff's office is supposed to be in town, and not over on the North Fork, but I'll leave two of these deputies with you. Some of you had better ride in to-morrow, for there may be overtures made looking towards a settlement; and treat those beeves well, so that there can be no charge of damage to the cattle. Good-night, everybody."

CHAPTER XV.

TOLLESTON BUTTS IN

Morning dawned on a scene of pastoral grandeur. The valley of the North Platte was dotted with cattle from hill and plain. The river, well confined within its low banks, divided an unsurveyed domain of green-swarded meadows like a boundary line between vast pastures. The exodus of cattle from Texas to the new Northwest was nearing flood-tide, and from every swell and knoll the solitary figure of the herdsman greeted the rising sun.

Sponsilier and I had agreed to rejoin our own outfits at the first opportunity. We might have exchanged places the evening before, but I had a horse and some ammunition at Dave's camp and was just contentious enough not to give up a single animal from my own mount. On the other hand, Mr. Dave Sponsilier would have traded whole remudas with me; but my love for a good horse was strong, and Fort Buford was many a weary mile distant. Hence there was no surprise shown as Sponsilier rode up to his own wagon that morning in time for breakfast. We were good friends when personal advantages did not conflict, and where our employer's interests were at stake we stood shoulder to shoulder like comrades. Yet Dave gave me a big jolly about being daffy over my horses, well knowing that there is an indescribable nearness between one of our craft and his own mount. But warding off his raillery, just the same and in due time, I cantered away on my own horse.

As I rode up the North Fork towards my outfit, the attached herd was in plain view across the river. Arriving at my own wagon, I saw a mute appeal in every face for permission to go to town, and consent was readily granted to all who had not been excused on a similar errand the day before. The cook and horse-wrangler were included, and the activities of the outfit in saddling and getting away were suggestive of a prairie fire or a stampede. I accompanied them across the river, and then turned upstream to my brother's camp, promising to join them later and make a full day of it. At Bob's wagon they had stretched a fly, and in its shade lounged half a dozen men, while an air of languid indolence pervaded the camp. Without dismounting, I announced myself as on the way to town, and invited any one who wished to accompany me. Lovell and Reed both declined; half of Bob's men had been excused and started an hour before, but my brother assured me that if I would wait until the deposed foreman returned, the latter's company could be counted on. I waited, and in the course of half an hour the trail boss came back from his cattle. During the interim, the two old cowmen reviewed Grant's siege of Vicksburg, both having been participants, but on opposite sides. While the guest was shifting his saddle to a loaned horse, I inquired if there was anything that I could attend to for any one at Ogalalla. Lovell could think of nothing; but as we mounted to start, Reed aroused himself, and coming over, rested the stub of his armless sleeve on my horse's neck, saying:

"You boys might drop into the sheriff's office as you go in and also again as you are starting back. Report the cattle as having spent a quiet night and ask Phillips if he has any word for me."

Turning to the trail boss he continued: "Young man, I would suggest that you hunt up your employer and have him stir things up. The cattle will be well taken care of, but we're just as anxious to turn them back to you as you are to receive them. Tell the seller that it would be well worth his while to see Lovell and myself before going any farther. We can put him in possession of a few facts that may save him time and trouble. I reckon that's about all. Oh, yes, I'll be at this wagon all evening."

My brother rode a short distance with us and introduced the stranger as Hugh Morris. He proved a sociable fellow, had made three trips up the trail as foreman, his first two herds having gone to the Cherokee Strip under contract. By the time we reached Ogalalla, as strong a fraternal level existed between us as though we had known each other for years. Halting for a moment at the sheriff's office, we delivered our messages, after which we left our horses at the same corral with the understanding that we would ride back together. A few drinks were indulged in before parting, then each went to attend to his own errands, but we met frequently during the day. Once my boys were provided with funds, they fell to gambling so eagerly that they required no further thought on my part until evening. Several times during the day I caught glimpses of Tolleston, always on horseback, and once surrounded by quite a cavalcade of horsemen. Morris and I took dinner at the hotel where the trio of government jobbers were stopping. They were in evidence, and amongst the jolliest of the guests, commanding and receiving the best that the hostelry afforded. Sutton was likewise present, but quiet and unpretentious, and I thought there was a false, affected note in the hilarity of the ringsters, and for effect. I was known to two of the trio, but managed to overhear any conversation which was adrift. After dinner and over fragrant cigars, they reared their feet high on an outer gallery, and the inference could be easily drawn that a contract, unless it involved millions, was beneath their notice.

Morris informed me that his employer's suspicions were aroused, and that he had that morning demanded a settlement in full or the immediate release of the herd. They had laughed the matter off as a mere incident that would right itself at the proper time, and flashed as references a list of congressmen, senators, and bankers galore. But Morris's employer had stood firm in his contentions, refusing to be overawed by flattery or empty promises. What would be the result remained to be seen, and the foreman and myself wandered aimlessly around town during the afternoon, meeting other trail bosses, nearly all of whom had heard more or less about the existing trouble. That we had the sympathy of the cattle interests on our side goes without saying, and one of them, known as "the kidgloved foreman," a man in the employ of Shanghai Pierce, invoked the powers above to witness what would happen if he were in Lovell's boots. This was my first meeting with the picturesque trail boss, though I had heard of him often and found him a trifle boastful but not a bad fellow. He distinguished himself from others of his station on the trail by always wearing white shirts, kid gloves, riding-boots, inlaid spurs, while a heavy silver chain was wound several times round a costly sombrero in lieu of a hatband. We spent an hour or more together, drinking sparingly, and at parting he begged that I would assure my employer that he sympathized with him and was at his command.

The afternoon was waning when I hunted up my outfit and started them for camp. With one or two exceptions, the boys were broke and perfectly willing to go. Morris and I joined them at the livery where they had left their horses, and together we started out of town. Ordering them to ride on to camp, and saying that I expected to return by way of Bob Quirk's wagon, Morris and myself stopped at the court-house. Sheriff Phillips was in his office and recognized us both at a glance. "Well, she's working," said he, "and I'll probably have some word for you late this evening. Yes, one of the local attorneys for your friends came in and we figured everything up. He thought that if this office would throw off a certain per cent. of its expense, and Reed would knock off the interest, his clients would consent to a settlement. I told him to go right back and tell his people that as long as they thought that way, it would only cost them one hundred and forty dollars every twenty-four hours. The lawyer was back within twenty minutes, bringing a draft, covering every item, and urged me to have it accepted by wire. The bank was closed, but I found the cashier in a poker-game and played his hand while he went over to the depot and sent the message. The operator has orders to send a duplicate of the answer to this office, and the moment I get it, if favorable, I'll send a deputy with the news over to the North Fork. Tell Reed that I think the check's all right this time, but we'll stand pat until we know for a certainty. We'll get an answer by morning sure."

The message was hailed with delight at Bob Quirk's wagon. On nearing the river, Morris rode by way of the herd to ask the deputies in charge to turn the cattle up the river towards his camp. Several of the foreman's men were waiting at my brother's wagon, and on Morris's return he ordered his outfit to meet the beeves the next morning and be in readiness to receive them back. Our foremen were lying around temporary headquarters, and as we were starting for our respective camps for the night, Lovell suggested that we hold our outfits all ready to move out with the herds on an hour's notice. Accordingly the next morning, I refused every one leave of absence, and gave special orders to the cook and horse-wrangler to have things in hand to start on an emergency order. Jim Flood had agreed to wait for me, and we would recross the river together and hear the report from the sheriff's office. Forrest and Sponsilier rode up about the same time we arrived at his wagon, and all four of us set out for headquarters across the North Fork. The sun was several hours high when we reached the wagon, and learned that an officer had arrived during the night with a favorable answer, that the cattle had been turned over to Morris without a count, and that the deputies had started for town at daybreak.

"Well, boys," said Lovell, as we came in after picketing our horses, "Reed, here, wins out, but we're just as much at sea as ever. I've looked the situation over from a dozen different viewpoints, and the only thing to do is graze across country and tender our cattle at Fort Buford. It's my nature to look on the bright side of things, and yet I'm old enough to know that justice, in a world so full of injustice, is a rarity. By allowing the earnest-money paid at Dodge to apply, some kind of a compromise might be effected, whereby I could get rid of two of these herds, with three hundred saddle horses thrown back on my hands at the Yellowstone River. I might dispose of the third herd here and give the remuda away, but at a total loss of at least thirty thousand dollars on the Buford cattle. But then there's my bond to The Western Supply Company, and if this herd of Morris's fails to respond on the day of delivery, I know who will have to make good. An Indian uprising, or the enforcement of quarantine against Texas fever, or any one of a dozen things might tie up the herd, and September the 15th come and go and no beef offered on the contract. I've seen outfits start out and never get through with the chuck-wagon, even. Sutton's advice is good; we'll tender the cattle. There is a chance that we'll get turned down, but if we do, I have enough indemnity money in my possession to temper the wind if the day of delivery should prove a chilly one to us. I think you had all better start in the morning."

The old man's review of the situation was a rational one, in which Jim Reed and the rest of us concurred. Several of the foremen, among them myself, were anxious to start at once, but Lovell urged that we kill a beef before starting and divide it up among the six outfits. He also proposed to Flood that they go into town during the afternoon and freely announce our departure in the morning, hoping to force any issue that might be smouldering in the enemy's camp. The outlook for an early departure was hailed with delight by the older foremen, and we younger and more impulsive ones yielded. The cook had orders to get up something extra for dinner, and we played cards and otherwise lounged around until the midday meal was announced as ready. A horse had been gotten up for Lovell to ride and was on picket, all the relieved men from the attached herd were at Bob's wagon for dinner, and jokes and jollity graced the occasion. But near the middle of the noon repast, some one sighted a mounted man coming at a furious pace for the camp, and shortly the horseman dashed up and inquired for Lovell. We all arose, when the messenger dismounted and handed my employer a letter. Tearing open the missive, the old man read it and turned ashy pale. The message was from Mike Sutton, stating that a fourth member of the ring had arrived during the forenoon, accompanied by a United States marshal from the federal court at Omaha; that the officer was armed with an order of injunctive relief; that he had deputized thirty men whom Tolleston had gathered, and proposed taking possession of the two herds in question that afternoon.

"Like hell they will," said Don Lovell, as he started for his horse. His action was followed by every man present, including the one-armed guest, and within a few minutes thirty men swung into saddles, subject to orders. The camps of the two herds at issue were about four and five miles down and across the river, and no doubt Tolleston knew of their location, as they were only a little more than an hour's ride from Ogalalla. There was no time to be lost, and as we hastily gathered around the old man, he said: "Ride for your outfits, boys, and bring along every man you can spare. We'll meet north of the river about midway between Quince's and Tom's camps. Bring all the cartridges you have, and don't spare your horses going or coming."

Priest's wagon was almost on a line with mine, though south of the river. Fortunately I was mounted on one of the best horses in my string, and having the farthest to go, shook the kinks out of him as old Paul and myself tore down the mesa. After passing The Rebel's camp, I held my course as long as the footing was solid, but on encountering the first sand, crossed the river nearly opposite the appointed rendezvous. The North Platte was fordable at any point, flowing but a midsummer stage of water, with numerous wagon crossings, its shallow channel being about one hundred yards wide. I reined in my horse for the first time near the middle of the stream, as the water reached my saddle-skirts; when I came out on the other side, Priest and his boys were not a mile behind me. As I turned down the river, casting a backward glance, squads of horsemen were galloping in from several quarters and joining a larger one which was throwing up clouds of dust like a column of cavalry. In making a cut-off to reach my camp, I crossed a sand dune from which I sighted the marshal's posse less than two miles distant. My boys were gambling among themselves, not a horse under saddle, and did not notice my approach until I dashed up. Three lads were on herd, but the rest, including the wrangler, ran for their mounts on picket, while Parent and myself ransacked the wagon for ammunition. Fortunately the supply of the latter was abundant, and while saddles were being cinched on horses, the cook and I divided the ammunition and distributed it among the men. The few minutes' rest refreshed my horse, but as we dashed away, the boys yelling like Comanches, the five-mile ride had bested him and he fell slightly behind. As we turned into the open valley, it was a question if we or the marshal would reach the stream first; he had followed an old wood road and would strike the river nearly opposite Forrest's camp. The horses were excited and straining every nerve, and as we neared our crowd the posse halted on the south side and I noticed a conveyance among them in which were seated four men. There was a moment's consultation held, when the posse entered the water and began fording the stream, the vehicle and its occupants remaining on the other side. We had halted in a circle about fifty yards back from the river-bank, and as the first two men came out of the water, Don Lovell rode forward several lengths of his horse, and with his hand motioned to them to halt. The leaders stopped within easy speaking distance, the remainder of the posse halting in groups at their rear, when Lovell demanded the meaning of this demonstration.

An inquiry and answer followed identifying the speakers. "In pursuance of an order from the federal court of this jurisdiction," continued the marshal, "I am vested with authority to take into my custody two herds, numbering nearly seven thousand beeves, now in your possession, and recently sold to Field, Radcliff & Co. for government purposes. I propose to execute my orders peaceably, and any interference on your part will put you and your men in contempt of government authority. If resistance is offered, I can, if necessary, have a company of United States cavalry here from Fort Logan within forty-eight hours to enforce the mandates of the federal court. Now my advice to you would be to turn these cattle over without further controversy."

"And my advice to you," replied Lovell, "is to go back to your federal court and tell that judge that as a citizen of these United States, and one who has borne arms in her defense, I object to having snap judgment rendered against me. If the honorable court which you have the pleasure to represent is willing to dispossess me of my property in favor of a ring of government thieves, and on only hearing one side of the question, then consider me in contempt. I'll gladly go back to Omaha with you, but you can't so much as look at a hoof in my possession. Now call your troops, or take me with you for treating with scorn the orders of your court."

Meanwhile every man on our side had an eye on Archie Tolleston, who had gradually edged forward until his horse stood beside that of the marshal. Before the latter could frame a reply to Lovell's ultimatum, Tolleston said to the federal officer:

"Didn't my employers tell you that the old - - - - - - would defy you without a demonstration of soldiers at your back? Now, the laugh's on you, and - "

"No, it's on you," interrupted a voice at my back, accompanied by a pistol report. My horse jumped forward, followed by a fusillade of shots behind me, when the hireling deputies turned and plunged into the river. Tolleston had wheeled his horse, joining the retreat, and as I brought my six-shooter into action and was in the act of leveling on him, he reeled from the saddle, but clung to the neck of his mount as the animal dashed into the water. I held my fire in the hope that he would right in the saddle and afford me a shot, but he struck a swift current, released his hold, and sunk out of sight. Above the din and excitement of the moment, I heard a voice which I recognized as Reed's, shouting, "Cut loose on that team, boys! blaze away at those harness horses!" Evidently the team had been burnt by random firing, for they were rearing and plunging, and as I fired my first shot at them, the occupants sprang out of the vehicle and the team ran away. A lull occurred in the shooting, to eject shells and refill cylinders, which Lovell took advantage of by ordering back a number of impulsive lads, who were determined to follow up the fleeing deputies.

"Come back here, you rascals, and stop this shooting!" shouted the old man. "Stop it, now, or you'll land me in a federal prison for life! Those horsemen may be deceived. When federal courts can be deluded with sugar-coated blandishments, ordinary men ought to be excusable."

Six-shooters were returned to their holsters. Several horses and two men on our side had received slight flesh wounds, as there had been a random return fire. The deputies halted well out of pistol range, covering the retreat of the occupants of the carriage as best they could, but leaving three dead horses in plain view. As we dropped back towards Forrest's wagon, the team in the mean time having been caught, those on foot were picked up and given seats in the conveyance. Meanwhile a remuda of horses and two chuck-wagons were sighted back on the old wood road, but a horseman met and halted them and they turned back for Ogalalla. On reaching our nearest camp, the posse south of the river had started on their return, leaving behind one of their number in the muddy waters of the North Platte.

Late that evening, as we were preparing to leave for our respective camps, Lovell said to the assembled foremen: "Quince will take Reed and me into Ogalalla about midnight. If Sutton advises it, all three of us will go down to Omaha and try and square things. I can't escape a severe fine, but what do I care as long as I have their money to pay it with? The killing of that fool boy worries me more than a dozen fines. It was uncalled for, too, but he would butt in, and you fellows were all itching for the chance to finger a trigger. Now the understanding is that you all start in the morning."

CHAPTER XVI.

CROSSING THE NIOBRARA

The parting of the ways was reached. On the morning of July 12, the different outfits in charge of Lovell's drive in '84 started on three angles of the compass for their final destination. The Rosebud Agency, where Flood's herd was to be delivered on September 1, lay to the northeast in Dakota. The route was not direct, and the herd would be forced to make quite an elbow, touching on the different forks of the Loup in order to secure water. The Rebel and my brother would follow up on the south side of the North Platte until near old Fort Laramie, when their routes would separate, the latter turning north for Montana, while Priest would continue along the same watercourse to within a short distance of his destination. The Buford herds would strike due north from the first tributary putting in from above, which we would intercept the second morning out.

An early start was the order of the day. My beeves were pushed from the bed-ground with the first sign of dawn, and when the relief overtook them, they were several miles back from the river and holding a northwest course. My camp being the lowest one on the North Fork, Forrest and Sponsilier, also starting at daybreak, naturally took the lead, the latter having fully a five-mile start over my outfit. But as we left the valley and came up on the mesa, there on an angle in our front, Flood's herd snailed along like an army brigade, anxious to dispute our advance. The point-men veered our cattle slightly to the left, and as the drag-end of Flood's beeves passed before us, standing in our stirrups we waved our hats in farewell to the lads, starting on their last tack for the Rosebud Agency. Across the river were the dim outlines of two herds trailing upstream, being distinguishable from numerous others by the dust-clouds which marked the moving from the grazing cattle. The course of the North Platte was southwest, and on the direction which we were holding, we would strike the river again during the afternoon at a bend some ten or twelve miles above.

Near the middle of the forenoon we were met by Hugh Morris. He was discouraged, as it was well known now that his cattle would be tendered in competition with ours at Fort Buford. There was no comparison between the beeves, ours being much larger, more uniform in weight, and in better flesh. He looked over both Forrest's and Sponsilier's herds before meeting us, and was good enough judge of cattle to know that his stood no chance against ours, if they were to be received on their merits. We talked matters over for fully an hour, and I advised him never to leave Keith County until the last dollar in payment for his beeves was in hand. Morris thought this was quite possible, as information had reached him that the buyers had recently purchased a remuda, and now, since they had failed to take possession of two of Lovell's herds, it remained to be seen what the next move would be. He thought it quite likely, though, that a settlement could be effected whereby he would be relieved at Ogalalla. Mutually hoping that all would turn out well, we parted until our paths should cross again.

We intercepted the North Fork again during the afternoon, watering from it for the last time, and the next morning struck the Blue River, the expected tributary. Sponsilier maintained his position in the lead, but I was certain when we reached the source of the Blue, David would fall to the rear, as thenceforth there was neither trail nor trace, map nor compass. The year before, Forrest and I had been over the route to the Pine Ridge Agency, and one or the other of us must take the lead across a dry country between the present stream and tributaries of the Niobrara. The Blue possessed the attributes of a river in name only, and the third day up it, Sponsilier crossed the tributary to allow either Forrest or myself to take the lead. Quince professed a remarkable ignorance and faulty memory as to the topography of the country between the Blue and Niobrara, and threw bouquets at me regarding my ability always to find water. It is true that I had gone and returned across this arid belt the year before, but on the back trip it was late in the fall, and we were making forty miles a day with nothing but a wagon and remuda, water being the least of my troubles. But a compromise was effected whereby we would both ride out the country anew, leaving the herds to lie over on the head waters of the Blue River. There were several shallow lakes in the intervening country, and on finding the first one sufficient to our needs, the herds were brought up, and we scouted again in advance. The abundance of antelope was accepted as an assurance of water, and on recognizing certain landmarks, I agreed to take the lead thereafter, and we turned back. The seventh day out from the Blue, the Box Buttes were sighted, at the foot of which ran a creek by the same name, and an affluent of the Niobrara. Contrary to expectations, water was even more plentiful than the year before, and we grazed nearly the entire distance. The antelope were unusually tame; with six-shooters we killed quite a number by flagging, or using a gentle horse for a blind, driving the animal forward with the bridle reins, tacking frequently, and allowing him to graze up within pistol range.

The Niobrara was a fine grazing country. Since we had over two months at our disposal, after leaving the North Platte, every advantage was given the cattle to round into form. Ten miles was a day's move, and the different outfits kept in close touch with each other. We had planned a picnic for the crossing of the Niobrara, and on reaching that stream during the afternoon, Sponsilier and myself crossed, camping a mile apart, Forrest remaining on the south side. Wild raspberries had been extremely plentiful, and every wagon had gathered a quantity sufficient to make a pie for each man. The cooks had mutually agreed to meet at Sponsilier's wagon and do the baking, and every man not on herd was present in expectation of the coming banquet. One of Forrest's boys had a fiddle, and bringing it along, the festivities opened with a stag dance, the "ladies" being designated by wearing a horse-hobble loosely around their necks. While the pies were baking, a slow process with Dutch ovens, I sat on the wagon-tongue and played the violin by the hour. A rude imitation of the gentler sex, as we had witnessed in dance-halls in Dodge and Ogalalla, was reproduced with open shirt fronts, and amorous advances by the sterner one.

The dancing ceased the moment the banquet was ready. The cooks had experienced considerable trouble in restraining some of the boys from the too free exercise of what they looked upon as the inalienable right of man to eat his pie when, where, and how it best pleased him. But Sponsilier, as host, stood behind the culinary trio, and overawed the impetuous guests. The repast barely concluded in time for the wranglers and first guard from Forrest's and my outfit to reach camp, catch night-horses, bed the cattle, and excuse the herders, as supper was served only at the one wagon. The relieved ones, like eleventh-hour guests, came tearing in after darkness, and the tempting spread soon absorbed them. As the evening wore on, the loungers gathered in several circles, and the raconteur held sway. The fact that we were in a country in which game abounded suggested numerous stories. The delights of cat-hunting by night found an enthusiast in each one present. Every dog in our memory, back to early boyhood, was properly introduced and his best qualities applauded. Not only cat-hounds but coon-dogs had a respectful hearing.

"I remember a hound," said Forrest's wrangler, "which I owned when a boy back in Virginia. My folks lived in the foot-hills of the Blue Ridge Mountains in that state. We were just as poor as our poorest neighbors. But if there was any one thing that that section was rich in it was dogs, principally hounds. This dog of mine was four years old when I left home to go to Texas. Fine hound, swallow marked, and when he opened on a scent you could always tell what it was that he was running. I never allowed him to run with packs, but generally used him

ANDY ADAMS

in treeing coon, which pestered the cornfields during roasting-ear season and in the fall. Well, after I had been out in Texas about five years, I concluded to go back on a little visit to the old folks. There were no railroads within twenty miles of my home, and I had to hoof it that distance, so I arrived after dark. Of course my return was a great surprise to my folks, and we sat up late telling stories about things out West. I had worked with cattle all the time, and had made one trip over the trail from Collin County to Abilene, Kansas.

"My folks questioned me so fast that they gave me no show to make any inquiries in return, but I finally eased one in and asked about my dog Keiser, and was tickled to hear that he was still living. I went out and called him, but he failed to show up, when mother explained his absence by saying that he often went out hunting alone now, since there was none of us boys at home to hunt with him. They told me that he was no account any longer; that he had grown old and gray, and father said he was too slow on trail to be of any use. I noticed that it was a nice damp night, and if my old dog had been there, I think I'd have taken a circle around the fields in the hope of hearing him sing once more. Well, we went back into the house, and after talking awhile longer, I climbed into the loft and went to bed. I didn't sleep very sound that night, and awakened several times. About an hour before daybreak, I awoke suddenly and imagined I heard a hound baying faintly in the distance. Finally I got up and opened the board window in the gable and listened. Say, boys, I knew that hound's baying as well as I know my own saddle. It was old Keiser, and he had something treed about a mile from the house, across a ridge over in some slashes. I slipped on my clothes, crept downstairs, and taking my old man's rifle out of the rack, started to him.

"It was as dark as a stack of black cats, but I knew every path and byway by heart. I followed the fields as far as I could, and later, taking into the timber, I had to go around a long swamp. An old beaver dam had once crossed the outlet of this marsh, and once I gained it, I gave a long yell to let the dog know that some one was coming. He answered me, and quite a little while before day broke I reached him. Did he know me? Why, he knew me as easy as the little boy knew his pap. Right now, I can't remember any simple thing in my whole life that moved me just as that little reunion of me and my dog, there in those woods that morning. Why, he howled with delight. He licked my face and hands and stood up on me with his wet feet and said just as plain as he could that he was glad to see me again. And I was glad to meet him, even though he did make me feel as mellow as a girl over a baby.

"Well, when daybreak came, I shot a nice big fat Mr. Zip Coon out of an old pin-oak, and we started for home like old pardners. Old as he was, he played like a puppy around me, and when we came in sight of the house, he ran on ahead and told the folks what he had found. Yes, you bet he told them. He came near clawing all the clothing off them in his delight. That's one reason I always like a dog and a poor man - you can't question their friendship."

A circus was in progress on the other side of the wagon. From a large rock, Jake Blair was announcing the various acts and introducing the actors and actresses. Runt Pickett, wearing a skirt made out of a blanket and belted with a hobble, won the admiration of all as the only living lady lion-tamer. Resuming comfortable positions on our side of the commissary, a lad named Waterwall, one of Sponsilier's boys, took up the broken thread where Forrest's wrangler had left off.

"The greatest dog-man I ever knew," said he, "lived on the Guadalupe River. His name was Dave Hapfinger, and he had the loveliest vagabond temperament of any man I ever saw. It mattered nothing what he was doing, all you had to do was to give old Dave a hint that you knew where there was fish to be caught, or a bee-course to hunt, and he would stop the plow and go with you for a week if necessary. He loved hounds better than any man I ever knew. You couldn't confer greater favor than to give him a promising hound pup, or, seeking the same, ask for one of his raising. And he was such a good fellow.

If any one was sick in the neighborhood, Uncle Dave always had time to kill them a squirrel every day; and he could make a broth for a baby, or fry a young squirrel, in a manner that would make a sick man's mouth water.

"When I was a boy, I've laid around many a camp-fire this way and listened to old Dave tell stories. He was quite a humorist in his way, and possessed a wonderful memory. He could tell you the day of the month, thirty years before, when he went to mill one time and found a peculiar bird's nest on the way. Colonel Andrews, owner of several large plantations, didn't like Dave, and threatened to prosecute him once for cutting a bee-tree on his land. If the evidence had been strong enough, I reckon the Colonel would. No doubt Uncle Dave was guilty, but mere suspicion isn't sufficient proof.

"Colonel Andrews was a haughty old fellow, blue-blooded and proud as a peacock, and about the only way Dave could get even with him was in his own mild, humorous way. One day at dinner at a neighboring log-rolling, when all danger of prosecution for cutting the bee-tree had passed, Uncle Dave told of a recent dream of his, a pure invention. 'I dreamt,' said he, 'that Colonel Andrews died and went to heaven. There was an unusually big commotion at St. Peter's gate on his arrival. A troop of angels greeted him, still the Colonel seemed displeased at his reception. But the welcoming hosts humored him forward, and on nearing the throne, the Almighty, recognizing the distinguished arrival, vacated the throne and came down to greet the Colonel personally. At this mark of appreciation, he relaxed a trifle, and when the Almighty insisted that he should take the throne seat, Colonel Andrews actually smiled for the first time on earth or in heaven.'

"Uncle Dave told this story so often that he actually believed it himself. But finally a wag friend of Colonel Andrews told of a dream which he had had about old Dave, which the latter hugely enjoyed. According to this second vagary, the old vagabond had also died and gone to heaven. There was some trouble at St. Peter's gate, as they refused to admit dogs, and

Uncle Dave always had a troop of hounds at his heels. When he found that it was useless to argue the matter, he finally yielded the point and left the pack outside. Once inside the gate he stopped, bewildered at the scene before him. But after waiting inside some little time unnoticed, he turned and was on the point of asking the gate-keeper to let him out, when an angel approached and asked him to stay. There was some doubt in Dave's mind if he would like the place, but the messenger urged that he remain and at least look the city over. The old hunter goodnaturedly consented, and as they started up one of the golden streets Uncle Dave recognized an old friend who had once given him a hound pup. Excusing himself to the angel, he rushed over to his former earthly friend and greeted him with warmth and cordiality. The two old cronies talked and talked about the things below, and finally Uncle Dave asked if there was any hunting up there. The reply was disappointing.

"Meanwhile the angel kept urging Uncle Dave forward to salute the throne. But he loitered along, meeting former hunting acquaintances, and stopping with each for a social chat. When they finally neared the throne, the patience of the angel was nearly exhausted; and as old Dave looked up and saw Colonel Andrews occupying the throne, he rebelled and refused to salute, when the angel wrathfully led him back to the gate and kicked him out among his dogs."

Jack Splann told a yarn about the friendship of a pet lamb and dog which he owned when a boy. It was so unreasonable that he was interrupted on nearly every assertion. Long before he had finished, Sponsilier checked his narrative and informed him that if he insisted on doling out fiction he must have some consideration for his listeners, and at least tell it within reason. Splann stopped right there and refused to conclude his story, though no one but myself seemed to regret it. I had a true incident about a dog which I expected to tell, but the audience had become too critical, and I kept quiet. As it was evident that no more dog stories would be told, the conversation was allowed to drift at will. The recent shooting on the North

Platte had been witnessed by nearly every one present, and was suggestive of other scenes.

"I have always contended," said Dorg Seay, "that the man who can control his temper always shoots the truest. You take one of these fellows that can smile and shoot at the same time - they are the boys that I want to stand in with. But speaking cf losing the temper, did any of you ever see a woman real angry, - not merely cross, but the tigress in her raging and thirsting to tear you limb from limb? I did only once, but I have never forgotten the occasion. In supreme anger the only superior to this woman I ever witnessed was Captain Cartwright when he shot the slayer of his only son. He was as cool as a cucumber, as his only shot proved, but years afterward when he told me of the incident, he lost all control of himself, and fire flashed from his eyes like from the muzzle of a six-shooter. 'Dorg,' said he, unconsciously shaking me like a terrier does a rat, his blazing eyes not a foot from my face, 'Dorg, when I shot that cowardly - - - - - - - -, I didn't miss the centre of his forehead the width of my thumb nail.' "But this woman defied a throng of men. Quite a few of the crowd had assisted the night before in lynching her husband, and this meeting occurred at the burying-ground the next afternoon. The woman's husband was a well-known horse-thief, a dissolute, dangerous character, and had been warned to leave the community. He lived in a little village, and after darkness the evening before, had crept up to a window and shot a man sitting at the supper-table with his family. The murderer had harbored a grudge against his victim, had made threats, and before he could escape, was caught red-handed with the freshly fired pistol in his hand. The evidence of guilt was beyond question, and a vigilance committee didn't waste any time in hanging him to the nearest tree. "The burying took place the next afternoon. The murdered man was a popular citizen, and the village and country turned out to pay their last respects. But when the services were over, a number of us lingered behind, as it was understood that the slayer as well as his victim would be interred in the same grounds. A second grave had been prepared, and within an hour a wagon containing a woman, three small children, and several Mexicans drove up to the rear side of the inclosure. There was no mistaking the party, the coffin was carried in to the open grave, when every one present went over to offer friendly services. But as we neared the little group the woman picked up a shovel and charged on us like a tigress. I never saw such an expression of mingled anger and anguish in a human countenance as was pictured in that woman's face. We shrank from her as if she had been a lioness, and when at last she found her tongue, every word cut like a lash. Livid with rage, the spittle frothing from her mouth, she drove us away, saying:

"'Oh, you fiends of hell, when did I ask your help? Like the curs you are, you would lick up the blood of your victim! Had you been friends to me or mine, why did you not raise your voice in protest when they were strangling the life out of the father of my children? Away, you cowardly hounds! I've hired a few Mexicans to help me, and I want none of your sympathy in this hour. Was it your hand that cut him down from the tree this morning, and if it was not, why do I need you now? Is my shame not enough in your eyes but that you must taunt me further? Do my innocent children want to look upon the faces of those who robbed them of a father? If there is a spark of manhood left in one of you, show it by leaving me alone! And you other scum, never fear but that you will clutter hell in reward for last night's work. Begone, and leave me with my dead!'"

The circus had ended. The lateness of the hour was unobserved by any one until John Levering asked me if he should bring in my horse. It lacked less than half an hour until the guards should change, and it was high time our outfit was riding for camp. The innate modesty of my wrangler, in calling attention to the time, was not forgotten, but instead of permitting him to turn servant, I asked him to help our cook look after his utensils. On my return to the wagon, Parent was trying to quiet a nervous horse so as to allow him to carry the Dutch oven returning. But as Levering was in the act of handing up the heavy oven, one of Forrest's men, hoping to make the animal buck, attempted to place a briar stem under the horse's tail. Sponsilier detected the movement in time to stop it, and turning to the culprit, said: "None of that, my bully boy. I have no objection to killing a cheap cow-hand, but these cooks have won me, hands down. If ever I run across a girl who can make as good pies as we had for supper, she can win the affections of my young and trusting heart."

CHAPTER XVII.

WATER-BOUND

Our route was carrying us to the eastward of the Black Hills. The regular trail to the Yellowstone and Montana points was by the way of the Powder River, through Wyoming; but as we were only grazing across to our destination, the most direct route was adopted. The first week after leaving the Niobrara was without incident, except the meeting with a band of Indians, who were gathering and drying the wild fruit in which the country abounded. At first sighting their camp we were uneasy, holding the herd close together; but as they proved friendly, we relaxed and shared our tobacco with the men. The women were nearly all of one stature, short, heavy, and repulsive in appearance, while the men were tall, splendid specimens of the aborigines, and as uniform in a dozen respects as the cattle we were driving. Communication was impossible, except by signs, but the chief had a letter of permission from the agent at Pine Ridge, allowing himself and band a month's absence from the reservation on a berrying expedition. The bucks rode with us for hours, silently absorbed in the beeves, and towards evening turned and galloped away for their encampment.

It must have been the latter part of July when we reached the South Fork of the Big Cheyenne River. The lead was first held by one and then the other herd, but on reaching that watercourse, we all found it more formidable than we expected. The stage of water was not only swimming, but where we struck it, the river had an abrupt cut-bank on one side or the other. Sponsilier happened to be in the lead, and

Forrest and myself held back to await the decision of the veteran foreman. The river ran on a northwest angle where we encountered it, and Dave followed down it some distance looking for a crossing. The herds were only three or four miles apart, and assistance could have been rendered each other, but it was hardly to be expected that an older foreman would ask either advice or help from younger ones. Hence Quince and myself were in no hurry, nor did we intrude ourselves on David the pathfinder, but sought out a crossing up the river and on our course. A convenient riffle was soon found in the river which would admit the passage of the wagons without rafting, if a cut-bank on the south side could be overcome. There was an abrupt drop of about ten feet to the water level, and I argued that a wagon-way could be easily cut in the bank and the commissaries lowered to the river's edge with a rope to the rear axle. Forrest also favored the idea, and I was authorized to cross the wagons in case a suitable ford could be found for the cattle. My aversion to manual labor was quite pronounced, yet John Q. Forrest wheedled me into accepting the task of making a wagon-road. About a mile above the riffle, a dry wash cut a gash in the bluff bank on the opposite side, which promised the necessary passageway for the herds out of the river. The slope on the south side was gradual, affording an easy inlet to the water, the only danger being on the other bank, the dry wash not being over thirty feet wide. But we both agreed that by putting the cattle in well above the passageway, even if the current was swift, an easy and successful ford would result. Forrest volunteered to cross the cattle, and together we returned to the herds for dinner.

Quince allowed me one of his men besides the cook, and detailed Clay Zilligan to assist with the wagons. We took my remuda, the spades and axes, and started for the riffle. The commissaries had orders to follow up, and Forrest rode away with a supercilious air, as if the crossing of wagons was beneath the attention of a foreman of his standing. Several hours of hard work were spent with the implements at hand in cutting the wagon-way through the bank, after which my saddle horses were driven up and down; and when it was pronounced finished, it looked more like a beaver-slide than a roadway. But a strong stake was cut and driven into the ground, and a corral-rope taken from the axle to it; without detaching the teams, the wagons were eased down the incline and crossed in safety, the water not being over three feet deep in the shallows. I was elated over the ease and success of my task, when Zilligan called attention to the fact that the first herd had not yet crossed. The chosen ford was out of sight, but had the cattle been crossing, we could have easily seen them on the mesa opposite. "Well," said Clay, "the wagons are over, and what's more, all the mules in the three outfits couldn't bring one of them back up that cliff."

We mounted our horses, paying no attention to Zilligan's note of warning, and started up the river. But before we came in view of the ford, a great shouting reached our ears, and giving our horses the rowel, we rounded a bend, only to be confronted with the river full of cattle which had missed the passageway out on the farther side. A glance at the situation revealed a dangerous predicament, as the swift water and the contour of the river held the animals on the farther side or under the cut-bank. In numerous places there was footing on the narrow ledges to which the beeves clung like shipwrecked sailors, constantly crowding each other off into the current and being carried downstream hundreds of yards before again catching a foothold. Above and below the chosen ford, the river made a long gradual bend, the current and deepest water naturally hugged the opposite shore, and it was impossible for the cattle to turn back, though the swimming water was not over forty yards wide. As we dashed up, the outfit succeeded in cutting the train of cattle and turning them back, though fully five hundred were in the river, while not over one fifth that number had crossed in safety. Forrest was as cool as could be expected, and exercised an elegant command of profanity in issuing his orders.

"I did allow for the swiftness of the current," said he, in reply to a criticism of mine, "but those old beeves just drifted downstream like a lot of big tubs. The horses swam it easy, and the first hundred cattle struck the mouth of the wash square in the eye, but after that they misunderstood it for a bath instead of a ford. Oh, well, it's live and learn, die and forget it. But since you're so d - strong on the sabe, suppose you suggest a way of getting those beeves out of the river."

It was impossible to bring them back, and the only alternative was attempted. About three quarters of a mile down the river the cut-bank shifted to the south side. If the cattle could swim that distance there was an easy landing below. The beeves belonged to Forrest's herd, and I declined the proffered leadership, but plans were outlined and we started the work of rescue. Only a few men were left to look after the main herds, the remainder of us swimming the river on our horses. One man was detailed to drive the contingent which had safely forded, down to the point where the bluff bank shifted and the incline commenced on the north shore. The cattle were clinging, in small bunches, under the cut-bank like swallows to a roof for fully a quarter-mile below the mouth of the dry wash. Divesting ourselves of all clothing, a squad of six of us, by way of experiment, dropped over the bank and pushed into the river about twenty of the lowest cattle. On catching the full force of the current, which ran like a mill-race, we swept downstream at a rapid pace, sometimes clinging to a beef's tail, but generally swimming between the cattle and the bluff. The force of the stream drove them against the bank repeatedly, but we dashed water in their eyes and pushed them off again and again, and finally landed every steer.

The Big Cheyenne was a mountain stream, having numerous tributaries heading in the Black Hills. The water was none too warm, and when we came out the air chilled us; but we scaled the bluff and raced back after more cattle. Forrest was in the river on our return, but I ordered his wrangler to drive all the horses under saddle down to the landing, in order that the men could have mounts for returning. This expedited matters, and the work progressed more rapidly. Four separate squads were drifting the cattle, but in the third contingent we cut off too many beeves and came near drowning two fine ones. The animals in question were large and strong, but had stood for nearly an hour on a slippery ledge, frequently being crowded into the water, and were on the verge of collapse from nervous exhaustion. They were trembling like leaves when we pushed them off. Runt Pickett was detailed to look especially after those two, and the little rascal nursed and toyed and played with them like a circus rider. They struggled constantly for the inshore, but Runt rode their rumps alternately, the displacement lifting their heads out of the water to good advantage. When we finally landed, the two big fellows staggered out of the river and dropped down through sheer weakness, a thing which I had never seen before except in wild horses.

A number of the boys were attacked by chills, and towards evening had to be excused for fear of cramps. By six o'clock we were reduced to two squads, with about fifty cattle still remaining in the river. Forrest and I had quit the water after the fourth trip; but Quince had a man named De Manse, a Frenchman, who swam like a wharf-rat and who stayed to the finish, while I turned my crew over to Runt Pickett. The latter was raised on the coast of Texas, and when a mere boy could swim all day, with or without occasion. Dividing the remaining beeves as near equally as possible, Runt's squad pushed off slightly in advance of De Manse, the remainder of us riding along the bank with the horses and clothing, and cheering our respective crews. The Frenchman was but a moment later in taking the water, and as pretty and thrilling a race as I ever witnessed was in progress. The latter practiced a trick, when catching a favorable current, of dipping the rump of a steer, thus lifting his fore parts and rocking him forward like a porpoise. When a beef dropped to the rear, this process was resorted to, and De Manse promised to overtake Pickett. From our position on the bank, we shouted to Runt to dip his drag cattle in swift water; but amid the din and splash of the struggling swimmers our messages failed to reach his ears. De Manse was gaining slowly, when Pickett's bunch were driven inshore, a number of them catching a footing, and before they could be again pushed off, the Frenchman's cattle were at their heels. A number of De Manse's men were swimming shoreward of their charges, and succeeded in holding their beeves off the ledge, which was the last one before the landing. The remaining hundred yards was eddy water; and though Pickett fought hard, swimming among the Frenchman's lead cattle, to hold the two bunches separate, they mixed in the river. As an evidence of victory, however, when the cattle struck a foothold, Runt and each of his men mounted a beef and rode out of the water some distance. As the steers recovered and attempted to dislodge their riders, they nimbly sprang from their backs and hustled themselves into their ragged clothing.

I breathed easier after the last cattle landed, though Forrest contended there was never any danger. At least a serious predicament had been blundered into and handled, as was shown by subsequent events. At noon that day, rumblings of thunder were heard in the Black Hills country to the west, a warning to get across the river as soon as possible. So the situation at the close of the day was not a very encouraging one to either Forrest or myself. The former had his cattle split in two bunches, while I had my wagon and remuda on the other side of the river from my herd. But the emergency must be met. I sent a messenger after our wagon, it was brought back near the river, and a hasty supper was ordered. Two of my boys were sent up to the dry wash to recross the river and drift our cattle down somewhere near the wagon-crossing, thus separating the herds for the night. I have never made claim to being overbright, but that evening I did have sense or intuition enough to take our saddle horses back across the river. My few years of trail life had taught me the importance of keeping in close touch with our base of subsistence, while the cattle and the saddle stock for handling them should under no circumstances ever be separated. Yet under existing conditions it was impossible to recross our commissary, and darkness fell upon us encamped on the south side of the Big Cheyenne.

The night passed with almost constant thunder and lightning in the west. At daybreak heavy dark clouds hung low in a semicircle all around the northwest, threatening falling weather, and hasty preparations were made to move down the stream in search of a crossing. In fording the river to breakfast, my outfit agreed that there had been no perceptible change in the stage of water overnight, which quickened our desire to move at once. The two wagons were camped close together, and as usual Forrest was indifferent and unconcerned over the threatening weather; he had left his remuda all night on the north side of the river, and had actually turned loose the rescued contingent of cattle. I did not mince my words in giving Mr. Forrest my programme, when he turned on me, saying: "Quirk, you have more trouble than a married woman. What do I care if it is raining in London or the Black Hills either? Let her rain; our sugar and salt are both covered, and we can lend you some if yours gets wet. But you go right ahead and follow up Sponsilier; he may not find a crossing this side of the Belle Fourche. I can take spades and axes, and in two hours' time cut down and widen that wagon-way until the herds can cross. I wouldn't be as fidgety as you are for a large farm. You ought to take something for your nerves."

I had a mental picture of John Quincy Forrest doing any manual labor with an axe or spade. During our short acquaintance that had been put to the test too often to admit of question; but I encouraged him to fly right at the bank, assuring him that in case his tools became heated, there was always water at hand to cool them. The wrangler had rustled in the wagon-mules for our cook, and Forrest was still ridiculing my anxiety to move, when a fusillade of shots was heard across and up the river. Every man at both wagons was on his feet in an instant, not one of us even dreaming that the firing of the boys on herd was a warning, when Quince's horsewrangler galloped up and announced a flood-wave coming down the river. A rush was made for our horses, and we struck for the ford, dashing through the shallows and up the farther bank without drawing rein. With a steady rush, a body of water, less than a mile distant, greeted our vision, looking like the falls of some river, rolling forward like an immense cylinder. We sat our horses in bewilderment of the scene, though I had often heard Jim Flood describe the sudden rise of streams which had mountain tributaries. Forrest and his men crossed behind us, leaving but the cooks and a horse-wrangler on the farther side. It was easily to be seen that all the lowlands along the river would be inundated, so I sent Levering back with orders to hook up the team and strike for tall timber. Following suit, Forrest sent two men to rout the contingent of cattle out of a bend which was nearly a mile below the wagons. The wave, apparently ten to twelve feet high, moved forward slowly, great walls lopping off on the side and flooding out over the bottoms, while on the farther shore every cranny and arroyo claimed its fill from the avalanche of water. The cattle on the south side were safe, grazing well back on the uplands, so we gave the oncoming flood our undivided attention. It was traveling at the rate of eight to ten miles an hour, not at a steady pace, but sometimes almost halting when the bottoms absorbed its volume, only to catch its breath and forge ahead again in angry impetuosity. As the water passed us on the bluff bank, several waves broke over and washed around our horses' feet, filling the wagon-way, but the main volume rolled across the narrow valley on the opposite side. The wagons had pulled out to higher ground, and while every eye was strained, watching for the rescued beeves to come out of the bend below, Vick Wolf, who happened to look upstream, uttered a single shout of warning and dashed away. Turning in our saddles, we saw within five hundred feet of us a second wave about half the height of the first one. Rowels and quirts were plied with energy and will, as we tore down the river-bank, making a gradual circle until the second bottoms were reached, outriding the flood by a close margin.

The situation was anything but encouraging, as days might elapse before the water would fall. But our hopes revived as we saw the contingent of about six hundred beeves stampede out of a bend below and across the river, followed by two men who were energetically burning powder and flaunting slickers in their rear. Within a quarter of an hour, a halfmile of roaring, raging torrent, filled with floating driftwood, separated us from the wagons which contained the staples of life. But in the midst of the travail of mountain and plain, the dry humor of the men was irrepressible, one of Forrest's own boys asking him if he felt any uneasiness now about his salt and sugar.

"Oh, this is nothing," replied Quince, with a contemptuous wave of his hand. "These freshets are liable to happen at any time; rise in an hour and fall in half a day. Look there how it is clearing off in the west; the river will be fordable this evening or in the morning at the furthest. As long as everything is safe, what do we care? If it comes to a pinch, we have plenty of stray beef; berries are ripe, and I reckon if we cast around we might find some wild onions. I have lived a whole month at a time on nothing but land-terrapin; they make larruping fine eating when you are cut off from camp this way. Blankets? Never use them; sleep on your belly and cover with your back, and get up with the birds in the morning. These Lovell outfits are getting so tony that by another year or two they'll insist on bathtubs, Florida water, and towels with every wagon. I like to get down to straight beans for a few days every once in a while; it has a tendency to cure a man with a whining disposition. The only thing that's worrying me, if we get cut off, is the laugh that Sponsilier will have on us."

We all knew Forrest was bluffing. The fact that we were water-bound was too apparent to admit of question, and since the elements were beyond our control, there was no telling when relief would come. Until the weather moderated in the hills to the west, there was no hope of crossing the river; but men grew hungry and nights were chilly, and bluster and bravado brought neither food nor warmth. A third wave was noticed within an hour, raising the water-gauge over a foot. The South Fork of the Big Cheyenne almost encircled the entire Black Hills country, and with a hundred mountain affluents emptying in their tribute, the waters commanded and we obeyed. Ordering my men to kill a beef, I rode down the river in the hope of finding Sponsilier on our side, and about noon sighted his camp and cattle on the opposite bank. A group of men were dallying along the shore, but being out of hearing, I turned back without exposing myself.

ANDY ADAMS

On my return a general camp had been established at the nearest wood, and a stray killed. Stakes were driven to mark the rise or fall of the water, and we settled down like prisoners, waiting for an expected reprieve. Towards evening a fire was built up and the two sides of ribs were spitted over it, our only chance for supper. Night fell with no perceptible change in the situation, the weather remaining dry and clear. Forrest's outfit had been furnished horses from my remuda for guard duty, and about midnight, wrapping ourselves in slickers, we lay down in a circle with our feet to the fire like cave-dwellers. The camp-fire was kept up all night by the returning guards, even until the morning hours, when we woke up shivering at dawn and hurried away to note the stage of the water. A four-foot fall had taken place during the night, another foot was added within an hour after sun-up, brightening our hopes, when a tidal wave swept down the valley, easily establishing a new high-water mark. Then we breakfasted on broiled beefsteak, and fell back into the hills in search of the huckleberry, which abounded in that vicinity.

A second day and night passed, with the water gradually falling. The third morning a few of the best swimmers, tiring of the diet of beef and berries, took advantage of the current and swam to the other shore. On returning several hours later, they brought back word that Sponsilier had been up to the wagons the afternoon before and reported an easy crossing about five miles below. By noon the channel had narrowed to one hundred yards of swimming water, and plunging into it on our horses, we dined at the wagons and did justice to the spread. Both outfits were anxious to move, and once dinner was over, the commissaries were started down the river, while we turned up it, looking for a chance to swim back to the cattle. Forrest had secured a fresh mount of horses, and some distance above the dry wash we again took to the water, landing on the opposite side between a quarter and half mile below. Little time was lost in starting the herds, mine in the lead, while the wagons got away well in advance, accompanied by Forrest's remuda and the isolated contingent of cattle.

Sponsilier was expecting us, and on the appearance of our wagons, moved out to a new camp and gave us a clear crossing. A number of the boys came down to the river with him, and several of them swam it, meeting the cattle a mile above and piloting us into the ford. They had assured me that there might be seventy-five yards of swimming water, with a gradual entrance to the channel and a half-mile of solid footing at the outcome. The description of the crossing suited me, and putting our remuda in the lead, we struck the muddy torrent and crossed it without a halt, the chain of swimming cattle never breaking for a single moment. Forrest followed in our wake, the one herd piloting the other, and within an hour after our arrival at the lower ford, the drag-end of the "Drooping T" herd kicked up their heels on the north bank of the Big Cheyenne. Meanwhile Sponsilier had been quietly sitting his horse below the main landing, his hat pulled down over his eye, nursing the humor of the situation. As Forrest came up out of the water with the rear guard of his cattle, the opportunity was too good to be overlooked.

"Hello, Quince," said Dave; "how goes it, old sport? Do you keep stout? I was up at your wagon yesterday to ask you all down to supper. Yes, we had huckleberry pie and venison galore, but your men told me that you had quit eating with the wagon. I was pained to hear that you and Tom have both gone plum hog-wild, drinking out of cowtracks and living on wild garlic and land-terrapin, just like Injuns. Honest, boys, I hate to see good men go wrong that way."

CHAPTER XVIII.

THE LITTLE MISSOURI

A week later we crossed the Belle Fourche, sometimes called the North Fork of the Big Cheyenne. Like its twin sister on the south, it was a mountain river, having numerous affluents putting in from the Black Hills, which it encircled on the north and west. Between these two branches of the mother stream were numerous tributaries, establishing it as the best watered country encountered in our long overland cruise. Besides the splendid watercourses which marked that section, numerous wagontrails, leading into the hills, were peopled with freighters. Long ox trains, moving at a snail's pace, crept over hill and plain, the common carrier between the mines and the outside world. The fascination of the primal land was there; the buttes stood like sentinels, guarding a king's domain, while the palisaded cliffs frowned down, as if erected by the hand Omnipotent to mark the boundary of nations.

Our route, after skirting the Black Hills, followed up the Belle Fourche a few days, and early in August we crossed over to the Little Missouri River. The divide between the Belle Fourche and the latter stream was a narrow one, requiring little time to graze across it, and intercepting the Little Missouri somewhere in Montana. The course of that river was almost due north, and crossing and recrossing it frequently, we kept constantly in touch with it on our last northward tack. The river led through sections of country now known as the Bad Lands, but we found an abundance of grass and an easy passage. Sponsilier held the lead all the way down the river, though I did most of the advance scouting, sometimes being as much as fifty miles in front of the herds. Near the last of the month we sighted Sentinel Butte and the smoke of railroad trains, and a few days later all three of us foremen rode into Little Missouri Station of the Northern Pacific Railway. Our arrival was expected by one man at least; for as we approached the straggling village, our employer was recognized at a distance, waving his hat, and a minute later all three of us were shaking hands with Don Lovell. Mutual inquiries followed, and when we reported the cattle fine as silk, having never known a hungry or thirsty hour after leaving the North Platte, the old man brightened and led the way to a well-known saloon.

"How did I fare at Omaha?" said old man Don, repeating Forrest's query. "Well, at first it was a question if I would be hung or shot, but we came out with colors flying. The United States marshal who attempted to take possession of the cattle on the North Platte went back on the same train with us. He was feeling sore over his defeat, but Sutton cultivated his acquaintance, and in mollifying that official, showed him how easily failure could be palmed off as a victory. In fact, I think Mike overcolored the story at my expense. He and the marshal gave it to the papers, and the next morning it appeared in the form of a sensational article. According to the report, a certain popular federal officer had gone out to Ogalalla to take possession of two herds of cattle intended for government purposes; he had met with resistance by a lot of Texas roughs, who fatally shot one of his deputies, wounding several others, and killing a number of horses during the assault; but the intrepid officer had added to his laurels by arresting the owner of the cattle and leader of the resisting mob, and had brought him back to face the charge of contempt in resisting service. The papers freely predicted that I would get the maximum fine, and one even went so far as to suggest that imprisonment might teach certain arrogant cattle kings a salutary lesson. But when the hearing came up, Sutton placed Jim Reed and me in the witness-box, taking the stand later himself, and we showed that federal court that it had been buncoed out of an order of injunctive relief, in favor of the biggest set of ringsters that ever missed stretching hemp. The result was, I walked out of that federal court scot free. And Judge Dundy, when he realized the injustice that he had inflicted, made all three of us take dinner with him, fully explaining the pressure which had been brought to bear at the time the order of relief was issued. Oh, that old judge was all right. I only hope we'll have as square a man as Judge Dundy at the final hearing at Fort Buford. Do you see that sign over there, where it says Barley Water and Bad Cigars? Well, put your horses in some corral and meet me there."

There was a great deal of news to review. Lovell had returned to Ogalalla; the body of Tolleston had been recovered and given decent burial; delivery day of the three Indian herds was at hand, bringing that branch of the season's drive to a close. But the main thing which absorbed our employer was the quarantine that the upper Yellowstone country proposed enforcing against through Texas cattle. He assured us that had we gone by way of Wyoming and down the Powder River, the chances were that the local authorities would have placed us under quarantine until after the first frost. He assured us that the year before, Texas fever had played sad havoc among the native and wintered Southern cattle, and that Miles City and Glendive, live-stock centres on the Yellowstone, were up in arms in favor of a rigid quarantine against all through cattle. If this proved true, it was certainly an ill wind to drovers on the Powder River route; yet I failed to see where we were benefited until my employer got down to details.

"That's so," said he; "I forgot to tell you boys that when Reed and I went back to Ogalalla, we found Field, Radcliff & Co. buying beeves. Yes, they had bought a remuda of horses, rigged up two wagons, and hired men to take possession of our 'Open A' and 'Drooping T herds. But meeting with disappointment and having the outfit on their hands, they concluded to buy cattle and go ahead and make the delivery at Buford. They simply had to do it or admit that I had called their hands. But Reed and I raised such a howl around that town that we posted every man with beeves for sale until the buyers had to pony up the cash for every hoof they bought. We even hunted up young Murnane, the seller of the herd that Jim Reed ran the attachment on; and before old Jim and I got through with him, we had his promise not to move out of Keith County until the last dollar was in hand. The buyers seemed to command all kinds of money, but where they expect to make anything, even if they do deliver, beats me, as Reed and I have got a good wad of their money. Since leaving there, I have had word that they settled with Murnane, putting a new outfit with the cattle, and that they have ten thousand beef steers on the way to Fort Buford this very minute. They are coming through on the North Platte and Powder River route, and if quarantine can be enforced against them until frost falls, it will give us a clear field at Buford on the day of delivery. Now it stands us in hand to see that those herds are isolated until after the 15th day of September."

The atmosphere cleared instantly. I was well aware of the ravages of splenic fever; but two decades ago every drover from Texas denied the possibility of a through animal in perfect health giving a disease to wintered Southerners or domestic cattle, also robust and healthy. Time has demonstrated the truth, yet the manner in which the germ is transmitted between healthy animals remains a mystery to this day, although there has been no lack of theories advanced. Even the theorists differed as to the manner of germ transmission, the sporule, tick, and ship fever being the leading theories, and each having its advocates. The latter was entitled to some consideration, for if bad usage and the lack of necessary rest, food, and water will produce fever aboard emigrant steamships, the same privations might do it among animals. The overdriving of trail cattle was frequently unavoidable, dry drives and the lack of grass on arid wastes being of common occurrence. However, the presence of fever among through cattle was never noticeable to the practical man, and if it existed, it must have been very mild in form compared to its virulent nature among natives. Time has demonstrated that it is necessary for the domestic animals to walk over and occupy the same ground to contract the disease, though they may drink from the same trough or stream of water, or inhale each other's breath in play across a wire fence, without fear of contagion. A peculiar feature of Texas fever was that the very cattle which would impart it on their arrival, after wintering in the North would contract it and die the same as natives. The isolation of herds on a good range for a period of sixty days, or the falling of frost, was recognized as the only preventive against transmitting the germ. Government rewards and experiments have never demonstrated a theory that practical experience does not dispute.

The only time on this drive that our attention had been called to the fever alarm was on crossing the wagon trail running from Pierre on the Missouri River to the Black Hills. I was in the lead when a large bull train was sighted in our front, and shortly afterward the wagon-boss met me and earnestly begged that I allow his outfit to pass before we crossed the wagon-road. I knew the usual form of ridicule of a herd foreman, but the boss bull-whacker must have anticipated my reply, for he informed me that the summer before he had lost ninety head out of two hundred yoke of oxen. The wagon-master's appeal was fortified by a sincerity which won his request, and I held up my cattle and allowed his train to pass in advance. Sponsilier's herd was out of sight in my rear, while Forrest was several miles to my left, and slightly behind me. The wagon-boss rode across and made a similar request of Forrest, but that worthy refused to recognize the right of way to a bull train at the expense of a trail herd of government beeves. Ungentlemanly remarks are said to have passed between them, when the boss bull-whacker threw down the gauntlet and galloped back to his train. Forrest pushed on, with ample time to have occupied the road in crossing, thus holding up the wagon train. My herd fell to grazing, and Sponsilier rode up to inquire the cause of my halting. I explained the request of the wagon-master, his loss the year before and present fear of fever, and called attention to the clash which was imminent between the long freight outfit in our front and Forrest's herd to the left, both anxious for the right of way. A number of us rode forward in clear view of the impending meeting. It was evident that Forrest would be the first to reach the freight road, and would naturally hold it while his cattle were crossing it. But when this also became apparent to the bull train, the lead teams drove out of the road and halted, the rear wagons passing on ahead, the two outfits being fully a mile apart. There were about twenty teams of ten yoke each, and when the first five or six halted, they unearthed old needle rifles and opened fire across Forrest's front. Once the range was found, those long-range buffalo guns threw up the dust in handfuls in the lead of the herd, and Forrest turned his cattle back, while the bull train held its way, undisputed. It was immaterial to Forrest who occupied the road first, and with the jeers of the freighters mingled the laughter of Sponsilier and my outfit, as John Quincy Forrest reluctantly turned back.

This incident served as a safety-valve, and whenever Forrest forged to the lead in coming down the Little Missouri, all that was necessary to check him was to inquire casually which held the right of way, a trail herd or a bull train.

Throughout the North, Texas fever was generally accepted as a fact, and any one who had ever come in contact with it once, dreaded it ever afterward. So when the devil was sick the devil a monk would be; and if there was any advantage in taking the contrary view to the one entertained by all drovers, so long as our herds were free, we were not like men who could not experience a change of opinion, if in doing so the wind was tempered to us. Also in this instance we were fighting an avowed enemy, and all is fair in love and war. And amid the fumes of bad cigars, Sponsilier drew out the plan of campaign.

"Now, let's see," said old man Don, "tomorrow will be the 25th day of August. I've got to be at the Crow Agency a few days before the 10th of next month, as you know we have a delivery there on that date. Flood will have to attend to matters at Rosebud on the 1st, and then hurry on west and be present at Paul's delivery at Fort Washakie. So you see I'll have to depend on two of you boys going up to Glendive and Miles and seeing that those cow-towns take the proper view of this quarantine matter. After dinner you'll fall back and bring up

ANDY ADAMS

your herds, and after crossing the railroad here, the outfits will graze over to Buford. We'll leave four of our best saddle horses here in a pasture, so as to be independent on our return. Since things have changed so, the chances are that I'll bring Bob Quirk back with me, as I've written Flood to help The Rebel sell his remuda and take the outfit and go home. Now you boys decide among yourselves which two of you will go up the Yellowstone and promote the enforcement of the quarantine laws. Don't get the impression that you can't do this, because an all-round cowman can do anything where his interests are at stake. I'll think the programme out a little more clearly by the time you bring up the cattle."

The herds were not over fifteen miles back up the river when we left them in the morning. After honoring the village of Little Missouri with our presence for several hours, we saddled up and started to meet the cattle. There was no doubt in my mind but that Sponsilier would be one of the two to go on the proposed errand of diplomacy, as his years, experience, and good solid sense entitled him to outrank either Forrest or myself. I knew that Quince would want to go, if for no other reason than to get out of working the few days that yet remained of the drive. All three of us talked the matter of quarantine freely as we rode along, yet no one ventured any proposition looking to an agreement as to who should go on the diplomatic mission. I was the youngest and naturally took refuge behind my years, yet perfectly conscious that, in spite of the indifferent and nonchalant attitude assumed, all three of us foremen were equally anxious for the chance. Matters remained undecided; but the next day at dinner, Lovell having met us before reaching the railroad, the question arose who should go up to Miles City. Dave and Quince were also eating at my wagon, and when our employer forced an answer, Sponsilier innocently replied that he supposed that we were all willing to leave it to him. Forrest immediately approved of Dave's suggestion. I gave my assent, and old man Don didn't qualify, hedge, or mince his words in appointing the committees to represent the firm of Lovell.

"Jealous of each other, ain't you? Very well; I want these herds grazed across to Buford at the rate of four miles a day. Nothing but a Mexican pastor, or a white man as lazy as Quince Forrest can fill the bill. You're listening, are you, Quince? Well, after the sun sets to-night, you're in charge of ten thousand beeves from here to the mouth of the Yellowstone. I want to put every ounce possible on those steers for the next twenty days. We may have to make a comparison of cattle, and if we should, I want ours to lay over the opposition like a double eagle does over a lead dime. We may run up against a lot of red tape at Fort Buford, but if there is a lick of cow-sense among the government representatives, we want our beeves to speak for themselves. Fat animals do their own talking. You remember when every one was admiring the fine horse, the blind man said, 'Isn't he fat?' Now, Dave, you and Tom appoint your segundos, and we'll all catch the 10:20 train west to-night."

I dared to risk one eye on Forrest. Inwardly I was chuckling, but Quince was mincing along with his dinner, showing that languid indifference which is inborn to the Texan. Lovell continued to monopolize the conversation, blowing on the cattle and ribbing up Forrest to see that the beeves thenceforth should never know tire, hunger, or thirst. The commissaries had run low; Sponsilier's cook had been borrowing beans from us for a week past, while Parent point-blank refused to share any more of our bacon. The latter was recognized as a staple in trail-work, and it mattered not how inviting the beef or venison might be, we always fell back to bacon with avidity. When it came time to move out on the evening lap, Forrest's herd took the lead, the other two falling in behind, the wagons pulling out for town in advance of everything. Jack Splann had always acted as segundo in my absence, and as he had overheard Lovell's orders to Forrest, there was nothing further for me to add, and Splann took charge of my "Open A's."

When changing mounts at noon, I caught out two of my best saddlers and tied one behind the chuckwagon, to be left with a liveryman in town. Leaving old man Don with the cattle, all three of us foremen went into the village in order to secure a few staple supplies with which to complete the journey.

It can be taken for granted that Sponsilier and myself were feeling quite gala. The former took occasion, as we rode along, to throw several bouquets at Forrest over his preferment, when the latter turned on us, saying: "You fellows think you're d – d smart, now, don't you? You're both purty good talkers, but neither one of you can show me where the rainbow comes in in rotting along with these measly cattle. It's enough to make a man kick his own dog. But I can see where the old man was perfectly right in sending you two up to Miles City. When you fellows work your rabbit's foot, it will be Katy with those Washington City schemers - more than likely they'll not draw cards when they see that you are in the game - When it comes to the real sabe, you fellows shine like a tree full of owls. Honest, it has always been a wonder to me that Grant didn't send for both of you when he was making up his cabinet."

The herds crossed the railroad about a mile west of Little Missouri Station. The wagons secured the needed supplies, and pulled out down the river, leaving Sponsilier and myself foot-loose and free.

Lovell was riding a livery horse, and as neither of us expected him to return until it was too dark to see the cattle, we amused ourselves by looking over the town. There seemed to be a great deal of freighting to outlying points, numerous ox and mule trains coming in and also leaving for their destinations. Our employer came in about dusk, and at once went to the depot, as he was expecting a message. One had arrived during his absence, and after reading it, he came over to Dave and me, saying:

"It's from Mike Sutton. I authorized him to secure the services of the best lawyer in the West, and he has just wired me that he has retained Senator Aspgrain of Sioux City, Iowa. They will report at Fort Buford on September the 5th and will take care of any legal complications which may arise. I don't know who this senator is, but Mike has orders not to spare any expense as long as we have the other fellow's money to fight with. Well, if the Iowa lawyers are as good stuff as the Iowa troops were down in Dixie, that's all I ask. Now, we'll get our suppers and then sack our saddles - why, sure, you'll need them; every good cowman takes his saddle wherever he goes, though he may not have clothes enough with him to dust a fiddle."

ANDY ADAMS

CHAPTER XIX.

IN QUARANTINE

We reached Miles City shortly after midnight. It was the recognized cattle centre of Montana at that time, but devoid of the high-lights which were a feature of the trail towns. The village boasted the usual number of saloons and dance-houses, and likewise an ordinance compelling such resorts to close on the stroke of twelve. Lovell had been there before, and led the way to a well-known hostelry. The house was crowded, and the best the night clerk could do was to give us a room with two beds. This was perfectly satisfactory, as it was a large apartment and fronted out on an open gallery. Old man Don suggested we take the mattresses outside, but as this was my first chance to sleep in a bed since leaving the ranch in March, I wanted all the comforts that were due me. Sponsilier likewise favored the idea of sleeping inside, and our employer yielded, taking the single bed on retiring. The night was warm, and after thrashing around for nearly an hour, supposing that Dave and I were asleep, old man Don arose and quietly dragged his mattress outside. Our bed was soft and downy, but in spite of the lateness of the hour and having been in our saddles at dawn, we tossed about, unable to sleep. After agreeing that it was the mattress, we took the covering and pillows and lay down on the floor, falling into a deep slumber almost instantly. "Well, wouldn't that jar your eccentric," said Dave to me the next morning, speaking of our inability to sleep in a bed. "I slept in one in Ogalalla, and I wasn't over-full either."

Lovell remained with us all the next day. He was well known in Miles City, having in other years sold cattle to resident cowmen. The day was spent in hunting up former acquaintances, getting the lay of the land, and feeling the public pulse on the matter of quarantine on Southern cattle. The outlook was to our liking, as heavy losses had been sustained from fever the year before, and steps had already been taken to isolate all through animals until frost fell. Report was abroad that there were already within the jurisdiction of Montana over one hundred and fifty thousand through Texas cattle, with a possibility of one third that number more being added before the close of the season. That territory had established a quarantine camp on the Wyoming line, forcing all Texas stock to follow down the eastern side of the Powder River. Fully one hundred miles on the north, a dead-line was drawn from Powderville on that watercourse eastward to a spur of the Powder River Mountains, thus setting aside a quarantine ground ample to accommodate half a million cattle. Local range-riders kept all the native and wintered Texas cattle to the westward of the river and away from the through ones, which was easily done by riding lines, the Southern herds being held under constant control and hence never straying. The first Texas herds to arrive naturally traveled north to the dead-line, and, choosing a range, went into camp until frost relieved them. It was an unwritten law that a herd was entitled to as much grazing land as it needed, and there was a report about Miles City that the quarantine ground was congested with cattle halfway from Powderville to the Wyoming line.

The outlook was encouraging. Quarantine was working a hardship to herds along the old Powder River route, yet their enforced isolation was like a tempered wind to our cause and cattle, the latter then leisurely grazing across Dakota from the Little Missouri to the mouth of the Yellowstone. Fortune favored us in many respects. About Miles City there was no concealment of our mission, resulting in an old acquaintance of Lovell's loaning us horses, while old man Don had no trouble in getting drafts cashed to the amount of two thousand dollars. What he expected to do with this amount of money was a mystery to Dave and myself, a mystery which instantly cleared when we were in the privacy of our room at the hotel.

"Here, boys," said old man Don, throwing the roll of money on the bed, "divide this wad between you. There might be such a thing as using a little here and there to sweeten matters up, and making yourselves rattling good fellows wherever you go. Now in the first place, I want you both to understand that this money is clear velvet, and don't hesitate to spend it freely. Eat and drink all you can, and gamble a little of it if that is necessary. You two will saddle up in the morning and ride to Powderville, while I will lie around here a few days and try the market for cattle next year, and then go on to Big Horn on my way to the Crow Agency. Feel your way carefully; locate the herds of Field, Radcliff & Co., and throw everything in their way to retard progress. It is impossible to foretell what may happen, and for that reason only general orders can be given. And remember, I don't want to see that money again if there is any chance to use it."

Powderville was a long day's ride from Miles City. By making an early start and resting a few hours at noon, we reached that straggling outpost shortly after nightfall. There was a road-house for the wayfaring man and a corral for his beast, a general store, opposition saloons, and the regulation blacksmith shop, constituting the business interests of Powderville. As arriving guests, a rough but cordial welcome was extended us by the keeper of the hostelry, and we mingled with the other travelers, but never once mentioning our business. I was uneasy over the money in our possession; not that I feared robbery, but my mind constantly reverted to it, and it was with difficulty that I refrained from continually feeling to see that it was safe. Sponsilier had concealed his in his boot, and as we rode along, contended that he could feel the roll chafing his ankle. I had tied two handkerchiefs together, and rolling my share in one of them, belted the amount between my overshirt and undershirt. The belt was not noticeable, but in making the ride that day, my hand involuntarily went to my side where the money lay, the action never escaping the notice of Sponsilier, who constantly twitted me over my nervousness. And although we were tired as dogs after our long ride, I awoke many times that night and felt to see if my money was safe; my partner slept like a log.

Several cowmen, ranching on the lower Powder River, had headquarters at this outpost. The next morning Sponsilier and I made their acquaintance, and during the course of the day got a clear outline of the situation. On the west the river was the recognized dead-line to the Wyoming boundary, while two camps of five men each patroled the dividing line on the north, drifting back the native stock and holding the through herds in quarantine. The nearest camp was some distance east of Powderville, and saddling up towards evening we rode out and spent the night at the first quarantine station. A wagon and two tents, a relay of saddle horses, and an arsenal of long-range firearms composed the outfit. Three of the five men on duty were Texans. Making ourselves perfectly at home, we had no trouble in locating the herds in question, they having already sounded the tocsin to clear the way, claiming government beef recognized no local quarantine. The herds were not over thirty miles to the south, and expectation ran high as to results when an attempt should be made to cross the deadline. Trouble had already occurred, where outfits respecting the quarantine were trespassed upon by three herds, making claim of being under government protection and entitled to the rights of eminent domain. Fortunately several of the herds on the immediate line had been bought at Ogalalla and were in possession of ranch outfits who owned ranges farther north, and were anxious to see quarantine enforced. These local cowmen would support the established authority, and trouble was expected. Sponsilier and I widened the breach by denouncing these intruders as the hirelings of a set of ringsters, who had no regard for the rights of any one, and volunteered our services in enforcing quarantine against them the same as others.

Our services were gratefully accepted. The next morning we were furnished fresh horses, and one of us was requested, as we were strangers, to ride down the country and reconnoitre the advance of the defiant drovers. As I was fearful that Field or Radcliff might be accompanying the herds, and recognize me, Sponsilier went instead, returning late that evening.

"Well, fellows," said Dave, as he dismounted at the quarantine camp, "I've seen the herds, and they propose to cross this dead-line of yours as easily as water goes through a gourd funnel. They'll be here by noon to-morrow, and they've got the big conversation right on tap to show that the government couldn't feed its army if it wasn't for a few big cowmen like them. There's a strange corporal over the three herds and they're working on five horses to the man. But the major-domo's the whole works; he's a windy cuss, and intimates that he has a card or two up his sleeve that will put these quarantine guards to sleep when he springs them. He's a new man to me; at least he wasn't with the gang at Ogalalla."

During the absence of my partner, I had ridden the dead-line on the north. A strip of country five miles wide was clear of cattle above the boundary, while below were massed four herds, claiming the range from the mountains to the Powder River. The leader of the quarantine guards, Fred Ullmer, had accompanied me on the ride, and on our return we visited three of the outfits, urging them to hold all their reserve forces subject to call, in case an attempt was made to force the dead-line. At each camp I took every possible chance to sow the seeds of dissension and hatred against the high-handed methods of The Western Supply Company. Defining our situation clearly, I asked each foreman, in case these herds defied local authority, who would indemnify the owners for the loss among native cattle by fever between Powderville and the mouth of the Yellowstone. Would the drovers? Would the government? Leaving these and similar thoughts for their consideration, Ullmer and I had arrived at the first quarantine station shortly before the return of my partner.

Upon the report of Sponsilier, Ullmer was appointed captain, and lost no time in taking action. After dark, a scout was sent to Camp No. 2, a meeting-place was appointed on Wolf Creek below, and orders were given to bring along every possible man from the local outfits and to meet at the rendezvous within an hour after sun-up the next morning. Ullmer changed horses and left for Powderville, assuring us that he would rally every man interested in quarantine, and have his posse below, on the creek by sunrise. The remainder of us at headquarters were under orders to bring all the arms and ammunition, and join the quarantine forces at the meeting-place some five miles from our camp. We were also to touch at and command the presence of one of the four outfits while en route. I liked the determined action of Captain Ullmer, who I learned had emigrated with his parents to Montana when a boy, and had grown into manhood on the frontier. Sponsilier was likewise pleased with the quarantine leader, and we lay awake far into the night, reviewing the situation and trying to anticipate any possible contingency that might thwart our plans. But to our best reasoning the horizon was clear, and if Field, Radcliff & Co.'s cattle reached Fort Buford on the day of delivery, well, it would be a miracle.

Fresh horses were secured at dawn, and breakfast would be secured en route with the cow outfit. There were a dozen large-calibre rifles in scabbards, and burdening ourselves with two heavy guns to the man and an abundance of ammunition, we abandoned Quarantine Station No. 1 for the time being. The camp which we were to touch at was the one nearest the river and north of Wolf Creek, and we galloped up to it before the sun had even risen. Since everything was coming our way, Sponsilier and I observed a strict neutrality, but a tow-headed Texan rallied the outfit, saying:

"Make haste, fellows, and saddle up your horses. Those three herds which raised such a rumpus up on Little Powder have sent down word that they're going to cross our dead-line to-day if they have to prize up hell and put a chunk under it. We have decided to call their bluff before they even reach the line, and make them show their hand for all this big talk. Here's half a dozen guns and cartridges galore, but hustle yourselves. Fred went into Powderville last night and will meet us above at the twin buttes this morning with every cowman in town. All the other outfits have been sent for, and we'll have enough men to make our bluff stand up, never fear. From what I learn, these herds belong to a lot of Yankee speculators, and they don't give a tinker's dam if all the cattle in Montana die from fever. They're no better than anybody else, and if we allow them to go through, they'll leave a trail of dead natives that will stink us out of this valley. Make haste, everybody."

I could see at a glance that the young Texan had touched their pride. The foreman detailed three men to look after the herd, and the balance made hasty preparations to accompany the quarantine guards. A relief was rushed away for the herders; and when the latter came in, they reported having sighted the posse from Powderville, heading across country for the twin buttes. Meanwhile a breakfast had been bolted by the guards, Sponsilier, and myself, and swinging into our saddles, we rounded a bluff bend of the creek and rode for the rendezvous, some three miles distant. I noticed by the brands that nearly every horse in that country had been born in Texas, and the short time in which we covered the intervening miles proved that the change of climate had added to their stability and bottom. Our first glimpse of the meeting-point revealed the summit of the buttes fairly covered with horsemen. From their numbers it was evident that ours was the last contingent to arrive; but before we reached the twin mounds, the posse rode down from the lookout and a courier met and turned us from our course. The lead herd had been sighted in trail formation but a few miles distant, heading north, and it was the intention to head them at the earliest moment. The messenger inquired our numbers, and reported those arrived at forty-five, making the posse when united a few over sixty men.

A juncture of forces was effected within a mile of the lead herd. It was a unique posse. Old frontiersmen, with patriarchal beards and sawed-off shotguns, chewed their tobacco complacently as they rode forward at a swinging gallop. Beardless youths, armed with the old buffalo guns of their fathers, led the way as if an Indian invasion had called them forth. Soldiers of fortune, with Southern accents, who were assisting in the conquest of a new empire, intermingled with the hurrying throng, and two men whose home was in Medina County, Texas, looked on and approved. The very horses had caught the inspiration of the moment, champing bits in their effort to forge to the front rank, while the blood-stained slaver coated many breasts or driveled from our boots. Before we met the herd a halt was called, and about a dozen men were deployed off on each flank, while the main body awaited the arrival of the cattle. The latter were checked by the point-men and turned back when within a few hundred yards of the main posse. Several horsemen from the herd rode forward, and one politely inquired the meaning of this demonstration. The question was met by a counter one from Captain Ullmer, who demanded to know the reason why these cattle should trespass on the rights of others and ignore local quarantine. The spokesman in behalf of the herd turned in his saddle and gave an order to send some certain person forward. Sponsilier whispered to me that this fellow was merely a segundo. "But wait till the 'major-domo' arrives," he added. The appearance of the posse and the halting of the herd summoned that personage from the rear to the front, and the next moment he was seen galloping up the column of cattle. With a plausible smile this high mogul, on his arrival, repeated the previous question, and on a similar demand from the captain of the posse, he broke into a jolly laugh from which he recovered with difficulty.

"Why, gentlemen," said he, every word dripping with honeyed sweetness, "this is entirely uncalled for. I assure you that it was purely an oversight on my part that I did not send you word in advance that these herds of mine are government cattle and not subject to local quarantine. My associates are the largest army contractors in the country, these cattle are due at Fort Buford on the 15th of this month, and any interference on your part would be looked upon as an insult to the government. In fact, the post commander at Fort Laramie insisted that he be permitted to send a company of cavalry to escort us across Wyoming, and assured us that a troop from Fort Keogh, if requested, would meet our cattle on the Montana line. The army is jealous over its supplies, but I declined all military protection, knowing that I had but to show my credentials to pass unmolested anywhere. Now, if you care to look over these papers, you will see that these cattle are en route to Fort Buford, on an assignment of the original contract, issued by the secretary of war to The Western Supply Company. Very sorry to put you to all this trouble, but these herds must not be interfered with. I trust that you gentlemen understand that the government is supreme."

As the papers mentioned were produced, Sponsilier kicked me on the shin, gave me a quiet wink, and nodded towards the documents then being tendered to Captain Ullmer. Groping at his idea, I rode forward, and as the papers were being returned with a mere glance on the part of the quarantine leader, I politely asked if I might see the assignment of the original contract. But a quizzical smile met my request, and shaking out the heavy parchment, he rapped it with the knuckles of his disengaged hand, remarking as he returned it to his pocket, "Sorry, but altogether too valuable to allow out of my possession." Just what I would have done with the beribboned document, except to hand it over to Sponsilier, is beyond me, yet I was vaguely conscious that its destruction was of importance to our side of the matter at issue. At the same instant in which my request was declined, the big medicine man turned to Captain Ullmer and suavely remarked, "You found everything as represented, did you?"

"Why, I heard your statement, and I have also heard it disputed from other sources. In fact I have nothing to do with you except to enforce the quarantine now established by the cattlemen of eastern Montana. If you have any papers showing that your herds were wintered north of latitude 37, you can pass, as this quarantine is only enforced against cattle from south of that degree. This territory lost half a million dollars' worth of native stock last fall from Texas fever, and this season they propose to apply the ounce of preventive. You will have ample time to reach your destination after frost falls, and your detention by quarantine will be a good excuse for your delay. Now, unless you can convince me that your herds are immune, I'll show you a good place to camp on the head of Wolf Creek. It will probably be a matter of ten to fifteen days before the quarantine is lifted, and we are enforcing it against citizens of Montana and Texas alike, and no exception can be made in your case."

"But, my dear sir, this is not a local or personal matter. Whatever you do, don't invite the frown of the government. Let me warn you not to act in haste. Now, remember -"

"You made your cracks that you would cross this quarantine line," interrupted Ullmer, bristlingly, "and I want you to find out your mistake. There is no occasion for further words, and you can either order your outfit to turn your cattle east, or I'll send men and do it myself."

The "major-domo" turned and galloped back to his men, a number of whom had congregated near at hand. The next moment he returned and haughtily threatened to surrender the cattle then and there unless he was allowed to proceed. "Give him a receipt for his beeves, Fred," quietly remarked an old cowman, gently stroking his beard, "and I'll take these boys over here on the right and start the cattle. That will be the safest way, unless the gentleman can indemnify us. I lost ten thousand dollars' worth of stock last fall, and as a citizen of Montana I have objections to leaving a trail of fever from here to the mouth of the Yellowstone. And tell him he can have a bond for his cattle," called back the old man as he rode out of hearing.

The lead herd was pointed to the east, and squads of men rode down and met the other two, veering them off on an angle to the right. Meanwhile the superintendent raved, pleaded, and threatened without avail, but finally yielded and refused the receipt and dispossession of his cattle. This was just what the quarantine captain wanted, and the dove of peace began to shake its plumage. Within an hour all three of the herds were moving out for the head of Wolf Creek, accompanied only by the quarantine guards, the remainder of the posse returning to their homes or their work. Having ample time on our hands, Sponsilier and I expected to remain at Station No. 1 until after the 10th of September, and accordingly made ourselves at home at that camp. To say that we were elated over the situation puts it mildly, and that night the two of us lost nearly a hundred dollars playing poker with the quarantine guards. A strict vigilance was maintained over the herds in question, but all reports were unanimous that they were contentedly occupying their allotted range.

But at noon on the third day of the enforced isolation, a messenger from Powderville arrived at the first station. A troop of cavalry from Fort Keogh, accompanied by a pack-train, had crossed the Powder River below the hamlet, their avowed mission being to afford an escort for certain government beef, then under detention by the local authorities. The report fell among us like a flash of lightning. Ample time had elapsed for a messenger to ride to the Yellowstone, and, returning with troops, pilot them to the camps of Field, Radcliff & Co. A consultation was immediately held, but no definite line of action had been arrived at when a horseman from one of the lower camps dashed up and informed us that the three herds were already trailing out for the dead-line, under an escort of cavalry. Saddling up, we rallied what few men were available, determined to make a protest, at least, in the interest of humanity to dumb brutes. We dispatched couriers to the nearest camps and the outer quarantine station; but before a posse of twenty men arrived, the lead herd was within a mile of the dead-line, and we rode out and met them. Fully eighty troopers, half of which rode in column formation in front, halted us as we approached. Terse and to the point were the questions and answers exchanged between the military arm of the government and the quarantine authorities of Montana. When the question arose of indemnity to citizens, in case of death to native cattle, a humane chord was touched in the young lieutenant in command, resulting in his asking several questions, to which the "major-domo" protested. Once atisfied of the justice of quarantine, the officer, in defense of his action, said:

"Gentlemen, I am under instructions to give these herds,

intended for use at Fort Buford, a three days' escort beyond this quarantine line. I am very much obliged to you all for making so clear the necessity of isolating herds of Texas cattle, and that little or no hardship may attend my orders, you may have until noon to-morrow to drift all native stock west of the Powder River. When these herds encamp for the night, they will receive instructions not to move forward before twelve to-morrow. I find the situation quite different from reports; nevertheless orders are orders."

CHAPTER XX.

ON THE JUST AND THE UNJUST

The quarantine guards returned to their camp. Our plans were suddenly and completely upset, and not knowing which way to turn, Sponsilier and I, slightly crestfallen, accompanied the guards. It was already late in the evening, but Captain Ullmer took advantage of the brief respite granted him to clear the east half of the valley of native cattle. Couriers were dispatched to sound the warning among the ranches down the river, while a regular round-up outfit was mustered among the camps to begin the drifting of range stock that evening. A few men were left at the two camps, as quarantine was not to be abandoned, and securing our borrowed horses, my partner and I bade our friends farewell and set out on our return for the Yellowstone. Merely touching at Powderville for a hasty supper, we held a northwest, cross-country course, far into the night, when we unsaddled to rest our horses and catch a few hours' sleep. But sunrise found us again in our saddles, and by the middle of the forenoon we were breakfasting with our friends in Miles City.

Fort Keogh was but a short distance up the river. That military interference had been secured through fraud and deception, there was not the shadow of a doubt. During the few hours which we spent in Miles, the cattle interests were duly aroused, and a committee of cowmen were appointed to call on the post commander at Keogh with a formidable protest, which would no doubt be supplemented later, on the return of the young lieutenant and his troopers. During our ride the night before, Sponsilier and I had discussed the possibility of arousing the authorities at Glendive. Since it was in the neighborhood of one hundred miles from Powderville to the former point on the railroad, the herds would consume nearly a week in reaching there. A freight train was caught that afternoon, and within twenty-four hours after leaving the quarantine camp on the Powder River, we had opened headquarters at the Stock Exchange Saloon in Glendive. On arriving, I deposited one hundred dollars with the proprietor of that bar-room, with the understanding that it was to be used in getting an expression from the public in regard to the question of Texas fever. Before noon the next day, Dave Sponsilier and Tom Quirk were not only the two most popular men in Glendive, but quarantine had been decided on with ringing resolutions.

Our standing was soon of the best. Horses were tendered us, and saddling one I crossed the Yellowstone and started down the river to arouse outlying ranches, while Sponsilier and a number of local cowmen rode south to locate a camp and a deadline. I was absent two days, having gone north as far as Wolf Island, where I recrossed the river, returning on the eastern side of the valley. At no ranch which was visited did my mission fail of meeting hearty approval, especially on the western side of the river, where severe losses from fever had been sustained the fall before. One ranch on Thirteen Mile offered, if necessary, to send every man in its employ, with their own wagon and outfit of horses, free of all charge, until quarantine was lifted. But I suggested, instead, that they send three or four men with their horses and blankets, leaving the remainder to be provided for by the local committee. In my two days' ride, over fifty volunteers were tendered, but I refused all except twenty, who were to report at Glendive not later than the morning of the 6th. On my return to the railroad, all arrangements were completed and the outlook was promising. Couriers had arrived from the south during my absence, bringing the news of the coming of the through Texas cattle, and warning the local ranches to clear the way or take the consequences. All native stock had been pushed west of the Powder and Yellowstone, as far north as Cabin Creek, which had been decided on as the second quarantine-line. Daily reports were being received of the whereabouts of the moving herds, and at the rate they were traveling, they would reach Cabin Creek about the 7th. Two wagons had been outfitted, cooks employed, and couriers dispatched to watch the daily progress of the cattle, which, if following the usual route, would strike the deadline some distance south of Glendive.

During the next few days, Sponsilier and I were social lions in that town, and so great was our popularity we could have either married or been elected to office. We limited our losses at poker to so much an evening, and what we won from the merchant class we invariably lost among the volunteer guards and cowmen, taking our luck with a sangfroid which proved us dead-game sports, and made us hosts of friends. We had contributed one hundred dollars to the general quarantine fund, and had otherwise made ourselves popular with all classes in the brief time at our command. Under the pretense that we might receive orders at any time to overtake our herds, we declined all leadership in the second campaign about to be inaugurated against Texas fever. Dave and I were both feeling rather chesty over the masterful manner in which we had aroused the popular feeling in favor of quarantine in our own interest, at the same time making it purely a local movement. We were swaggering about like ward-heelers, when on the afternoon of the 5th the unexpected again happened. The business interests of the village usually turned out to meet the daily passenger trains, even the poker-games taking a recess until the cars went past. The arrival and departure of citizens of the place were noted by every one, and strangers were looked upon with timidity, very much as in all simple communities. Not taking any interest in the passing trains, Sponsilier was writing a letter to his girl in Texas, while I was shaking dice for the cigars with the bartender of the Stock Exchange, when the Eastbound arrived. After the departure of the train, I did not take any notice of the return of the boys to the abandoned games, or the influx of patrons to the house, until some one laid a hand on my shoulder and quietly said, "Isn't your name Quirk?"

Turning to the speaker, I was confronted by Mr. Field and Mr.

Radcliff, who had just arrived by train from the west. Admitting my identity, I invited them to have a cigar or liquid refreshment, inquiring whence they had come and where their cattle were. To my surprise, Fort Keogh was named as their last refuge, and the herds were reported to cross the railroad within the next few days. Similar questions were asked me, but before replying, I caught Sponsilier's eye and summoned him with a wink. On Dave's presenting himself, I innocently asked the pair if they did not remember my friend as one of the men whom they had under arrest at Dodge. They grunted an embarrassed acknowledgment, which was returned in the same coin, when I proceeded to inform them that our cattle crossed the railroad at Little Missouri ten days before, and that we were only waiting the return of Mr. Lovell from the Crow Agency before proceeding to our destination. With true Yankee inquisitiveness, other questions followed, the trend of which was to get us to admit that we had something to do with the present activities in quarantining Texas cattle. But I avoided their leading queries, and looked appealingly at Sponsilier, who came to my rescue with an answer born of the moment.

"Well, gentlemen," said Dave, seating himself on the bar and leisurely rolling a cigarette, "that town of Little Missouri is about the dullest hole that I was ever water-bound in. Honestly, I'd rather be with the cattle than loafing in it with money in my pocket. Now this town has got some get-up about it; I'll kiss a man's foot if he complains that this burg isn't sporty enough for his blood. They've given me a run here for my white alley, and I still think I know something about that game called draw-poker. But you were speaking about quarantine. Yes; there seems to have been a good many cattle lost through these parts last fall. You ought to have sent your herds up through Dakota, where there is no native stock to interfere. I'd hate to have cattle coming down the Powder River. A friend of mine passed through here yesterday; his herd was sold for delivery on the Elkhorn, north of here, and he tells me he may not be able to reach there before October. He saw your herds and tells me you are driving the guts out of them.

So if there's anything in that old 'ship-fever theory,' you ought to be quarantined until it snows. There's a right smart talk around here of fixing a dead-line below somewhere, and if you get tied up before reaching the railroad, it won't surprise me a little bit. When it comes to handling the cattle, old man Don has the good hard cow-sense every time, but you shorthorns give me a pain."

"What did I tell you?" said Radcliff, the elder one, to his partner, as they turned to leave.

On nearing the door, Mr. Field halted and begrudgingly said, "See you later, Quirk."

"Not if I see you first," I replied; "you ain't my kind of cowmen."

Not even waiting for them to pass outside, Sponsilier, from his elevated position, called every one to the bar to irrigate. The boys quit their games, and as they lined up in a double row, Dave begged the bartenders to bestir themselves, and said to his guests: "Those are the kid-gloved cowmen that I've been telling you about - the owners of the Texas cattle that are coming through here. Did I hang it on them artistically, or shall I call them back and smear it on a shade deeper? They smelt a mouse all right, and when their cattle reach Cabin Creek, they'll smell the rat in earnest. Now, set out the little and big bottle and everybody have a cigar on the side. And drink hearty, lads, for to-morrow we may be drinking branch water in a quarantine camp."

The arrival of Field and Radcliff was accepted as a defiance to the local cattle interests. Popular feeling was intensified when it was learned that they were determined not to recognize any local quarantine, and were secretly inquiring for extra men to guard their herds in passing Glendive. There was always a rabble element in every frontier town, and no doubt, as strangers, they could secure assistance in quarters that the local cowmen would spurn. Matters were approaching a white heat, when late that night an expected courier arrived, and reported the cattle coming through at the rate of twenty miles a day. They were not following any particular trail, traveling almost due north, and if the present rate of travel was maintained, Cabin Creek would be reached during the forenoon of the 7th. This meant business, and the word was quietly passed around that all volunteers were to be ready to move in the morning. A cowman named Retallac, owner of a range on the Yellowstone, had previously been decided on as captain, and would have under him not less than seventy-five chosen men, which number, if necessary, could easily be increased to one hundred.

Morning dawned on a scene of active operations. The two wagons were started fully an hour in advance of the cavalcade, which was to follow, driving a remuda of over two hundred saddle horses. Sponsilier and I expected to accompany the outfit, but at the last moment our plans were changed by an incident and we remained behind, promising to overtake them later. There were a number of old buffalo hunters in town, living a precarious life, and one of their number had quietly informed Sheriff Wherry that they had been approached with an offer of five dollars a day to act as an escort to the herds while passing through. The quarantine captain looked upon that element as a valuable ally, suggesting that if it was a question of money, our side ought to be in the market for their services. Heartily agreeing with him, the company of guards started, leaving their captain behind with Sponsilier and myself. Glendive was a county seat, and with the assistance of the sheriff, we soon had every buffalo hunter in the town corralled. They were a fine lot of rough men, inclined to be convivial, and with the assistance of Sheriff Wherry, coupled with the high standing of the quarantine captain, on a soldier's introduction Dave and I made a good impression among them. Sponsilier did the treating and talking, his offer being ten dollars a day for a man and horse, which was promptly accepted, when the question naturally arose who would stand sponsor for the wages. Dave backed off some distance, and standing on his left foot, pulled off his right boot, shaking out a roll of money on the floor.

"There's the long green, boys," said he, "and you fellows can name your own banker. I'll make it up a thousand, and whoever you say goes with me. Shall it be the sheriff, or Mr. Retallac, or the proprietor of the Stock Exchange?"

Sheriff Wherry interfered, relieving the embarrassment in appointing a receiver, and vouched that these two Texans were good for any reasonable sum. The buffalo hunters approved, apologizing to Sponsilier, as he pulled on his boot, for questioning his financial standing, and swearing allegiance in every breath. An hour's time was granted in which to saddle and make ready, during which we had a long chat with Sheriff Wherry and found him a valuable ally. He had cattle interests in the country, and when the hunters appeared, fifteen strong, he mounted his horse and accompanied us several miles on the way. "Now, boys," said he, at parting, "I'll keep an eye over things around town, and if anything important happens, I'll send a courier with the news. If those shorthorns attempt to offer any opposition, I'll run a blazer on them, and if necessary I'll jug the pair. You fellows just buffalo the herds, and the sheriff's office will keep cases on any happenings around Glendive. It's understood that night or day your camp can be found on Cabin Creek, opposite the old eagle tree. Better send me word as soon as the herds arrive. Good luck to you, lads. '

Neither wagons nor guards were even sighted during our three hours' ride to the appointed campground. On our arrival tents were being pitched and men were dragging up wood, while the cooks were busily preparing a late dinner, the station being fully fifteen miles south of the railroad. Scouts were thrown out during the afternoon, corrals built, and evening found the quarantine camp well established for the comfort of its ninety-odd men. The buffalo hunters were given special attention and christened the "Sponsilier Guards;" they took again to outdoor life as in the old days. The report of the scouts was satisfactory; all three of the herds had been seen and would arrive on schedule time. A hush of expectancy greeted this news, but Sponsilier and I ridiculed the idea that there would be any opposition, except a big talk and plenty of bluffing.

"Well, if that's what they rely on," said Captain Retallac, "then they're as good as in quarantine this minute. If you feel certain they can't get help from Fort Keogh a second time, those herds will be our guests until further orders. What we want to do now is to spike every possible chance for their getting any help, and the matter will pass over like a summer picnic. If you boys think there's any danger of an appeal to Fort Buford, the military authorities want to be notified that the Yellowstone Valley has quarantined against Texas fever and asks their cooperation in enforcing the same."

"I can fix that," replied Sponsilier. "We have lawyers at Buford right now, and I can wire them the situation fully in the morning. If they rely on the military, they will naturally appeal to the nearest post, and if Keogh and Buford turn them down, the next ones are on the Missouri River, and at that distance cavalry couldn't reach here within ten days. Oh, I think we've got a grapevine twist on them this time."

Sponsilier sat up half the night wording a message to our attorneys at Fort Buford. The next morning found me bright and early on the road to Glendive with the dispatch, the sending of which would deplete my cash on hand by several dollars, but what did we care for expense when we had the money and orders to spend it? I regretted my absence from the quarantine camp, as I was anxious to be present on the arrival of the herds, and again watch the "major-domo" run on the rope and fume and charge in vain. But the importance of blocking assistance was so urgent that I would gladly have ridden to Buford if necessary. In that bracing atmosphere it was a fine morning for the ride, and I was rapidly crossing the country, when a vehicle, in the dip of the plain, was sighted several miles ahead. I was following no road, but when the driver of the conveyance saw me he turned across my front and signaled. On meeting the rig, I could hardly control myself from laughing outright, for there on the rear seat sat Field and Radcliff, extremely gruff and uncongenial. Common courtesies were exchanged between the driver and myself, and I was able to answer clearly his leading questions: Yes; the herds would reach Cabin Creek before noon; the old eagle tree, which could be seen from the first swell of the plain beyond, marked the quarantine camp, and it was the intention to isolate the herds on the South Fork of Cabin. "Drive on," said a voice, and, in the absence of any gratitude expressed, I inwardly smiled in reward.

I was detained in Glendive until late in the day, waiting for an acknowledgment of the message. Sheriff Wherry informed me that the only move attempted on the part of the shorthorn drovers was the arrest of Sponsilier and myself, on the charge of being accomplices in the shooting of one of their men on the North Platte. But the sheriff had assured the gentlemen that our detention would have no effect on quarantining their cattle, and the matter was taken under advisement and dropped. It was late when I started for camp that evening. The drovers had returned, accompanied by their superintendent, and were occupying the depot, burning the wires in every direction. I was risking no chances, and cultivated the company of Sheriff Wherry until the acknowledgment arrived, when he urged me to ride one of his horses in returning to camp, and insisted on my taking a carbine. Possibly this was fortunate, for before I had ridden one third the distance to the quarantine camp, I met a cavalcade of nearly a dozen men from the isolated herds. When they halted and inquired the distance to Glendive, one of their number recognized me as having been among the quarantine guards at Powderville. I admitted that I was there, turning my horse so that the carbine fell to my hand, and politely asked if any one had any objections. It seems that no one had, and after a few common-place inquiries were exchanged, we passed on our way.

There was great rejoicing on Cabin Creek that night. Songs were sung, and white navy beans passed current in numerous poker-games until the small hours of morning. There had been nothing dramatic in the meeting between the herds and the quarantine guards, the latter force having been augmented by visiting ranchmen and their help, until protest would have been useless. A routine of work had been outlined, much stricter than at Powderville, and a surveillance of the camps was constantly maintained. Not that there was any danger of escape, but to see that the herds occupied the country allotted to them, and did not pollute any more territory than was necessary. The Sponsilier Guards were given an easy day shift, and held a circle of admirers at night, recounting and living over again "the good old days." Visitors from either side of the Yellowstone were early callers, and during the afternoon the sheriff from Glendive arrived. I did not know until then that Mr. Wherry was a candidate for reelection that fall, but the manner in which he mixed with the boys was enough to warrant his election for life. What endeared him to Sponsilier and myself was the fund of information he had collected, and the close tab he had kept on every movement of the opposition drovers. He told us that their appeal to Fort Keogh for assistance had been refused with a stinging rebuke; that a courier had started the evening before down the river for Fort Buford, and that Mr. Radcliff had personally gone to Fort Abraham Lincoln to solicit help. The latter post was fully one hundred and fifty miles away, but that distance could be easily covered by a special train in case of government interference.

It rained on the afternoon of the 9th. The courier had returned from Fort Buford on the north, unsuccessful, as had also Mr. Radcliff from Fort Lincoln on the Missouri River to the eastward. The latter post had referred the request to Keogh, and washed its hands of intermeddling in a country not tributary to its territory. The last hope of interference was gone, and the rigors of quarantine closed in like a siege with every gun of the enemy spiked. Let it be a week or a month before the quarantine was lifted, the citizens of Montana had so willed it, and their wish was law. Evening fell, and the men drew round the fires. The guards buttoned their coats as they rode away, and the tired ones drew their blankets around them as they lay down to sleep. Scarcely a star could be seen in the sky overhead, but before my partner or myself sought our bed, a great calm had fallen, the stars were shining, and the night had grown chilly.

ANDY ADAMS

The old buffalo hunters predicted a change in the weather, but beyond that they were reticent. As Sponsilier and I lay down to sleep, we agreed that if three days, even two days, were spared us, those cattle in quarantine could never be tendered at Fort Buford on the appointed day of delivery. But during the early hours of morning we were aroused by the returning guards, one of whom halted his horse near our blankets and shouted, "Hey, there, you Texans; get up - a frost has fallen!"

Sure enough, it had frosted during the night, and the quarantine was lifted. When day broke, every twig and blade of grass glistened in silver sheen, and the horses on picket stood humped and shivering. The sun arose upon the herds moving, with no excuse to say them nay, and orders were issued to the guards to break camp and disperse to their homes. As we rode into Glendive that morning, sullen and defeated by a power beyond our control, in speaking of the peculiarity of the intervention, Sponsilier said: "Well, if it rains on the just and the unjust alike, why shouldn't it frost the same."

CHAPTER XXI.

FORT BUFORD

We were at our rope's end. There were a few accounts to settle in Glendive, after which we would shake its dust from our feet. Very few of the quarantine guards returned to town, and with the exception of Sheriff Wherry, none of the leading cowmen, all having ridden direct for their ranches. Long before the train arrived which would carry us to Little Missouri, the opposition herds appeared and crossed the railroad west of town. Their commissaries entered the village for supplies, while the "majordomo," surrounded by a body-guard of men, rode about on his miserable palfrey. The sheriff, fearing a clash between the victorious and the vanquished, kept an eye on Sponsilier and me as we walked the streets, freely expressing our contempt of Field, Radcliff & Co., their henchmen and their methods. Dave and I were both nerved to desperation; Sheriff Wherry, anxious to prevent a conflict, counciled with the opposition drovers, resulting in their outfits leaving town, while the principals took stage across to Buford.

Meanwhile Sponsilier had wired full particulars to our employer at Big Horn. It was hardly necessary, as the frost no doubt was general all over Montana, but we were anxious to get into communication with Lovell immediately on his return to the railroad. We had written him from Miles of our failure at Powderville, and the expected second stand at Glendive, and now the elements had notified him that the opposition herds were within striking distance, and would no doubt appear at Buford on or before the day of delivery. An irritable man like our employer would neither eat nor sleep, once the delivery at the Crow Agency was over, until reaching the railroad, and our message would be awaiting him on his return to Big Horn. Our train reached Little Missouri early in the evening, and leaving word with the agent that we were expecting important messages from the west, we visited the liveryman and inquired about the welfare of our horses. The proprietor of the stable informed us that they had fared well, and that he would have them ready for us on an hour's notice. It was after dark and we were at supper when the first message came. An immediate answer was required, and arising from the table, we left our meal unfinished and hastened to the depot. From then until midnight, messages flashed back and forth, Sponsilier dictating while I wrote. As there was no train before the regular passenger the next day, the last wire requested us to have the horses ready to meet the Eastbound, saying that Bob Quirk would accompany Lovell.

That night it frosted again. Sponsilier and I slept until noon the next day without awakening. Then the horses were brought in from pasture, and preparation was made to leave that evening. It was in the neighborhood of ninety miles across to the mouth of the Yellowstone, and the chances were that we would ride it without unsaddling. The horses had had a two weeks' rest, and if our employer insisted on it, we would breakfast with the herds the next morning. I was anxious to see the cattle again and rejoin my outfit, but like a watched pot, the train was an hour late. Sponsilier and I took advantage of the delay and fortified the inner man against the night and the ride before us. This proved fortunate, as Lovell and my brother had supper en route in the dining-car. A running series of questions were asked and answered; saddles were shaken out of gunny-sacks and cinched on waiting horses as though we were starting to a prairie fire. Bob Quirk's cattle had reached the Crow Agency in splendid condition, the delivery was effected without a word, and old man Don was in possession of a letter from Flood, saying everything had passed smoothly at the Rosebud Agency.

Contrary to the expectation of Sponsilier and myself, our

employer was in a good humor, fairly walking on the clouds over the success of his two first deliveries of the year. But amid the bustle and rush, in view of another frosty night, Sponsilier inquired if it would not be a good idea to fortify against the chill, by taking along a bottle of brandy. "Yes, two of them if you want to," said old man Don, in good-humored approval. "Here, Tom, fork this horse and take the pitch out of him," he continued; "I don't like the look of his eye." But before I could reach the horse, one of my own string, Bob Quirk had mounted him, when in testimony of the nutritive qualities of Dakota's grasses, he arched his spine like a true Texan and outlined a worm-fence in bucking a circle.

The start was made during the gathering dusk. Sponsilier further lifted the spirits of our employer, as we rode along, by a clear-cut description of the opposition cattle, declaring that had they ever equaled ours, the handling they had received since leaving Ogalalla, compared to his, would class them with short twos in the spring against long threes in the fall. Within an hour the stars shone out, and after following the river some ten miles, we bore directly north until Beaver Creek was reached near midnight. The pace was set at about an eight-mile, steady clip, with an occasional halt to tighten cinches or shift saddles. The horses were capable of a faster gait without tiring, but we were not sure of the route and were saving them for the finish after daybreak. Early in the night we were conscious that a frost was falling, and several times Sponsilier inquired if no one cared for a nip from his bottle. Bob Quirk started the joke on Dave by declining; old man Don uncorked the flask, and, after smelling of the contents, handed it back with his thanks. I caught onto their banter, and not wishing to spoil a good jest, also declined, leaving Sponsilier to drink alone. During the night, whenever conversation lagged, some one was certain to make reference to the remarks which are said to have passed between the governors of the Carolinas, or if that failed to provoke a rise, ask direct if no one had something to ward off the chilly air. After being refused several times, Dave had thrown the bottle away, meeting these jests with the reply that he had a private flask, but its quality was such that he was afraid of offending our cultivated tastes by asking us to join him.

Day broke about five in the morning. We had been in the saddle nearly ten hours, and were confident that sunrise would reveal some landmark to identify our location. The atmosphere was frosty and clear, and once the gray of dawn yielded to the rising sun, the outline of the Yellowstone was easily traced on our left, while the bluffs in our front shielded a view of the mother Missouri. In attempting to approach the latter we encountered some rough country and were compelled to turn towards the former, crossing it, at O'Brien's roadhouse, some seven miles above the mouth. The husbanded reserves of our horses were shaken out, and shortly afterward smoke-clouds from camp-fires, hanging low, attracted our attention. The herds were soon located as they arose and grazed away from their bed-grounds. The outfits were encamped on the eastern side of the Yellowstone; and before leaving the government road, we sighted in our front a flag ascending to greet the morning, and the location of Fort Buford was established. Turning towards the cattle, we rode for the lower wagon and were soon unsaddling at Forrest's camp. The latter had arrived two days before and visited the post; he told us that the opposition were there in force, as well as our own attorneys. The arrival of the cattle under contract for that military division was the main topic of discussion, and Forrest had even met a number of civilian employees of Fort Buford whose duties were to look after the government beeves. The foreman of these unenlisted attaches, a Texan named Sanders, had casually ridden past his camp the day before, looking over the cattle, and had pronounced them the finest lot of beeves tendered the government since his connection with that post

"That's good news," said Lovell, as he threw his saddle astride the front wheel of the wagon; "that's the way I like to hear my cattle spoken about. Now, you boys want to make friends with all those civilians, and my attorneys and Bob and I will hobnob around with the officers, and try and win the good will of the entire post. You want to change your camp every few days and give your cattle good grazing and let them speak for themselves. Better kill a beef among the outfits, and insist on all callers staying for meals. We're strangers here, and we want to make a good impression, and show the public that we were born white, even if we do handle cattle for a living. Quince, tie up the horses for us, and after breakfast Bob and I will look over the herds and then ride into Fort Buford. - Trout for breakfast? You don't mean it!"

It was true, however, and our appetites did them justice. Forrest reported Splann as having arrived a day late, and now encamped the last herd up the valley. Taking our horses with us, Dave and I set out to look up our herds and resume our former positions. I rode through Sponsilier's cattle while en route to my own, and remembered the first impression they had made on my mind, - their uniformity in size and smoothness of build, - and now found them fatted into finished form, the herd being a credit to any drover. Continuing on my way, I intercepted my own cattle, lying down over hundreds of acres, and so contented that I refused to disturb them. Splann reported not over half a dozen sore-footed ones among them, having grazed the entire distance from Little Missouri, giving the tender cattle a good chance to recover. I held a circle of listeners for several hours, in recounting Sponsilier's and my own experiences in the quarantine camps, and our utter final failure, except that the opposition herds had been detained, which would force them to drive over twenty miles a day in order to reach Buford on time. On the other hand, an incident of more than ordinary moment had occurred with the cattle some ten days previous. The slow movement of the grazing herds allowed a great amount of freedom to the boys and was taken advantage of at every opportunity. It seems that on approaching Beaver Creek, Owen Ubery and Runt Pickett had ridden across to it for the purpose of trout-fishing. They were gone all day, having struck the creek some ten or twelve miles west of the cattle, expecting to fish down it and overtake the herds during the evening. But about noon they discovered where a wagon had been burned, years before, and near by were five human skeletons, evidently a family. It was possibly the work of Indians, or a blizzard, and to prove the discovery, Pickett had brought in one of the skulls and proposed taking it home with him as a memento of the drive. Parent objected to having the reminder in the wagon, and a row resulted between them, till Splann interfered and threw the gruesome relic away.

The next morning a dozen of us from the three herds rode into the post. Fort Buford was not only a military headquarters, but a supply depot for other posts farther west on the Missouri and Yellowstone rivers. The nearest railroad connection was Glend-ive, seventy-six miles up the latter stream, though steamboats took advantage of freshets in the river to transport immense supplies from lower points on the Missouri where there were rail connections. From Buford westward, transportation was effected by boats of lighter draft and the regulation wagon train. It was recognized as one of the most important supply posts in the West; as early as five years previous to this date, it had received in a single summer as many as ten thousand beeves. Its provision for cavalry was one of its boasted features, immense stacks of forage flanking those quarters, while the infantry barracks and officers' quarters were large and comfortable. A stirring little town had sprung up on the outside, affording the citizens employment in wood and hay contracts, and becoming the home of a large number of civilian employees, the post being the mainstay of the village.

After settling our quarantine bills, Sponsilier and I each had money left. Our employer refused even to look at our expense bills until after the delivery, but urged us to use freely any remaining funds in cultivating the good will of the citizens and soldiery alike. Forrest was accordingly supplied with funds, with the understanding that he was to hunt up Sanders and his outfit and show them a good time. The beef foreman was soon located in the quartermaster's office, and, having been connected with the post for several years, knew the ropes. He had come to Buford with Texas cattle, and after their delivery had accepted a situation under the acting quartermaster, easily rising to the foremanship through his superior abilities as a cowman. It was like a meeting of long-lost brothers to mingle again with a cow outfit, and the sutler's bar did a flourishing business during our stay in the post. There were ten men in Sanders's outfit, several of whom besides himself were Texans, and before we parted, every rascal had promised to visit us the next day and look over all the cattle.

The next morning Bob Quirk put in an early appearance at my wagon. He had passed the other outfits, and notified us all to have the cattle under convenient herd, properly watered in advance, as the post commandant, quartermaster, and a party of minor officers were going to ride out that afternoon and inspect our beeves. Lovell, of course, would accompany them, and Bob reported him as having made a ten-strike with the officers' mess, not being afraid to spend his money. Fortunately the present quartermaster at Buford was a former acquaintance of Lovell, the two having had business transactions. The quartermaster had been connected with frontier posts from Fort Clark, Texas, to his present position. According to report, the opposition were active and waging an aggressive campaign, but not being Western men, were at a disadvantage. Champagne had flowed freely at a dinner given the night before by our employer, during which Senator Aspgrain, in responding to a toast, had paid the army a high tribute for the part it had played in reclaiming the last of our western frontier. The quartermaster, in replying, had felicitously remarked, as a matter of his own observation, that the Californian's love for a horse was only excelled by the Texan's love for a cow, to which, amid uproarious laughter, old man Don arose and bowed his acknowledgment.

My brother changed horses and returned to Sponsilier's wagon. Dave had planned to entertain the post beef outfit for dinner, and had insisted on Bob's presence. They arrived at my herd near the middle of the forenoon, and after showing the cattle and remuda, we all returned to Sponsilier's camp. These civilian employees furnished their own mounts, and were anxious to buy a number of our best horses after the delivery was over. Not even a whisper was breathed about any uncertainty of our filling the outstanding contract, yet Sanders was given to understand that Don Lovell would rather, if he took a fancy to him, give a man a horse than sell him one. Not a word was said about any opposition to our herds; that would come later, and Sanders and his outfit were too good judges of Texas cattle to be misled by any bluster or boastful talk. Sponsilier acted the host, and after dinner unearthed a box of cigars, and we told stories and talked of our homes in the sunny South until the arrival of the military party. The herds had been well watered about noon and drifted out on the first uplands, and we intercepted the cavalcade before it reached Sponsilier's herd. They were mounted on fine cavalry horses, and the only greeting which passed, aside from a military salute, was when Lovell said: "Dave, show these officers your beeves. Answer any question they may ask to the best of your ability. Gentlemen, excuse me while you look over the cattle."

There were about a dozen military men in the party, some of them veterans of the civil war, others having spent their lifetime on our western frontier, while a few were seeing their first year's service after leaving West Point. In looking over the cattle, the post commander and quartermaster were taken under the wing of Sanders, who, as only a man could who was born to the occupation, called their attention to every fine point about the beeves. After spending fully an hour with Sponsilier's herd, the cavalcade proceeded on to mine, Lovell rejoining the party, but never once attempting to draw out an opinion, and again excusing himself on reaching my cattle. I continued with the military, answering every one's questions, from the young lieutenant's to the veteran commandant's, in which I was ably seconded by the quartermaster's foreman. My cattle had a splendid fill on them and eloquently spoke their own praises, yet Sanders lost no opportunity to enter a clincher in their favor. He pointed out beef after beef, and vouched for the pounds net they would dress, called attention to their sameness in build, ages, and general thrift, until one would have supposed that he was a salesman instead of a civilian employee.

My herd was fully ten miles from the post, and it was necessary for the military to return that evening. Don Lovell and a number of the boys had halted at a distance, and once the inspection was over, we turned and rode back to the waiting group of horsemen. On coming up, a number of the officers dismounted to shift saddles, preparatory to starting on their return, when the quartermaster halted near our employer and said:

"Colonel Lovell, let me say to you, in all sincerity, that in my twenty-five years' experience on this frontier, I never saw a finer lot of beeves tendered the government than these of yours. My position requires that I should have a fair knowledge of beef cattle, and the perquisites of my office in a post of Buford's class enable me to employ the best practical men available to perfect the service. I remember the quality of cattle which you delivered four years ago to me at Fort Randall, when it was a six-company post, yet they were not as fine a lot of beeves as these are. I have always contended that there was nothing too good in my department for the men who uphold the colors of our country, especially on the front line. You have been a soldier yourself and know that I am talking good horsesense, and I want to say to you that whatever the outcome of this dispute may be, if yours are the best cattle, you may count on my support until the drums beat tattoo. The government is liberal and insists on the best; the rank and file are worthy, and yet we don't always get what is ordered and well paid for. Now, remember, comrade, if this difference comes to an issue, I'm right behind you, and we'll stand or be turned down together."

"Thank you, Colonel," replied Mr. Lovell. "It does seem rather fortunate, my meeting up with a former business acquaintance, and at a time when I need him bad. If I am successful in delivering on this Buford award, it will round out, during my fifteen years as a drover, over a hundred thousand cattle that I have sold to the government for its Indian and army departments. There are no secrets in my business; the reason of my success is simple - my cattle were always there on the appointed day, humanely handled, and generally just a shade better than the specifications. My home country has the cattle for sale; I can tell within two bits a head what it will cost to lay them down here, and it's music to my ear to hear you insist on the best. I agree with you that the firing-line is entitled to special consideration, yet you know that there are ringsters who fatten at the expense of the rank and file. At present I haven't a word to say, but at noon to-morrow I shall tender the post commander at Ford Buford, through his quarter-master, ten thousand beeves, as a sub-contractor on the original award to The Western Supply Company." The post commander, an elderly, white-haired officer, rode over and smilingly said: "Now, look here, my Texas friend, I'm afraid you are borrowing trouble. True enough, there has been a protest made against our receiving your beeves, and I don't mince my words in saying that some hard things have been said about you. But we happen to know something about your reputation and don't give credit for all that is said. Your beeves are an eloquent argument in your favor, and if I were you I wouldn't worry. It is always a good idea in this Western country to make a proviso; and unless the unforeseen happens, the quartermaster's cattle foreman will count your beeves to-morrow afternoon; and for the sake of your company, if we keep you a day or two longer settling up, I don't want to hear you kick. Now, come on and go back with us to the post, as I promised my wife to bring you over to our house this evening. She seems to think that a man from Texas with ten thousand cattle ought to have horns, and I want to show her that she's mistaken. Come on, now, and not a damned word of protest out of you."

The military party started on their return, accompanied by Lovell. The civilian attaches followed at a respectful distance, a number of us joining them as far as Sponsilier's camp. There we halted, when Sanders insisted on an explanation of the remarks which had passed between our employer and his. Being once more among his own, he felt no delicacy in asking for information - which he would never think of doing with his superiors. My brother gave him a true version of the situation, but it remained for Dave Sponsilier to add an outline of the opposition herds and outfits.

"With humane treatment," said Dave, "the cattle would have qualified under the specifications. They were bought at Ogalalla, and any of the boys here will tell you that the first one was a good herd. The market was all shot to pieces, and they picked them up at their own price. But the owners didn't have cow-sense enough to handle the cattle, and put one of their own gang over the herds as superintendent. They left Cabin Creek, below Glendive, on the morning of the 10th, and they'll have to travel nearly twenty miles a day to reach here by noon to-morrow. Sanders, you know that gait will soon kill heavy cattle. The outfits were made up of short-card men and dance-hall ornaments, wild enough to look at, but shy on cattle sabe. Just so they showed up bad and wore a six-shooter, that was enough to win a home with Field and Radcliff. If they reach here on time, I'll gamble there ain't ten horses in the entire outfit that don't carry a nigger brand. And when it comes to the big conversation - well, they've simply got the earth faded."

It was nearly sundown when we mounted our horses and separated for the day. Bob Quirk returned to the post with the civilians, while I hastened back to my wagon. I had left orders with Splann to water the herd a second time during the evening and thus insure an easy night in holding the cattle. On my return, they were just grazing out from the river, their front a mile wide, making a pretty picture with the Yellowstone in the background. But as I sat my horse and in retrospect reviewed my connection with the cattle before me and the prospect of soon severing it, my remuda came over a near-by hill in a swinging trot for their second drink. Levering threw them into the river below the herd, and turning, galloped up to me and breathlessly asked: "Tom, did you see that dust-cloud up the river? Well, the other cattle are coming. The timber cuts off your view from here, besides the sun's gone down, but I watched their signal for half an hour from that second hill yonder. Oh, it's cattle all right; I know the sign, even if they are ten miles away."

CHAPTER XXII.

A SOLDIER'S HONOR

Delivery day dawned with a heavy fog hanging over the valley of the Yellowstone. The frosts had ceased, and several showers had fallen during the night, one of which brought our beeves to their feet, but they gave no serious trouble and resumed their beds within an hour. There was an autumn feeling in the atmosphere, and when the sun arose, dispelling the mists, a glorious September day was ushered in. The foliage of the timber which skirted either river was coloring from recent frosts, while in numerous places the fallen leaves of the cottonwood were littering the ground. Enough rain had fallen to settle the dust, and the signal of the approaching herds, seen the evening before, was no longer visible.

The delay in their appearance, however, was only temporary. I rode down to Sponsilier's camp early that morning and reported the observations of my wrangler at sundown. No one at the lower wagon had noticed the dust-clouds, and some one suggested that it might be a freight outfit returning unloaded, when one of the men on herd was seen signaling the camp's notice. The attention of the day-herders, several miles distant, was centered on some object up the river; and mounting our horses, we rode for the nearest elevation, from which two herds were to be seen on the opposite side, traveling in trail formation. There was no doubting their identity; and wondering what the day would bring forth, we rode for a better point of observation, when from behind a timbered bend of the river the lead of the last herd appeared. At last the Yellowstone Valley held over twenty thousand beef cattle, in plain sight of each other, both factions equally determined on making the delivery on an award that required only half that number. Dismounting, we kept the herds in view for over an hour, or until the last one had crossed the river above O'Brien's roadhouse, the lead one having disappeared out of sight over on the main Missouri.

This was the situation on the morning of September 15. As we returned to Sponsilier's wagon, all the idle men about the camp joined our cavalcade, and we rode down and paid Forrest's outfit a social visit. The latter were all absent, except the cook, but shortly returned from down the river and reported the opposition herds to be crossing the Missouri, evidently going to camp at Alkali Lake.

"Well, I've been present at a good many deliveries," said Quince Forrest, as he reined in his horse, "but this one is in a class by itself. We always aimed to get within five or ten miles of a post or agency, but our friends made a worthy effort to get on the parade-ground. They did the next best thing and occupied the grazing where the cavalry horses have been herded all summer. Oh, their cattle will be hog-fat in a few days. Possibly they expect to show their cattle in town, and not trouble the quartermaster and comandante to even saddle up - they're the very kind of people who wouldn't give anybody trouble if they could help it. It wouldn't make so much difference about those old frontier officers or a common cowman, but if one of those young lieutenants was to get his feet wet, the chances are that those Washington City contractors would fret and worry for weeks. Of course, any little inconvenience that any one incurred on their account, they'd gladly come all the way back from Europe to make it right - I don't think.'

While we were discussing the situation, Bob Quirk arrived at camp. He reported that Lovell, relying on the superiority of our beeves, had waived his right to deliver on the hour of high noon, and an inspection of the other cattle would be made that evening. The waiver was made at the request of the leading officers of Fort Buford, all very friendly to the best interests of the service and consequently ours, and the object was to silence all subsequent controversy. My brother admitted that some outside pressure had been brought to bear during the night, very antagonistic to the post commander, who was now more determined than ever to accept none but the best for their next year's meat supply. A well-known congressman, of unsavory reputation as a lobbyist in aiding and securing government contracts for his friends, was the latest addition to the legal forces of the opposition. He constantly mentioned his acquaintances in the War Department and maintained an air of assurance which was very disconcerting. The younger officers in the post were abashed at the effrontery of the contractors and their legal representatives, and had even gone so far as to express doubts as to the stability of their positions in case the decision favored Lovell's cattle. Opinion was current that a possible shake-up might occur at Buford after the receipt of its beef supply, and the more timorous ones were anxious to get into the right wagon, instead of being relegated to some obscure outpost.

It was now evident that the decisive issue was to occur over the delivery of the contending herds. Numerous possibilities arose in my imagination, and the various foremen advanced their views. A general belief that old man Don would fight to the last was prevalent, and amidst the discussions pro and con, I remarked that Lovell could take a final refuge behind the indemnity in hand.

"Indemnity, hell!" said Bob Quirk, giving me a withering look; "what is sixty-five thousand dollars on ten thousand beeves, within an hour of delivery and at thirty-seven and a half a head? You all know that the old man has strained his credit on this summer's drive, and he's got to have the money when he goes home. A fifteen or twenty per cent. indemnity does him no good. The Indian herds have paid out well, but if this delivery falls down, it will leave him holding the sack. On the other hand, if it goes through, he will be, financially, an independent man for life. And while he knows the danger of delay, he consented as readily as any of us would if asked for a cigarette-paper. He may come out all right, but he's just about white enough to get the worst of it. I've read these Sunday-school stories, where the good little boy always came out on top, but in real life, especially in cattle, it's quite different."

My brother's words had a magical effect. Sponsilier asked for suggestions, when Bob urged that every man available go into the post and accompany the inspection party that afternoon. Since Forrest and himself were unknown, they would take about three of the boys with them, cross the Missouri, ride through and sum up the opposition cattle. Forrest approved of the idea, and ordered his cook to bestir himself in getting up an early dinner. Meanwhile a number of my boys had ridden down to Forrest's wagon, and I immediately dispatched Clay Zilligan back to my cattle to relieve Vick Wolf and inform the day-herders that we might not return before dark. Wolf was the coolest man in my employ, had figured in several shooting scrapes, and as he was a splendid shot, I wanted to send him with Forrest and my brother. If identified as belonging to Lovell's outfits, there was a possibility that insult might be offered the boys; and knowing that it mattered not what the odds were, it would be resented, I thought it advisable to send a man who had smelt powder at short range. I felt no special uneasiness about my brother, in fact he was the logical man to go, but a little precaution would do no harm, and I saw to it that Sponsilier sent a good representative.

About one o'clock we started, thirty strong. Riding down the Yellowstone, the three detailed men, Quince Forrest, and my brother soon bore off to the left and we lost sight of them. Continuing on down the river, we forded the Missouri at the regular wagon-crossing, and within an hour after leaving Forrest's camp cantered into Fort Buford. Sanders and his outfit were waiting in front of the quartermaster's office, the hour for starting having been changed from two to three, which afforded ample time to visit the sutler's bar. Our arrival was noticed about the barracks, and evidently some complaint had been made, as old man Don joined us in time for the first round, after which he called Dave and me aside. In reply to his inquiry regarding our presence, Sponsilier informed him that we had come in to afford him an escort, in case he wished to attend the inspection of the opposition herds; that if there was any bulldozing going on he needn't stand behind the door. Dave informed him that Bob and Quince and three of the other boys would meet us at the cattle, and that he need feel no hesitancy in going if it was his wish. It was quite evident that Mr. Lovell was despondent, but he took courage and announced his willingness to go along.

"It was my intention not to go," said he, "though Mr. Aspgrain and Sutton both urged that I should. But now since you boys all feel the same way, I believe I'll go. Heaven and earth are being moved to have the other cattle accepted, but there are a couple of old war-horses at the head of this post that will fight them to the last ditch, and then some. I'm satisfied that my beeves, in any market in the West, are worth ten dollars a head more than the other ones, yet there is an effort being made to turn us down. Our claims rest on two points, - superiority of the beef tendered, and the legal impossibility of a transfer from themselves, a corporation, to themselves as individuals. If there is no outside interference, I think we will make the delivery before noon to-morrow. Now, I'll get horses for both Mr. Sutton and Senator Aspgrain, and you see that none of the boys drink too much. Sanders and his outfit are all right, and I want you lads to remind me to remember him before we leave this post. Now, we'll all go in a little party by ourselves, and I don't want a word out of a man, unless we are asked for an opinion from the officers, as our cattle must argue our cause."

A second drink, a cigar all round, and we were ready to start. As we returned to our mounts, a bustle of activity pervaded the post. Orderlies were leading forth the best horses, officers were appearing in riding-boots and gauntlets, while two conveyances from a livery in town stood waiting to convey the contractors and their legal representatives. Our employer and his counsel were on hand, awaiting the start, when the quartermaster and his outfit led off. There was some delay among the officers over the change of a horse, which had shown lameness, while the ringsters were all seated and waiting in their vehicles. Since none of us knew the trail to Alkali Lake, some one suggested that we follow up the quartermaster and allow the military and conveyances to go by the wagon-road. But Lovell objected, and ordered me forward to notice the trail and course, as the latter was a cut-off and much nearer than by road. I rode leisurely past the two vehicles, carefully scanning every face, when Mr. Field recognized and attempted to halt me, but I answered him with a contemptuous look and rode on. Instantly from the rigs came cries of "Stop that man!" "Halt that cowboy!" etc., when an orderly stepped in front of my horse and I reined in. But the shouting and my detention were seen and heard, and the next instant, led by Mike Sutton, our men dashed up, scaring the teams, overturning both of the conveyances, and spilling their occupants on the dusty ground. I admit that we were a hard-looking lot of cow-hands, our employer's grievance was our own, and just for an instant there was a blue, sulphuric tinge in the atmosphere as we accented our protest. The congressman scrambled to his feet, sputtering a complaint to the post commander, and when order was finally restored, the latter coolly said:

"Well, Mr. Y - - -, when did you assume command at Fort Buford? Any orders that you want given, while on this military reservation, please submit them to the proper authorities, and if just, they will receive attention. What right have you or any of your friends to stop a man without due process? I spent several hours with these men a few days ago and found them to my liking. I wish we could recruit the last one of them into our cavalry. But if you are afraid, I'll order out a troop of horse to protect you. Shall I?"

"I'm not at all afraid," replied Mr. Raddiff, "but feel under obligation to protect my counsel. If you please, Colonel."

"Captain O'Neill," said the commandant, turning to that officer, "order out your troop and give these conveyances ample protection from now until their return from this cattle inspection. Mr. Lovell, if you wish to be present, please ride on ahead with your men. The rest of us will proceed at once, and as soon as the escort arrives, these vehicles will bring up the rear."

As we rode away, the bugles were calling the troopers.

"That's the way to throw the gaff into them," said Sutton, when we had ridden out of hearing. "Every time they bluff, call their hand, and they'll soon get tired running blazers. I want to give notice right now that the first mark of disrespect shown me, by client or attorney, I'll slap him then and there, I don't care if he is as big as a giant. We are up against a hard crowd, and we want to meet them a little over halfway, even on a hint or insinuation. When it comes to buffaloing the opposite side, that's my long suit. The history of this case shows that the opposition has no regard for the rights of others, and it is up to us to try and teach them that a love of justice is universal. Personally, I'm nothing but a frontier lawyer from Dodge, but I'm the equal of any lobbyist that ever left Washington City."

Alkali Lake was some little distance from the post. All three of the herds were holding beyond it, a polite request having reached them to vacate the grazing-ground of the cavalry horses. Lovell still insisted that we stand aloof and give the constituted authorities a free, untrammeled hand until the inspection was over. The quartermaster and his assistants halted on approaching the first herd, and giving them a wide berth, we rode for the nearest good point of observation. The officers galloped up shortly afterward, reining in for a short conversation, but entering the first herd before the arrival of the conveyances and their escort. When the latter party arrived, the nearest one of the three herds had been passed upon, but the contractors stood on the carriage seats and attempted to look over the cordon of troopers, formed into a hollow square, which surrounded them. The troop were mounted on chestnut horses, making a pretty sight, and I think they enjoyed the folly and humor of the situation fully as much as we did. On nearing the second herd, we were met by the other boys, who had given the cattle a thorough going-over and reported finding two "Circle Dot" beeves among the opposition steers. The chances are that they had walked off a bed-ground some night while holding at Ogalalla and had been absorbed into another herd before morning. My brother announced his intention of taking them back with us, when Sponsilier taunted him with the fact that there might be objections offered.

"That'll be all right, Davy," replied Bob; "it'll take a bigger and better outfit than these pimps and tin-horns to keep me from claiming my own. You just watch and notice if those two steers don't go back with Forrest. Why, they had the nerve to question our right even to look them over. It must be a trifle dull with the GIRLS down there in Ogalalla when all these 'babies' have to turn out at work or go hungry."

Little time was lost in inspecting the last herd. The cattle were thrown entirely too close together to afford much opportunity in looking them over, and after riding through them a few times, the officers rode away for a consultation. We had kept at a distance from the convoy, perfectly contented so long as the opposition were prisoners of their own choosing. Captain O'Neill evidently understood the wishes of his superior officer, and never once were his charges allowed within hailing distance of the party of inspection. As far as exerting any influence was concerned, for that matter, all of us might have remained back at the post and received the report on the commander's return. Yet there was a tinge of uncertainty as to the result, and all concerned wanted to hear it at the earliest moment. The inspection party did not keep us long in waiting, for after a brief conference they turned and rode for the contractors under escort. We rode forward, the troop closed up in close formation about the two vehicles, and the general tension rose to that of rigidity. We halted quietly within easy hearing distance, and without noticing us the commandant addressed himself to the occupants of the conveyances, who were now standing on the seats.

"Gentlemen," said he, with military austerity, "the quality and condition of your cattle places them beyond our consideration. Beef intended for delivery at this post must arrive here with sufficient flesh to withstand the rigors of our winter. When possible to secure them, we prefer Northern wintered cattle, but if they are not available, and we are compelled to receive Southern ones, they must be of the first quality in conformation and flesh. It now becomes my duty to say to you that your beeves are rough, have been over-driven, are tender-footed and otherwise abused, and, having in view the best interests of the service, with the concurrence of my associates, I decline them."

The decision was rendered amid breathless silence. Not a word of exultation escaped one of our party, but the nervous strain rather intensified.

Mr. Y - -, the congressman, made the first move. Quietly alighting from the vehicle, he held a whispered conversation with his associates, very composedly turned to the commandant, and said:

"No doubt you are aware that there are higher authorities than the post commander and quartermaster of Fort Buford. This higher court to which I refer saw fit to award a contract for five million pounds of beef to be delivered at this post on foot. Any stipulations inserted or omitted in that article, the customary usages of the War Department would govern. If you will kindly look at the original contract, a copy of which is in your possession, you will notice that nothing is said about the quality of the cattle, just so the pounds avoirdupois are there. The government does not presume, when contracting for Texas cattle, that they will arrive here in perfect order; but so long as the sex, age, and weight have been complied with, there can be no evasion of the contract. My clients are sub-contractors, under an assignment of the original award, are acting in good faith in making this tender, and if your decision is against them, we will make an appeal to the War Department. I am not presuming to tell you your duty, but trust you will take this matter under full advisement before making your decision final."

"Mr. Y - , I have received cattle before without any legal advice or interference of higher authority. Although you have ignored his presence, there is another man here with a tender of beef who is entitled to more than passing consideration. He holds a sub-contract under the original award, and there is no doubt but he is also acting in good faith. My first concern as a receiving agent of this government is that the goods tendered must be of the first quality. Your cattle fall below our established standards here, while his will take rank as the finest lot of beeves ever tendered at this post, and therefore he is entitled to the award. I am not going to stand on any technicalities as to who is legally entitled to make this delivery; there have been charges and counter-charges which have reached me, the justice of which I cannot pass on, but with the cattle it is quite different. I lack but five years of being retired on my rank, the greater portion of which service has been spent on this frontier, and I feel justified in the decision made. The government buys the best, insists on its receiving agents demanding the same, and what few remaining years I serve the flag, there will be no change in my policy."

There was a hurried conference. The "major-domo" was called into the consultation, after which the congressman returned to the attack.

"Colonel, you are forcing us to make a protest to the War Department. As commander at Fort Buford, what right have you to consider the tender of any Tom, Dick, or Harry who may have cattle to sell? Armed with an assignment of the original award, we have tendered you the pounds quantity required by the existing contract, have insisted on the acceptance of the same, and if refused, our protest will be in the War Office before that sun sets. Now, my advice is -"

"I don't give a damn for you nor your advice. My reputation as a soldier is all I possess, and no man can dictate to nor intimidate me. My past record is an open book and one which I am proud of; and while I have the honor to command at Fort Buford, no threats can terrify nor cause me to deviate from my duty. Captain O'Neill, attend orders and escort these vehicles back to their quarters."

The escort loosened out, the conveyances started, and the inspection was over. We were a quiet crowd, though inwardly we all felt like shouting. We held apart from the military party, and when near the herd which held the "Circle Dot" steers, my brother and a number of the boys galloped on ahead and cut out the animals before our arrival. On entering the wagon-road near the post, the military cavalcade halted a moment for us to come up. Lovell was in the lead, and as we halted the commandant said to him: "We have decided to receive your cattle in the morning - about ten o'clock if that hour will be convenient. I may not come over, but the quartermaster's Mr. Sanders will count for us, and you cowmen ought to agree on the numbers. We have delayed you a day, and if you will put in a bill for demurrage, I will approve it. I believe that is all. We'll expect you to spend the night with us at the post. I thought it best to advise you now, so that you might give your men any final orders."

CHAPTER XXIII.

KANGAROOED

Lovell and his attorneys joined the cavalcade which returned to the post, while we continued on south, fording the Missouri above Forrest's camp. The two recovered beeves were recognized by their ranch brands as belonging in Bee County, thus identifying them as having escaped from Bob Quirk's herd, though he had previously denied all knowledge of them. The cattle world was a small one, and it mattered little where an animal roamed, there was always a man near by who could identify the brand and give the bovine's past history. With the prospects bright for a new owner on the morrow, these two wayfarers found lodgment among our own for the night.

But when another day dawned, it brought new complications. Instead of the early arrival of any receiving party, the appointed hour passed, noon came, and no one appeared. I had ridden down to the lower camps about the latter hour, yet there was no one who could explain, neither had any word from the post reached Forrest's wagon. Sponsilier suggested that we ride into Buford, and accordingly all three of us foremen started. When we sighted the ford on the Missouri, a trio of horsemen were just emerging from the water, and we soon were in possession of the facts. Sanders, my brother, and Mike Sutton composed the party, and the latter explained the situation. Orders from the War Department had reached Fort Buford that morning, temporarily suspending the post commander and his quartermaster from receiving any cattle intended for that post, and giving notice that a special commissioner was then en route from Minneapolis with full authority in the premises. The order was signed by the first quartermaster and approved by the head of that department; there was no going behind it, which further showed the strength that the opposition were able to command. The little attorney was wearing his war-paint, and we all dismounted, when Sanders volunteered some valuable points on the wintering of Texas cattle in the North. Sutton made a memorandum of the data, saying if opportunity offered he would like to submit it in evidence at the final hearing. The general opinion was that a court of inquiry would be instituted, and if such was the case, our cause was not by any means hopeless.

"The chances are that the opposition will centre the fight on an assignment of the original contract which they claim to hold," said the lawyer, in conclusion. "The point was advanced yesterday that we were intruders, while, on the other hand, the government was in honor bound to recognize its outstanding obligation, no matter in whose hands it was presented, so long as it was accompanied by the proper tender. A great deal will depend on the viewpoint of this special commissioner; he may be a stickler for red tape, with no concern for the service, as were the post commander and quartermaster. Their possession of the original document will be self-evident, and it will devolve on us to show that that assignment was illegal. This may not be as easy as it seems, for the chances are that there may be a dozen men in the gang, with numerous stool-pigeons ready and willing to do their bidding. This contract may demonstrate the possibility of a ring within a ring, with everything working to the same end. The absence of Honest John Griscom at this delivery is significant as proving that his presence at Dodge and Ogalalla was a mistake. You notice, with the exception of Field and Radcliff, they are all new men. Well, another day will tell the story."

The special commissioner could not arrive before the next morning. An ambulance, with relay teams, had left the post at daybreak for Glendive, and would return that night. Since the following promised to be a decisive day, we were requested to bring every available man and report at Fort Buford at an early hour. The trio returned to the post and we foremen to our herds. My outfit received the news in anything but a cheerful mood. The monotony of the long drive had made the men restless, and the delay of a single day in being finally relieved, when looked forward to, was doubly exasperating. It had been over six months since we left the ranch in Medina, and there was a lurking suspicion among a number of the boys that the final decision would be against our cattle and that they would be thrown back on our hands. There was a general anxiety among us to go home, hastened by the recent frosty nights and a common fear of a Northern climate. I tried to stem this feeling, promising a holiday on the morrow and assuring every one that we still had a fighting chance.

We reached the post at a timely hour the next morning. Only three men were left with each herd, my wrangler and cook accompanying us for the day. Parent held forth with quite a dissertation on the legal aspects of the case, and after we forded the river, an argument arose between him and Jake Blair. "Don't talk to me about what's legal and what isn't," said the latter; "the man with the pull generally gets all that he goes after. You remember the Indian and the white man were at a loss to know how to divide the turkey and the buzzard, but in the end poor man got the buzzard. And if you'll just pay a little more attention to humanity, you may notice that the legal aspects don't cut so much figure as you thought they did. The moment that cattle declined five to seven dollars a head, The Western Supply Company didn't trouble themselves as to the legality or the right or wrong, but proceeded to take advantage of the situation at once. Neal, when you've lived about twenty-five years on the cold charity of strangers, you'll get over that blind confidence and become wary and cunning. It might be a good idea to keep your eye open to-day for your first lesson. Anyhow don't rely too strong on the right or justice of anything, but keep a good horse on picket and your powder dry."

The commissioner had arrived early that morning and would take up matters at once. Nine o'clock was set for the hearing, which would take place in the quartermaster's office. Consultations were being held among the two factions, and the only ray of light was the reported frigidity of the special officer. He was such a superior personage that ordinary mortals felt a chill radiating from his person on their slightest approach. His credentials were from the War Department and were such as to leave no doubt but that he was the autocrat of the situation, before whom all should render homage. A rigid military air prevailed about the post and grounds, quite out of the ordinary, while the officers' bar was empty and silent.

The quartermaster's office would comfortably accommodate about one hundred persons. Fort Buford had been rebuilt in 1871, the adobe buildings giving place to frame structures, and the room in which the hearing was to be held was not only commodious but furnished with good taste. Promptly on the stroke of the hour, and escorted by the post adjutant, the grand mogul made his appearance. There was nothing striking about him, except his military bearing; he was rather young and walked so erect that he actually leaned backward a trifle. There was no prelude; he ordered certain tables rearranged, seated himself at one, and called for a copy of the original contract. The post adjutant had all the papers covering the situation in hand, and the copy was placed at the disposal of the special commissioner, who merely glanced at the names of the contracting parties, amount and date, and handed the document back. Turning to the table at which Lovell and his attorneys sat, he asked for the credentials under which they were tendering beeves at Fort Buford. The sub-contract was produced, some slight memorandum was made, and it was passed back as readily as was the original. The opposition were calmly awaiting a similar request, and when it came, in offering the papers, Congressman Y - took occasion to remark: "Our tender is not only on a sub-contract, but that agreement is fortified by an assignment of the original award, by and between the War Department and The Western Supply Company. We rely on the latter; you will find everything regular."

The customary glance was given the bulky documents. Senator Aspgrain was awaiting the opportune moment to attack the assignment. When it came, the senator arose with dignity and, addressing the commissioner, attempted to enter a protest, but was instantly stopped by that high functionary. A frozen silence pervaded the room. "There is no occasion for any remarks in this matter," austerely replied the government specialist. "Our department regularly awarded the beef contract for this post to The Western Supply Company. There was ample competition on the award, insuring the government against exorbitant prices, and the required bonds were furnished for the fulfillment of the contract. Right then and there all interest upon the part of the grantor ceased until the tender was made at this post on the appointed day of delivery. In the interim, however, it seems that for reasons purely their own, the grantees saw fit to sub-let their contract, not once but twice. Our department amply protected themselves by requiring bonds, and the sub-contractors should have done the same. That, however, is not the matter at issue, but who is entitled to deliver on the original award. Fortunately that point is beyond question; an assignment of the original has always been recognized at the War Office, and in this case the holders of the same are declared entitled to deliver. There is only one provision, - does the article of beef tendered qualify under the specifications? That is the only question before making this decision final. If there is any evidence to the contrary, I am ready to hear it."

This afforded the opportunity of using Sanders as a witness, and Sutton grasped the opportunity of calling him to testify in regard to wintering Southern cattle in the North. After stating his qualifications as a citizen and present occupation, he was asked by the commissioner regarding his experience with cattle to entitle his testimony to consideration. "I was born to the occupation in Texas," replied the witness. "Five years ago this summer I came with beef cattle from Uvalde County, that State, to this post, and after the delivery, accepted a situation under the quartermaster here in locating and holding the government's beeves. At present I am foreman and have charge of all cattle delivered at or issued from this post. I have had five years' experience in wintering Texas cattle in this vicinity, and have no hesitancy in saying that it is a matter of the utmost importance that steers should be in the best possible flesh to withstand our winters. The losses during the most favorable seasons have averaged from one to five per cent., while the same cattle in a severe season will lose from ten to twenty-five, all depending on the condition of the stock with the beginning of cold weather. Since my connection with this post we have always received good steers, and our losses have been light, but above and below this military reservation the per cent. loss has run as high as fifty among thin, weak animals."

"Now, Mr. Sanders," said the special commissioner, "as an expert, you are testifying as to the probable loss to the government in this locality in buying and holding beef on its own account. You may now state if you have seen the tender of beef made by Field, Radcliff & Co., and if so, anticipating the worst, what would be the probable loss if their cattle were accepted on this year's delivery?"

"I was present at their inspection by the officers of this post," replied the witness, "and have no hesitancy in saying that should the coming one prove as hard a winter as '82 was, there would be a loss of fully one half these cattle. At least that was my opinion as expressed to the post commander and quartermaster at the inspection, and they agreed with me. There are half a dozen other boys here whose views on wintering cattle can be had - and they're worth listening to."

This testimony was the brutal truth, and though eternal, was sadly out of place. The opposition lawyers winced; and when Sutton asked if permission would be given to hear the testimony of the post commander and quartermaster, both familiar with the quality of cattle the government had been receiving for years, the commissioner, having admitted damaging testimony, objected on the ground that they were under suspension, and military men were not considered specialists outside their own vocation. Other competent witnesses were offered and objected to, simply because they would not admit they were experts. Taking advantage of the opening, Congressman Y -- called attention to a few facts in passing. This unfortunate situation, he said, in substance, was deeply regretted by his clients and himself. The War Department was to be warmly commended for sending a special commissioner to hear the matter at issue, otherwise unjust charges might have been preferred against old and honored officers in the service. However, if specialists were to be called to testify, and their testimony considered, as to what per cent. of cattle would survive a winter, why not call on the weather prophets to testify just what the coming one would be? He ridiculed the attestations of Sanders as irrelevant, defiantly asserting that the only question at issue was, were there five million pounds of dressed beef in the tender of cattle by Field, Radcliff & Co. He insisted on the letter in the bond being observed. The government bought cattle one year with another, and assumed risks as did other people. Was there any man present to challenge his assertion that the pounds quantity had been tendered?

There was. Don Lovell arose, and addressing the special commissioner, said: "Sir, I am not giving my opinion as an expert but as a practical cowman. If the testimony of one who has delivered over ninety thousand cattle to this government, in its army and Indian departments, is of any service to you, I trust you will hear me patiently. No exception is taken to your ruling as to who is entitled to deliver on the existing award; that was expected from the first. I have been contracting beef to this government for the past fifteen years, and there may be tricks in the trade of which I am ignorant. The army has always demanded the best, while lower grades have always been acceptable to the Indian Department. But in all my experience, I have never tendered this government for its gut-eating wards as poor a lot of cattle as I am satisfied that you are going to receive at the hands of Field, Radcliff & Co. I accept the challenge that there are not five million pounds of dressed beef in their tender to-day, and what there is would be a disgrace to any commonwealth to feed its convicts. True, these cattle are not intended for immediate use, and I make the counter-assertion that this government will never kill out fifty per cent. of the weight that you accept to-day. Possibly you prefer the blandishments of a lobbyist to the opinion of a practical cowman like Sanders. That's your privilege. You refuse to allow us to show the relationship between The Western Supply Company and the present holders of its assignment, and in doing so I charge you with being in collusion with these contractors to defraud the government!"

"You're a liar!" shouted Congressman Y - - , jumping to his feet. The only reply was a chair hurled from the hand of Sutton at the head of the offender, instantly followed by a rough house. Several officers present sprang to the side of the special commissioner, but fortunately refrained from drawing revolvers. I was standing at some distance from the table, and as I made a lunge forward, old man Don was hurled backward into my arms. He could not whip a sick chicken, yet his uncontrollable anger had carried him into the general melee and he had been roughly thrown out by some of his own men. They didn't want him in the fight; they could do all that was necessary. A number of soldiers were present, and while the officers were frantically commanding them to restore order, the scrap went merrily on. Old man Don struggled with might and main, cursing me for refusing to free him, and when one of the contractors was knocked down within easy reach, I was half tempted to turn him loose. The "major-domo" had singled out Sponsilier and was trying issues with him, Bob Quirk was dropping them right and left, when the deposed commandant sprang upon a table, and in a voice like the hiss of an adder, commanded peace, and the disorder instantly ceased.

The row had lasted only a few seconds. The opposing sides stood glaring daggers at each other, when the commissioner took occasion to administer a reproof to all parties concerned, referring to Texas in not very complimentary terms. Dave Sponsilier was the only one who had the temerity to offer any reply, saying, "Mr. Yank, I'll give you one hundred dollars if you'll point me out the grave of a man, woman, or child who starved to death in that state."

A short recess was taken, after which apologies followed, and the commissioner resumed the hearing. A Western lawyer, named Lemeraux, made a very plausible plea for the immediate acceptance of the tender of Field, Radcliff & Co. He admitted that the cattle, at present, were not in as good flesh as his clients expected to offer them; that they had left the Platte River in fine condition, but had been twice quarantined en route. He was cautious in his remarks, but clearly intimated that had there been no other cattle in competition for delivery on this award, there might have been no quarantine. In his insinuations, the fact was adroitly brought out that the isolation of their herds, if not directly chargeable to Lovell and his men, had been aided and abetted by them, retarding the progress of his clients' beeves and forcing them to travel as fast as twenty-five miles a day, so that they arrived in a jaded condition. Had there been no interference, the tender of Field, Radcliff & Co. would have reached this post ten days earlier, and rest would soon have restored the cattle to their normal condition. In concluding, he boldly made the assertion that the condition of his client's tender of beef was the result of a conspiracy to injure one firm, that another drover might profit thereby; that right and justice could be conserved only by immediately making the decision final, and thus fearlessly silencing any and all imputations reflecting on the character of this government's trusted representatives.

The special commissioner assumed an air of affected dignity and announced that a conclusion had been arrived at. Turning to old man Don, he expressed the deepest regret that a civilian was beyond his power to punish, otherwise he would have cause to remember the affront offered himself; not that he personally cared, but the department of government which he had the honor to serve was jealous of its good name. Under the circumstances he could only warn him to be more guarded hereafter in choosing his language, and assured Lovell that it was in his power to escort any offender off that military reservation. Pausing a moment, he resumed a judicial air, and summed up the situation:

"There was no occasion," said he, in an amiable mood, "to refer this incident to the War Department if the authorities here had gone about their work properly. Fortunately I was in Minneapolis adjusting some flour accounts, when I was ordered here by the quartermaster-general. Instead of attempting to decide who had the best tender of cattle, the one with the legal right alone should have been considered. Our department is perfectly familiar with these petty jealousies, which usually accompany awards of this class, and generally emanate from disappointed and disgruntled competitors. The point is well taken by counsel that the government does not anticipate the unforeseen, and it matters not what the loss may be from the rigors of winter, the contractor is exempt after the day of delivery. If the cattle were delayed en route, as has been asserted, and it was necessary to make forced drives in order to reach here within the specified time, all this should be taken into consideration in arriving at a final conclusion. On his reinstatement, I shall give the quartermaster of this post instructions, in receiving these cattle, to be governed, not so much by their present condition as by what they would have been had there been no interference. Now in behalf of the War Department, I declare the award to The Western Supply Company, and assigned to Field, Radcliff, and associates, to have been fulfilled to the satisfaction of all parties concerned. This closes the incident, and if there is nothing further, the inquiry will stand adjourned without date."

"One moment, if you please," said Don Lovell, addressing the commissioner and contractors; "there is a private matter existing between Field, Radcliff & Co. and myself which demands an understanding between us. I hold a sum of money, belonging to them, as indemnity against loss in driving ten thousand cattle from Southern Texas to this post. That I will sustain a heavy loss, under your decision, is beyond question. I am indemnified to the amount of about six dollars and a half a head, and since the government is exempt from garnishment and the contractors are wholly irresponsible, I must content myself with the money in hand. To recover th_s amount, held as indemnity, suit has been threatened against me. Of course I can't force their hands, but I sincerely hope they will feel exultant enough over your kangaroo decision to file their action before taking their usual outing in Europe. They will have no trouble in securing my legal address, my rating can be obtained from any commercial agency, and no doubt their attorneys are aware of the statute of limitation in my state. I believe that's all, except to extend my thanks to every one about Fort Buford for the many kind attentions shown my counsel, my boys, and myself. To my enemies, I can only say that I hope to meet them on Texas soil, and w_ll promise them a fairer hearing than was accorded me here to-day. Mr. Commissioner, I have always prided myself on being a good citizen, have borne arms in defense of my country, and in taking exception to your decision I brand you as the most despicable member of The Western Supply Company. Any man who will prostitute a trust for a money consideration - "

"That's enough!" shouted the special commissioner, rising. "Orderly, call the officer of the day, and tell him I want two companies of cavalry to furnish an escort for this man and his herds beyond the boundaries of this military reservation." Looking Lovell in the face, he said: "You have justly merited a severe punishment, and I shall report your reflections to the War and Indian departments, and you may find it more difficult to secure contracts in the future. One of you officers detail men and take charge of this man until the escort is ready. The inquiry is adjourned."

CHAPTER XXIV.

THE WINTER OF OUR DISCONTENT

The inquiry was over before noon. A lieutenant detailed a few men and made a pretense of taking possession of Lovell. But once the special commissioner was out of sight, the farce was turned into an ovation, and nearly every officer in the post came forward and extended his sympathy. Old man Don was visibly affected by the generous manifestations of the military men in general, and after thanking each one personally, urged that no unnecessary demonstration should be made, begging that the order of escort beyond the boundary of the reservation be countermanded. No one present cared to suggest it, but gave assurance that it would be so modified as not in any way to interfere with the natural movement of the herds. Some little time would be required to outfit the forage-wagons to accommodate the cavalry companies, during which my brother rode up, leading Lovell's horse, permission was given to leave in advance of the escort, and we all mounted and quietly rode away.

The sudden turn of affairs had disconcerted every man in the three outfits. Just what the next move would be was conjecture with most of us, though every lad present was anxious to know. But when we were beyond the immediate grounds, Lovell turned in his saddle and asked which one of us foremen wanted to winter in the North. No one volunteered, and old man Don continued: "Anticipating the worst, I had a long talk this morning with Sanders, and he assured me that our cattle would go through any winter without serious loss. He suggested the Little Missouri as a good range, and told me of a hay ranch below the mouth of the Beaver. If it can be bought reasonably, we would have forage for our horses, and the railroad is said to be not over forty miles to the south. If the government can afford to take the risk of wintering cattle in this climate, since there is no other choice, I reckon I'll have to follow suit. Bob and I will take fresh horses and ride through to the Beaver this afternoon, and you fellows follow up leisurely with the cattle. Sanders says the winters are dry and cold, with very little if any snowfall. Well, we're simply up against it; there's no hope of selling this late in the season, and nothing is left us but to face the music of a Northern winter.'

As we turned in to ford the Missouri, some one called attention to a cavalry company riding out from their quarters at the post. We halted a moment, and as the first one entered the road, the second one swung into view, followed by forage-wagons. From maps in our possession we knew the southern boundary of the Fort Buford military reservation must be under twenty miles to the south, and if necessary, we could put it behind us that afternoon. But after crossing the river, and when the two troops again came in view, they had dropped into a walk, passing entirely out of sight long before we reached Forrest's camp. Orders were left with the latter to take the lead and make a short drive that evening, at least far enough to convince observers that we were moving. The different outfits dropped out as their wagons were reached, and when my remuda was sighted, old man Don ordered it brought in for a change of horses. One of the dayherders was at camp getting dinner, and inviting themselves to join him, my employer and my brother helped themselves while their saddles were shifted to two of my well-rested mounts. Inquiry had been made of all three of the outfits if any ranch had been sighted on the Beaver while crossing that creek, but the only recollection among the forty-odd men was that of Burl Van Vedder, who contended that a dim trail, over which horses had passed that summer, ran down on the south side of the stream.

With this meagre information Lovell and my brother started. A late dinner over and the herders relieved, we all rode for the nearest eminence which would afford us a view. The cavalry were just going into camp below O'Brien's ranch, their forage-train in sight, while Forrest's cattle were well bunched and heading south. Sponsilier was evidently going to start, as his team was tied up and the saddle stock in hand, while the herd was crossing over to the eastern side of the Yellowstone. We dismounted and lay around for an hour or so, when the greater portion of the boys left to help in the watering of our herd, the remainder of us doing outpost duty. Forrest had passed out of sight, Sponsilier's wagon and remuda crossed opposite us, going up the valley, followed by his cattle in loose grazing order, and still we loitered on the hill. But towards evening I rode down to where the cavalry was encamped, and before I had conversed very long with the officers, it was clear to me that the shorter our moves the longer it would extend their outing. Before I left the soldier camp, Sanders arrived, and as we started away together, I sent him back to tell the officers to let me know any time they could use half a beef. On reaching our wagon, the boys were just corralling the saddle stock for their night-horses, when Sanders begged me to sell him two which had caught his fancy. I dared not offer them; but remembering the fellow's faithful service in our behalf, and that my employer expected to remember him, I ordered him to pick, with Don Lovell's compliments, any horse in the remuda as a present.

The proposition stunned Sanders, but I insisted that if old man Don was there, he would make him take something. He picked a good horse out of my mount and stayed until morning, when he was compelled to return, as the probabilities were that they would receive the other cattle some time during the day. After breakfast, and as he was starting to return, he said, "Well, boys, tell the old man that I don't expect ever to be able to return his kindness, though I'd ride a thousand miles for the chance. One thing sure, there isn't a man in Dakota who has money enough to tempt me to part with my pelon. If you locate down on the Little Missouri, drop me a line where you are at, and if Lovell wants four good men, I can let him have them about the first of December. You through lads are liable to be scared over the coming winter, and a few acclimated ones will put backbone in his outfit. And tell the old man that if I can ever do him a good turn just to snap his fingers and I'll quit the government - he's a few shades whiter than it, anyhow."

The herd had already left the bed-ground, headed south. About five miles above O'Brien's, we recrossed to the eastern side of the Yellowstone, and for the next three days moved short distances, the military always camped well in our rear. The fourth morning I killed a beef, a forage-wagon came forward and took half of it back to the cavalry camp with our greetings and farewell, and we parted company. Don Lovell met us about noon, elated as a boy over his purchase of the hay ranch. My brother had gone on to the railroad and thence by train to Miles City to meet his remuda and outfit. "Boys, I have bought you a new home," was the greeting of old man Don, as he dismounted at our noon camp. "There's a comfortable dugout, stabling for about ten horses, and seventy-five tons of good hay in the stack. The owner was homesick to get back to God's country, and he'll give us possession in ten days. Bob will be in Little Missouri to-day and order us a car of sacked corn from Omaha, and within a month we'll be as snug as they are down in old Medina. Bob's outfit will go home from Miles, and if he can't sell his remuda he'll bring it up here. Two of these outfits can start back in a few days, and afterward the camp will be reduced to ten men."

Two days later Forrest veered off and turned his cattle loose below the junction of the Beaver with the Little Missouri. Sponsilier crossed the former, scattering his beeves both up and down the latter, while I cut mine into a dozen bunches and likewise freed them along the creek. The range was about ten miles in length along the river, and a camp was established at either end where men would be stationed until the beeves were located. The commissaries had run low, there was a quiet rivalry as to which outfits should go home, and we all waited with bated breath for the final word. I had Dorg Seay secretly inform my employer that I had given Sanders a horse without his permission, hoping that it might displease him. But the others pointed out the fact that my outfit had far the best remuda, and that it would require well-mounted men to locate and hold that number of cattle through the winter. Old man Don listened to them all, and the next morning, as all three of us foremen were outlining certain improvements about the hay ranch with him, he turned to me and said:

"Tom, I hear you gave Sanders a horse. Well, that was all right, although it strikes me you were rather liberal in giving him the pick of a choice remuda. But it may all come right in the long run, as Bob and I have decided to leave you and your outfit to hold these cattle this winter. So divide your men and send half of them down to Quince's camp, and have your cook and wrangler come over to Dave's wagon to bring back provision and the horses, as we'll start for the railroad in the morning. I may not come back, but Bob will, and he'll see that you are well fixed for the winter before he goes home. After he leaves, I want you to write me every chance you have to send a letter to the railroad. Now, I don't want any grumbling out of you or your men; you're a disgrace to the state that raised you if you can't handle cattle anywhere that any other man can."

I felt all along it would fall to me, the youngest of six foremen; and my own dear brother consigning me to a winter in the North, while he would bask in the sunshine of our own sunny South! It was hard to face; but I remembered that the fall before it had been my lot to drive a thousand saddle horses home to the ranch, and that I had swaggered as a trail foreman afterward as the result. It had always been my luck to have to earn every little advance or promotion, while others seemed to fall into them without any effort. Bob Quirk never saw the day that he was half the all-round cowman that I was; yet he was above me and could advise, and I had to obey.

On the morning of the 25th of September, 1884, the two outfits started for the railroad, leaving the remainder of us in a country, save for the cattle, so desolate that there was no chance even to spend our wages. I committed to memory a curtain lecture for my brother, though somehow or other it escaped me and was never delivered. We rode lines between the upper and lower wagons, holding the cattle loosely on a large range. A delightful fall favored us, and before the first squall of winter came on, the beeves had contented themselves as though they had been born on the Little Missouri. Meanwhile Bob's wagon and remuda arrived, the car of corn was hauled to our headquarters, extra stabling was built, and we settled down like banished exiles. Communication had been opened with Fort Buford, and in the latter part of October the four promised men arrived, when Bob Quirk took part of my outfit and went home, leaving me ten men. Parent remained as cook, the new men assimilated easily, a fiddle was secured, and in fulfillment of the assertion of Sanders, we picked up courage. Two grain-fed horses, carefully stabled, were allowed to each man, the remainder of our large number of saddle stock running free on the range.

To that long winter on the Little Missouri a relentless memory turns in retrospect. We dressed and lived like Eskimos. The first blizzard struck us early in December, the thermometer dropped sixty degrees in twelve hours, but in the absence of wind and snow the cattle did not leave the breaks along the river. Three weeks later a second one came, and we could not catch the lead animals until near the railroad; but the storm drove them up the Little Missouri, and its sheltering banks helped us to check our worst winter drift. After the first month of wintry weather, the dread of the cold passed, and men and horses faced the work as though it was springtime in our own loved southland. The months rolled by scarcely noticed. During fine weather Sanders and some of his boys twice dropped down for a few days, but we never left camp except to send letters home.

An early spring favored us. I was able to report less than one per cent. loss on the home range, with the possibility of but few cattle having escaped us during the winter. The latter part of May we sold four hundred saddle horses to some men from the upper Yellowstone. Early in June a wagon was rigged out, extra men employed, and an outfit sent two hundred miles up the Little Missouri to attend the round-ups. They were gone a month and came in with less than five hundred beeves, which represented our winter drift. Don Lovell reached the ranch during the first week in July. One day's ride through the splendid cattle, and old man Don lost his voice, but the smile refused to come off. Everything was coming his way. Field, Radcliff & Co. had sued him, and the jury awarded him one-hundred thousand dollars. His bankers had unlimited confidence in his business ability; he had four Indian herds on the trail and three others of younger steers, intended for the Little Missouri ranch. Cattle prices in Texas had depreciated nearly one half since the spring before - "a good time for every cowman to strain his credit and enlarge his holdings," my employer assured me.

Orders were left that I was to begin shipping out the beeves early in August. It was the intention to ship them in two and three train-load lots, and I was expecting to run a double outfit, when a landslide came our way. The first train-load netted sixty dollars a head at Omaha - but they were beeves; cods like an ox's heart and waddled as they walked. We had just returned from the railroad with the intention of shipping two train-loads more, when the quartermaster and Sanders from Fort Buford rode into the ranch under an escort. The government had lost forty per cent. of the Field-Radcliff cattle during the winter just passed, and were in the market to buy the deficiency. The quartermaster wanted a thousand beeves on the first day of September and October each, and double that number for the next month. Did we care to sell that amount? A United States marshal, armed with a search-warrant, could not have found Don Lovell in a month, but they were promptly assured that our beef steers were for sale. It is easy to show prime cattle. The quartermaster, Sanders, and myself rode down the river, crossed over and came up beyond our camp, forded back and came down the Beaver, and I knew the sale was made. I priced the beeves, delivered at Buford, at sixty-five dollars a head, and the quartermaster took them.

Then we went to work in earnest. Sanders remained to receive the first contingent for Buford, which would leave our range on the 25th of each month. A single round-up and we had the beeves in hand. The next morning after Splann left for the mouth of the Yellowstone, I started south for the railroad with two train-loads of picked cattle. Professional shippers took them off our hands at the station, accompanied them en route to market, and the commission house in Omaha knew where to remit the proceeds. The beef shipping season was on with a vengeance. Our saddle stock had improved with a winter in the North, until one was equal to two Southern or trail horses. Old man Don had come on in the mean time, and was so pleased with my sale to the army post that he returned to Little Missouri Station at once and bought two herds of three-year-olds at Ogalalla by wire. This made sixteen thousand steer cattle en route from the latter point for Lovell's new ranch in Dakota.

"Tom," said old man Don, enthusiastically, "this is the making of a fine cattle ranch, and we want to get in on the flood-tide. There is always a natural wealth in a new country, and the goldmines of this one are in its grass. The instinct that taught the buffalo to choose this as their summer and winter range was unerring, and they found a grass at hand that would sustain them in any and all kinds of weather. This country to-day is just what Texas was thirty years ago. All the early settlers at home grew rich without any effort, but once the cream of the virgin land is gone, look out for a change. The early cowmen of Texas flatter themselves on being shrewd and far-seeing - just about as much as I was last fall, when I would gladly have lost twenty-five thousand dollars rather than winter these cattle. Now look where I will come out, all due to the primitive wealth of the land. From sixty to sixty-five dollars a head beats thirty-seven and a half for our time and trouble."

The first of the through cattle arrived early in September. They avoided our range for fear of fever, and dropped in about fifteen miles below our headquarters on the Little Missouri. Dorg Seay was one of the three foremen, Forrest and

Sponsilier being the other two, having followed the same route as our herds of the year before. But having spent a winter in the North, we showed the through outfits a chilling contempt. I had ribbed up Parent not even to give them a pleasant word about our wagon or headquarters; and particularly if Bob Quirk came through with one of the purchased herds, he was to be given the marble heart. One outfit loose-herded the new cattle, the other two going home, and about the middle of the month, my brother and The Rebel came trailing in with the last two herds. I was delighted to meet my old bunkie, and had him remain over until the last outfit went home, when we reluctantly parted company. Not so, however, with Bob Quirk, who haughtily informed me that he came near slapping my cook for his effrontery. "So you are another one of these lousy through outfits that think we ought to make a fuss over you, are you?" I retorted. "Just you wait until we do. Every one of you except old Paul had the idea that we ought to give you a reception and ask you to sleep in our beds. I'm glad that Parent had the gumption to give you a mean look; he'll ride for me next year."

The month of October finished the shipping. There was a magic in that Northern climate that wrought wonders in an animal from the South. Little wonder that the buffalo could face the blizzard, in a country of his own choosing, and in a climate where the frost king held high revel five months out of the twelve. There was a tonic like the iron of wine in the atmosphere, absorbed alike by man and beast, and its possessor laughed at the fury of the storm. Our loss of cattle during the first winter, traceable to season, was insignificant, while we sold out over two hundred head more than the accounts called for, due to the presence of strays, which went to Buford. And when the last beef was shipped, the final delivery concluded to the army, Don Lovell was a quarter-million dollars to the good, over and above the contract price at which he failed to deliver the same cattle to the government the fall before.

As foreman of Lovell's beef ranch on the Little Missouri I spent five banner years of my life. In '89 the stock, good-will,

ANDY ADAMS

and range were sold to a cattle syndicate, who installed a superintendent and posted rules for the observance of its employees. I do not care to say why, but in a stranger's hands it never seemed quite the same home to a few of us who were present when it was transformed into a cattle range. Late that fall, some half-dozen of us who were from Texas asked to be relieved and returned to the South. A traveler passing through that country to-day will hear the section about the mouth of the Beaver called only by the syndicate name, but old-timers will always lovingly refer to it as the Don Lovell Ranch.

Choose from Thousands of 1stWorldLibrary Classics By

Adolphus WilliamWard
Aesop
Agatha Christie
Alexander Aaronsohn
Alexander Kielland
Alexandre Dumas
Alfred Gatty
Alfred Ollivant
Alice Duer Miller
Alice Turner Curtis
Alice Dunbar
Ambrose Bierce
Amelia E. Barr
Andrew Lang
Andrew McFarland Davis
Anna Sewell
Annie Besant
Annie Hamilton Donnell
Annie Payson Call
Anton Chekhov
Arnold Bennett
Arthur Conan Doyle
Arthur Ransome
Atticus
B. M. Bower
Basil King
Bayard Taylor
Ben Macomber
Booth Tarkington
Bram Stoker
C. Collodi
C. E. Orr
C. M. Ingleby
Carolyn Wells
Catherine Parr Traill
Charles A. Eastman
Charles Dickens
Charles Dudley Warner
Charles Farrar Browne
Charles Ives
Charles Kingsley
Charles Lathrop Pack
Charles Whibley
Charles Willing Beale
Charlotte M. Braeme
Charlotte M.Yonge
Clair W. Hayes
Clarence Day Jr.
Clarence E. Mulford

Clemence Housman
Confucius
Cornelis DeWitt Wilcox
Cyril Burleigh
D. H. Lawrence
Daniel Defoe
David Garnett
Don Carlos Janes
Donald Keyhole
Dorothy Kilner
Dougan Clark
E. Nesbit
E.P.Roe
E. Phillips Oppenheim
Edgar Allan Poe
Edgar Rice Burroughs
Edith Wharton
Edward J. O'Biren
John Cournos
Edwin L. Arnold
Eleanor Atkins
Elizabeth Cleghorn
Gaskell
Elizabeth Von Arnim
Ellem Key
Emily Dickinson
Erasmus W. Jones
Ernie Howard Pie
Ethel Turner
Ethel Watts Mumford
Eugenie Foa
Eugene Wood
Evelyn Everett-Green
Everard Cotes
F. J. Cross
Federick Austin Ogg
Ferdinand Ossendowski
Francis Bacon
Francis Darwin
Frances Hodgson Burnett
Frank Gee Patchin
Frank Harris
Frank Jewett Mather
Frank L. Packard
Frederick Trevor Hill
Frederick Winslow Taylor
Friedrich Kerst
Friedrich Nietzsche
Fyodor Dostoyevsky

Gabrielle E. Jackson
Garrett P. Serviss
Gaston Leroux
George Ade
Geroge Bernard Shaw
George Ebers
George Eliot
George MacDonald
George Orwell
George Tucker
George W. Cable
George Wharton James
Gertrude Atherton
Grace E. King
Grant Allen
Guillermo A. Sherwell
Gulielma Zollinger
Gustav Flaubert
H. A. Cody
H. B. Irving
H. G. Wells
H. H. Munro
H. Irving Hancock
H. Rider Haggard
H. W. C. Davis
Hamilton Wright Mabie
Hans Christian Andersen
Harold Avery
Harold McGrath
Harriet Beecher Stowe
Harry Houidini
Helent Hunt Jackson
Helen Nicolay
Hendy David Thoreau
Henrik Ibsen
Henry Adams
Henry Ford
Henry Frost
Henry James
Henry Jones Ford
Henry Seton Merriman
Henry Wadsworth
Longfellow
Henry W Longfellow
Herbert A. Giles
Herbert N. Casson
Herman Hesse
Homer
Honore De Balzac

Horace Walpole
Horatio Alger, Jr.
Howard Pyle
Howard R. Garis
Hugh Lofting
Hugh Walpole
Humphry Ward
Ian Maclaren
Israel Abrahams
J.G.Austin
J. Henri Fabre
J. M. Barrie
J. Macdonald Oxley
J. S. Knowles
J. Storer Clouston
Jack London
Jacob Abbott
James Allen
James Lane Allen
James Andrews
James Baldwin
James DeMille
James Joyce
James Oliver Curwood
James Oppenheim
James Otis
Jane Austen
Jens Peter Jacobsen
Jerome K. Jerome
John Burroughs
John F. Kennedy
John Gay
John Glasworthy
John Habberton
John Joy Bell
John Milton
John Philip Sousa
Jonathan Swift
Joseph Carey
Joseph Conrad
Joseph Jacobs
Julian Hawthrone
Julies Vernes
Justin Huntly McCarthy
Kakuzo Okakura
Kenneth Grahame
Kate Langley Bosher
L. A. Abbot
L. T. Meade
L. Frank Baum
Laura Lee Hope

Laurence Housman
Leo Tolstoy
Leonid Andreyev
Lewis Carroll
Lilian Bell
Lloyd Osbourne
Louis Tracy
Louisa May Alcott
Lucy Fitch Perkins
Lucy Maud Montgomery
Lydia Miller Middleton
Lyndon Orr
M. H. Adams
Margaret E. Sangster
Margaret Vandercook
Maria Edgeworth
Maria Thompson Daviess
Mariano Azuela
Marion Polk Angellotti
Mark Overton
Mark Twain
Mary Austin
Mary Cole
Mary Rowlandson
Mary Wollstonecraft
Shelley
Max Beerbohm
Myra Kelly
Nathaniel Hawthrone
O. F. Walton
Oscar Wilde
Owen Johnson
P.G.Wodehouse
Paul and Mable Thorn
Paul G. Tomlinson
Paul Severing
Peter B. Kyne
Plato
R. Derby Holmes
R. L. Stevenson
Rabindranath Tagore
Rahul Alvares
Ralph Waldo Emmerson
Rene Descartes
Rex E. Beach
Richard Harding Davis
Richard Jefferies
Robert Barr
Robert Frost
Robert Gordon Anderson
Robert L. Drake

Robert Lansing
Robert Michael Ballantyne
Robert W. Chambers
Rosa Nouchette Carey
Ross Kay
Rudyard Kipling
Samuel B. Allison
Samuel Hopkins Adams
Sarah Bernhardt
Selma Lagerlof
Sherwood Anderson
Sigmund Freud
Standish O'Grady
Stanley Weyman
Stella Benson
Stephen Crane
Stewart Edward White
Stijn Streuvels
Swami Abhedananda
Swami Parmananca
T. S. Ackland
The Princess Der Ling
Thomas A. Janvier
Thomas A Kempis
Thomas Anderton
Thomas Bailey Aldrich
Thomas Bulfinch
Thomas De Quincey
Thomas H. Huxley
Thomas Hardy
Thomas More
Thornton W. Burgess
U. S. Grant
Valentine Williams
Victor Appleton
Virginia Woolf
Walter Scott
Washington Irving
Wilbur Lawton
Wilkie Collins
Willa Cather
Willard F. Baker
William Makepeace
Thackeray
William W. Walter
Winston Churchill
Yei Theodora Ozaki
Young E. Allison
Zane Grey